BirthDate

LA PATRON SERIES – BOOK FIVE
The Alphas Alpha

Sydney Addae

BirthDate: Book Five of the La Patron Series
Sydney Addae
Copyright 2014 by Addae, Sydney
First Edition Electronic March 2014

This is a work of fiction. Names, places, characters, and incidents are either the product of the author's imagination or are used fictitiously, and any resemblance to any actual persons, living or dead, businesses, organizations, events, or locales is entirely coincidental. All trademarks, service marks, registered trademarks, and registered service marks are the property of their respective owners and are used herein for identification purposes only. The publisher does not have any control over or assume any responsibility for the author or third-party websites or their contents.

All rights reserved under the International and Pan-American Copyright Conventions. No part of this book may be reproduced or transmitted in any form or by any means, electronic or mechanical, including photocopying, recording, or by any information storage and retrieval system, without permission in writing from Sydney Addae

BirthDate

Book 5 of
The Patron, the Alphas Alpha

When you're the top wolf on the continent with the backing of the Goddess, how does an enemy topple your kingdom? By challenging you to a fight?

No.

By changing the rules.

In BirthDate, Silas goes to destroy the laboratory that has been a hub of wolf experiments and Asia's former residence. Jasmine and Asia are linked in a way that no one can explain. But their connection proves to be critical to saving the young warrior as well as destroying one of the enemy's strongholds. Leaving Jasmine in charge of the compound is risky but necessary for her to realize her role in his life. Through ups and downs, new threats, and the name of their enemies, Silas and Jasmine's love and commitment to each other is tried, tested, and renewed in BirthDate.

This is the fifth book in the La Patron series.

Book one is BirthRight,
Book two is BirthControl
Book three is BirthMark
Book four is BirthStone

I want to thank everyone who enjoys the La Patron Series, you are the best. I appreciate your kind words and thoughts. A special shout out to Karen M. and Karen J., and Kelly, you ladies rock and I appreciate you so much for your hard work and efforts!

Thanks
Sydney

Chapter 1

"YOU CAN LEAVE TO die, but I need you to return here to live," Jasmine, mate of La Patron, said sternly to Asia while sitting in the small steel-encased cubicle. Asia's bowed head nodded slowly. It was obvious this conversation distressed her, but Jasmine's mate, Silas, was concerned over Asia's reckless, ready-to-die attitude since the last attempt on her life outside this very cell.

"I will try, Mistress. But the people we are going to destroy have a lot of tricks and there is no way to be prepared for them all. I have sworn to serve La Patron with my life and I consider it an honor to greet the Goddess on the battlefield."

Boiling energy shot through Jasmine's core as she stared at the honey-brown complexioned warrior. She tamped it down as she grabbed Asia's arm to gain her attention and shake sense into her if possible. "The Goddess doesn't want your life forfeited in this battle. You'll assist the La Patron to defeat his enemies, but not with your life. Do. You. Understand. Me?" Jasmine growled as her fingers pressed into Asia's flesh.

The warrior bitch's head flew up sending her long braids flying over her shoulder. If she were not still blindfolded, their gazes would have collided. Instead, Jasmine stared into the dark half mask covering Asia's eyes, trying to find the words to express how important it was to everyone that she not go all kamikaze in the field.

"But... I am not important, Mistress. I am still connected to them in some way, that is how the assassin found me."

Jasmine thought of Mark and his unerring movements toward Asia's cell. He had known exactly which cell the young bitch was in, which was why the blindfold was still in place. They had no idea what was the true state of Asia's mind.

"And this life I have is not living. I do not wish to live without my mind being free, wondering if I am a threat to those I serve." She shook her head. "I have little knowledge of who I am, where I have been, or where I am going. The real me has been stolen –"

"Then steal it back," Jasmine said quickly as she warmed to the idea. "A part of your mission will be to seek out a way to restore your mind, your memories, and your family." The idea had merit. This way Asia would be free to live a semi-normal life.

Jasmine tightened her grip again intent on gaining a promise. "If this lab is the place you spent most of your time, then start there. Let the prisoner you've become die. Take what you need to live free, but under no circumstances are you to cease to exist." Her heart raced as she thought of the discussion she would have with Silas over this conversation. He might not be pleased that she'd added that assignment, but Asia needed a purpose to live and she'd just given her one.

"Steal my mind...from...they would have records stored somewhere, they never fully erase everything...the trick would be finding where...hmmm...it's possible," Asia murmured as she sat straighter.

Jasmine imagined the light of battle that had just entered her charge's eyes and smiled. "There is so much we need to know that'll be stored in those hidden databases. Silas has set upload capabilities for you and the rest of the team."

"Yes, Mistress. I am aware," Asia said in a distracted tone. "It sounds like a good plan and Jacques is capable."

Jasmine bit back a laugh at the compliment that her mother's mate would no doubt consider an insult. In some circles, Jacques was considered a strategic genius, his ability to see patterns out of piles of data was legendary. His expertise had been sought by every Alpha in their nation at one time or another over the years.

"Yes, he is good at what he does." Thinking her work was done, Jasmine released Asia's arm and went to stand. Asia grabbed her hand, fell to her knees, and rested her forehead against Jasmine's arm.

"I pledge my life to you, Mistress."

Jasmine stiffened.

"You saved my life once and seek to save it again. I am unworthy of your care and yet honored that you notice such a one as me. I swear to do as you requested. I will return."

Concerned over the solemnity of the vow, Jasmine nodded and fought the awkwardness of the moment. When she remembered Asia could not see her, she cleared her throat and spoke. "Stand up, Asia." She waited until they stood facing each other. Similar heights and builds, Jasmine had always thought of Asia as a friend and not the servant the female kept insisting she was. She reached out and pulled a few braids from Asia's hair and placed them behind her ear while wracking her mind for the politically correct thing to say. To have someone pledge their life to you wasn't an everyday occurrence. There was nothing in any book of manners that covered this. But she now lived in a world where full and half breed wolves took these vows seriously so she needed to string her words together carefully. As the mate of La Patron, she had to represent him regardless of how weird it felt to her.

"I accept your promise and will hold you to it. I know you are more than capable of meeting every challenge that'll come up in this mission and it will be a success. I've met few people, let alone women, who can think as quickly on their feet as you. I expect you to use everything you've been taught to take back what our enemies took from you and destroy those bastards." She wondered if there was more she should say or do to make this more official and started to ask Silas when Asia spoke.

"I am honored you think so highly of me and have permitted me to destroy those who stole from me. It will be done, Mistress."

Jasmine blinked a couple of times. Wasn't that what Silas and his team going to do anyway? Weren't they all the same people? Was Asia just repeating what Jasmine said or was there more to it? Somebody needed to write a book on vow-taking and appropriate responses because it could get confusing. Rather than sound ignorant, Jasmine stepped back and nodded. "Okay...good. Silas is waiting for me and you have a team meeting soon. I...I'm glad we had this private conversation." She emphasized the word private. This conversation confused her on a few levels and she needed to go over everything in her mind before she shared it with Silas.

"Yes, Mistress. I understand."

Their talk had an unfinished quality to it, but Jasmine could not think of anything else to say. She had Asia's promise to return to the compound after the success of the mission, which was what Silas had been concerned about. Still, there was a nagging feeling that she needed to make something clear, but she couldn't pinpoint what that was.

"*Sweet Bitch*," Silas called her through their link.

"*I am leaving Asia now. We're done and she has committed to return to the compound, alive,*" Jasmine said, giving him that brief overview as she left the cubicle and headed toward the elevator.

"*Good. We will need her if this is not the only lab. Leon's a lot younger and his memories are limited. I have a meeting with Matt and then Froggy in the gym with Tomas. The young pup is still angry over his mother's death.*"

"*His mother was insane,*" Jasmine said, remembering the bitter woman.

"*Yes, she killed her own children and tried to kill his wolf, which would've killed him. But he is young and scared. Corrinna Griggs will have a lot to answer for when she meets the Goddess.*"

"*Hmmm. I doubt that fazed her. She was all about ruling the world.*" Jasmine stepped out of the elevator onto their private floor and headed to the nursery. The previous month her children had been deathly ill from some type of poison her mother innocently transmitted to them. She shivered thinking back on that time. Her relationship with Silas took a few hits and there were moments she hadn't been sure they'd make it. But they survived and so did their babies. It took weeks for their systems to fight off the parasitic toxin. Silas refused to leave to destroy the lab until he deemed them well and healthy. Three days ago, he made that decree and planned to take a small group to work with Alpha Samuel in Pennsylvania.

"*She wasn't the only one,*" Silas said with feeling.

Jasmine nodded as she walked slowly into the nursery and inhaled. The fresh scent of her children never failed to calm and soothe her.

"*True.*" She moved toward the large penned area and watched them play. Since the christening last month, Renee and Mandy had sent something for the kids every week. Renee believed all of her nieces and nephews were geniuses and constantly sent items that were for much older children.

Adam threw his new ball against the same spot on the wall of the pen with accuracy and laughed hysterically when it rolled back to him. Jasmine smiled at his excitement, knowing he hadn't seen her yet. Renee lay on her stomach coloring a picture in a large book her aunt sent her. Her dark hair spilled over her shoulders, brushing the page as she added to the delightful palette of colors. Jasmine leaned forward hoping to see what her daughter worked on but couldn't see without showing herself and she wasn't ready to do that yet.

On the other side of the pen, Jackie played with something that looked remarkably like a Rubik's cube. Leave it to Renee to send something like that to her baby. Her daughter's long black ponytail barely moved as her hands manipulated the puzzle. Jasmine shook her head at the concentrated look David gave to the cube as he sat quietly near Jackie. His gaze slid toward her, settled for a moment, and then returned to Jackie's manipulation of the toy.

Jasmine shook her head at him. "So much like your daddy," she murmured, taking another look around the room.

"You may as well come on in so they can have lunch and take naps if we're lucky," her mom, Victoria, said from across the room. The large play pen had been her idea and contribution to the play room. She noticed the children functioned best when they were close to each other and got into less trouble, fewer fights.

Pleased to see her mother, Jasmine walked further into the room and smiled as loud gibberish accompanied the word, Mama. Warmth filled her as the children scampered over. She entered the semi-transparent pen and sat on the floor so she could hug and kiss each child. David crawled onto her lap and sat after she kissed him. Renee showed the picture she worked on. Jasmine was floored by the combination of colors and how well her baby stayed within the lines.

"It's so beautiful," she crooned gazing at the page. "Mommies' little artist." She handed the book back to Renee, whose blue eyes gleamed as she settled close and continued to color.

Jackie handed her the Rubik's and she turned it over in her hand, hoping the child didn't expect her to fix it. Jasmine had never been good with these types of toys. "Auntie sent it for you sweetie. You have to fix it by yourself." She returned the cube under serious scrutiny from her daughter.

David chuckled and she had the disquieting notion that he knew she could not work the cube.

Jackie sat next to her leg and went back to working on the puzzle. Adam gave David his ball and waited. A moment later the ball was airborne and to her surprise, Adam caught it.

"That's great, Adam, you're getting good at that." He said something she didn't quite understand but ended with "here." He handed her the ball. She took it and tossed it to him. He scrambled and caught it. His face lit with pleasure and then he stood. Jasmine stared as he walked unassisted to her and dropped the ball in her lap.

Renee and Jackie stopped what they were doing and looked up at him. The next thing she knew, all four kids were running around the pen, unassisted. Tears pooled in her eyes as she laughed at their antics. Glancing around the room, she noticed the nurses standing in the distance smiling. Her babies weren't even one and were playing tag with each other. Tyrone and Tyrese walked a month before they turned one.

"Jasmine?"

"What?"

"What's wrong?"

"The babies are running around playing tag."

"You mean scooting around the pen?"

"No, I mean on their feet, running. They're too young for this. I wanted them to stay babies a little longer, damn it."

He chuckled. "The only reason they weren't walking before now is that they're half-breeds. Most full-blooded pups walk within three to six months. You've had them as babies longer than most."

Thinking it was his blood that made the difference, she snorted. "That's not what I want to hear."

"I am on my way, I know what you want...to hear." He sent a caress through their link that sent tingles down her spine.

"Why the long face?" her mom asked from across the room.

"Nothing, not really... I just... they're growing up so fast, that's all. I want them to be babies longer." She listened with mixed emotions as they all ran after the ball as if testing their limbs. The laughter, their joyful expressions touched off a feeling of melancholy inside her.

"Well, they are half-wolf," her mom said dryly. "They develop differently, so you'll have to adapt."

Jasmine bit back the smart remark on the tip of her tongue. Her mom's recent brush with death seemed to spur the woman onto a new track that Jasmine wasn't so sure she appreciated. The woman had always been an upfront, shoot from the hip kind of person. But lately, there was a brutal edge to her honesty.

"I know. It doesn't change how I feel though."

"Feelings change all the time. I was in love with a man whose mission was to kill me; he claimed to love me and left the medicine to heal me. See… definitely a change of feelings."

Jasmine rolled her eyes. Lately, no matter what they discussed all roads seemed to return to Mark, her mom's deceased fiancé, and his betrayal. How her mom worked it into a conversation dealing with her babies growing up showed just how creative the woman could be.

"Definitely," Jasmine murmured. Another discussion on the folly of loving Mark was not on her agenda today. Her husband and sons were leaving on a dangerous mission in a few hours, which captured all her attention. Nervous energy zipped up and down her spine as she went over all the instructions Silas had been giving her the past few days on how to secure the compound. On the one hand, she was proud to be in charge, and on the other, her stomach quivered in fear of making a mistake.

"You're ignoring me now, too?" her mom said standing.

"Huh?" Jasmine pulled her thoughts back to the present and stared in her mom's direction.

"I asked you a question… a couple of times. Are you ignoring me like Jacques?" There was a smidgen of concern in her mom's voice that surprised Jasmine. Jacques had stuck close to her mom throughout her recent illness, never allowing his mates' brutal words to affect him. As far as Jasmine knew, Jacques could not leave her mom or ever deliberately hurt her.

"My mind was on my mate and sons leaving to take out our enemies today, what did you say?" Jasmine asked as calmly as possible.

Her mom's hand flew to her throat as she walked closer swinging her hips before stopping near the high pen. Jasmine gazed up into hazel eyes similar to hers and waited. The purple velour jogging suit her mom wore hugged her full curves and complemented her short chic hair style. "You're worried."

Duh… she wanted to say. "There's been threats to our lives since day one, yes, I am very worried."

Her mom nodded. "I hope they return the same way they leave, healthy and whole. I cannot imagine a world without my grandsons. I need to kiss them before they leave."

"I'll make sure and tell them or call you before they leave. Are you going to your room?" She moved over as David returned to her lap, Renee picked up her art book, and Jackie grabbed the Rubik's cube from Adam.

"No, I thought… well Jacques has been inviting me to have lunch with him and I've… I haven't had time before. I figured I'd join him today, you want anything?"

Jasmine smothered a grin. Her mom had been rebuffing Jacques since the debacle with Mark. Once Silas set a date for their departure, Jacques had been working around the clock making sure everything in their database was current. Chances are he hadn't been as attentive to her mom which appears to have worked in Jacque's favor.

"No, thanks. Silas is on the way and we'll eat together."

Her mom snorted as she left the nursery. "I was talking about food, not the two of you…eating."

Chapter 2

SILAS FOLLOWED HIS MATE into their suite. His gaze locked on her perfectly rounded hips, small waist, and a peek of her high full breast made his mouth water. If the Goddess granted him another three hundred years, he wanted to spend each day with his mahogany Queen. He had no idea how she'd done it, but somewhere along their journey, she captured his heart and soul, giving a fresh new meaning to his existence. They argued like political adversaries coming from different perspectives, but at the end of the day, whatever was best for their nuclear family, and his family of wolves undergirded their decisions. A leader could not ask for better. After closing and locking their door, he grabbed her around the waist before she took another step forward.

"Mine," he growled near her ear, his wolf rising to the surface. Her hand touched the side of his face as she leaned back against him.

"Mine," she said as stroked him, easing his beast.

Turning her so that she faced him, they met each other's gaze and he opened himself completely, allowing her to see him as he was. Needing her to bathe in his love for her, to accept and cherish him, to recognize that she owned him; he tightened his grip as a shudder ripped through her.

"Sweet Bitch," he whispered as a euphoric wave of caring, understanding, patience, and lust slammed into him. He faltered beneath the onslaught of feeling roiling through their link. Her admiration of his strength pleased him. Her confidence in his wisdom and abilities to always care for his family and people humbled him. Her desire to be with him above all others set him aflame. Pulling her close, he leaned down and kissed her, telling her with his body how much he loved and trusted her.

Her hands pulled his head down, smashing their mouths together. Breaking for air, he gasped as her hands grabbed his face for another kiss. His wolf howled, picking up the need for their mate to join with them.

"Love you, love you so much," she said, her words muffled against his lips. He picked her up and laid her on the couch without breaking their physical connection. When they stopped to take in air, her hands were all over him, pulling up his shirt and pulling down his pants.

"I got this, take off your clothes," he panted, seeing the feral lusty gleam in her eyes. In a few moves, she removed her dress and undergarments but left her heels on. He smiled, sensing her mood. This was gonna be a wild ride.

She opened her legs in invitation. His gums itched as his eyes watered as the scent of her arousal hit him. The feel of her leg rubbing against his outer thigh cost him a breath. His wolf batted against his skin edging him to take her now. But experience had taught him to allow her to tease him until he broke and they would hit the level of completeness they both needed. Gritting his teeth, he tried to think of anything except the way her hands rubbed across his hypersensitive nipples. Pings of need shot straight to his core. He pulsed with the need to be sheathed inside her tight, heat.

Her teeth nipped across his chest, lingered on each nipple, and then laved the tiny bites with her tongue. He shuddered beneath her onslaught. Each touch, each caress, each kiss took him higher. He could not hold out much longer. When her fingers wrapped around his long length, he snapped. Pulling her beneath him, he surged into her.

She moaned as he settled his weight, and willed his throbbing dick to be patient just a bit longer. When the immediate eruption was no longer a threat, he moved. There was no way to describe the delicious pleasure enveloping him at this moment. Her silken walls accepted him as owner and pulled him deeper inside. As he thrust in and out, she tightened her legs across his back as if to hold him in place when there was no place he would rather be. She shifted and he slid deeper, her heel dug into his back as he picked up the pace.

"Yesssss," she moaned as he continued to slam into her.

Sensing her nearness to the peak, he howled his pleasure as they collided and took the leap together. Waves of inexplicable bliss shot through and flowed over him as he exploded into ecstasy.

His entire being shook from the strength of his release. It took a moment for him to realize Jasmine shook as well beneath him. When he could breathe, he rolled to the side and pulled her into him. Inhaling their combined scents calmed his wolf. They had claimed their mate again and all was well in his beast's mind.

"Ummmm, thank you, baby," Jasmine murmured as she wiggled closer into him. Cuddling was totally human and one of the best things his mate insisted they do. He always looked forward to the times when they were simply close to each other for no specific reason.

"You're welcome, Sweet Bitch." His palm ran up and down her back a few times before resting on her hip. As much as he hated to break the mood, they only had so much time before he had to leave. "How was the discussion with Asia? She isn't going to become a sacrificial lamb is she?"

She patted his chest and then slowly ran her fingertips across it. "No. She promised to return. It was…an interesting conversation."

Hearing her hesitation made him pause. "What happened?"

"She kneeled, told me she would serve me, and promised to return."

That sounded normal to him, but he sensed it bothered his mate for some reason. "There was a problem?" He placed his hand over hers, stopping her movement so he could concentrate.

"Yeah… I mean she pledged her all to me…"

"So have I."

"And I have returned that pledge to you. But…there was no reciprocity with her pledge, I feel as though it's all one-sided like she gave me her life and all I said was thank you. I mean who does that? I didn't know what was appropriate to say." She shrugged. Her confusion buffeted him.

"You are her Mistress, mate of La Patron. I am the ruler and caregiver of all wolves in this country. Your vow to protect and cherish her as a wolf is included in your title, you don't have to say it, she knows."

She relaxed against him.

He smiled as he rubbed his chin on the top of her head. This was one of the many things he loved about her, she genuinely cared about representing him correctly, and about the people he had sworn to lead and protect.

"I am sure you handled it well, and she is ready for our mission. Cameron and Lilly will be here when I leave later. He thought to travel with me to clear the lab. But I gave him instructions to seek out the rest of Corrina Griggs followers and detain them just in case one of them decided to take over where she left off."

The feel of her lips on his naked chest as she chuckled warmed him. "He's been the Alpha of West Virginia for what, a week? Two? Does he want more responsibilities? I'm glad he'll be here today because I'm locking this place down until you come back. No one in or out."

He nodded. "You've put that notice on broadcast and people have been scampering to load up on supplies. I think they are taking you seriously." Which made him happy. Wolves were all about strength and ability. His mate had proven she had both.

She snorted. "They'd better. I meant what I said. The only person who gave me any problems was Mama. She acted as if not being able to go shopping in town would kill her or something, like there's a real mall within fifty miles of here. Anyway, she pissed me off. Jacques promised to keep her close to him so I can be available to you."

Pulling her close, he pressed his lips against her forehead and inhaled. "This is all new to her, she's struggling to believe and make sense of our lifestyle just like you did. Don't take it personally; once she mates with Jacques, things will change."

She snorted again, this time she rolled over in his arms. "You and your everything is better when people are mated theory. I hope you're right this time because she is getting on my nerves and I'm afraid we're going to bump heads."

He heard the regret beneath her words and held her tighter. "You'll do the right thing at the right time. She'd been poisoned by someone she thought she loved and dumped into a new reality. Eventually, she'll turn to her mate, but in the meantime the personal demons she's fighting… we can only imagine."

She nodded and sighed. "I know, I know. I need to make sure she sees the boys before you leave."

"Yeah?"

"Oh, guess what?" she laid her hand on his and threaded their fingers as she told him about her mom going to see Jacques.

He chuckled. "He has been busy, but so have I. Let me just say, no one is ever too busy to see their mate. Perhaps he's doing this so that she can get an idea of what it feels like for them to be apart."

"Hmmm, can a mate do that?" she asked in a considering tone.

He pinched her arm lightly, laughing when she swatted him. "Yes, but there's a price… which you know." She had locked him out before and his wolf could not tolerate it. Breeders were not affected the same as wolves. He had begged her to keep their links open for his peace of mind and she had ended his suffering by reopening their links.

"Yeah, but they aren't at the same point we are, so it's not affecting them the same, right?"

He thought about everything he had to do in a short amount of time and nodded. Discussing Jacques and his problems with his mate was nowhere on his list. "They'll both feel some discomfort, like an incompleteness, or emptiness until they mate. Once connected, things will escalate. I placed Tomas with Matt and Davian until I return."

She stilled for a second and then turned in his arms to look up at him. "Who? What? Davian?"

"Griggs youngest son. He's been giving Froggy a hard time and I can't deal with it right now so I gave him to your ex-husband to hang onto for the time being."

"Oh… how did he respond?"

"Davian?"

"No, the kid…Tomas. How did he react being placed with gay men?"

Silas chuckled. "Your human thinking is showing. Those … gay men are mates, so the relationship is respected the same as any other in our world."

"What made you choose them?"

"Davian has experience with teenage breeds. I figure he can

shake some sense into Tomas. Froggy threatened to kill him if I did not intervene."

She nodded. "Am I going to have to deal with him while you're gone?"

Silas stilled at the thought of his bitch in the company of her former husband. A sliver of dark energy snaked through him as his wolf snapped pressing to break free. "Only if you want him to die."

She jerked and turned to face him. "Baby." She placed her hands on the sides of his face and kissed his clamped lips gently. "I was talking about Tomas. Not Davian. He knows better than to come on the grounds when you're not here. That's why Matt lives in town." She kissed him again and again until he could see her clearly.

"Tomas will live in town as well; you won't have anything to do with him. If he runs away and comes here, he's on his own. Have Rose call Davian to pick him up. I do not want Tomas here while I'm away." He paused, staring into her concerned eyes. "Froggy really will kill him."

"Got that. I'm not worried over that." She kissed him lightly and looked away.

"What worries you?"

"Failing you. I have nightmares about it."

He pulled her closer and kissed the top of her head. "You won't fail."

"I made bad decisions before. Like the christening, having it at the wrong time. I made a mess of that." She turned her face into the crook of his neck.

He ran his palm down her back to soothe her. "You can look at it in that manner or you can see the events this way. The christening brought your mom and Jacques together and saved her life. Flushed out an assassin, which alerted us that our enemies can still pinpoint Asia. With the upcoming assignment in Pennsylvania, that's critical knowledge that Matt used to create a collar that will block anything, which gives us an edge. Plus, you realized you had super powers."

She laughed and hit his chest as he intended. "Not super powers. Just poorly channeled energy."

"Which you handle much better now." He'd been teaching her how to manipulate her power surges into more manageable streams.

She nodded and curled into him. "Thanks, Wolfie."

He stroked the side of her face with his fingertips, enjoying the softness of her skin. "Remember, however you want to be treated by the Pack, while I am away is your time to train them. I am simply telling everyone, my mate is in charge."

Chapter 3

SILAS SAT IN THE large conference room with Alpha Samuel, Asia, Tyrone, Tyrese, Leon and Borian, Samuels' beta.
"I've sent a couple of my top wolves to scout the area Jacques suggests the underground lab is buried. Flat land for the most part. We cut down the few trees within that area. Most of it is brush, not very dense, although the trees grow thicker not far from there. Very little wildlife which is surprising considering the river's not that far." He tapped his pen on the table. "They found nothing. Not even a hint of fuel, or gases released in the air. That area appeared dead and my team has been unable to substantiate anything Jacques has sent," Alpha Samuel said, his dark gaze meeting Silas' for a brief moment before settling on his beta.
Silas nodded as his eyes lowered to the wicked scar on his Alpha's chin, a permanent reminder of why humans and wolves did not mix. Or at least why they hadn't before. Silas's gaze shifted to Borian, remembering the Siberian wolf from one of the Alpha training groups. The large white wolf had been a fierce fighter and rose through the ranks quickly. Unfortunately, there were no Alpha positions available at that time and Samuel had offered him the beta position.

Turning slightly Silas realized anger rolled off Leon in waves which could cause problems within such a small group. Leon's golden-colored eyes flashed and long gold-blond dreads brushed against his face as he glared at the Alpha but remained silent for the moment. But that would not last. Silas always thought the tawny complexioned breed resembled a lion and was aptly named. The young wolf worked long hours with Jacques in locating the lab, no wonder he was pissed at the Alpha's words.

"The lab is there, hidden like most things, but it's there," Asia said into the silence earning a frown from Borian. He did not appreciate anyone disagreeing with his Alpha.

"And you are an expert on hidden things?" Samuel asked in a conversational tone.

"Yes, I am," Asia said, looking across the table, meeting the Alpha's stare.

"So what is the best way to get to this area?" Tyrone said after a few moments passed with no one speaking.

"Let's hear from the expert," Samuel said, leaning back in his chair as he continued holding Asia's gaze.

She nodded and leaned forward. "Where is your map?"

Samuel's gaze slid to Borian's and he nodded slightly. Silas remained quiet as they jockeyed for positions within the group. He knew the twins wouldn't join in the pissing contest and was surprised Asia had spoken up. Once they landed in Pennsylvania and were in the limousine, he had removed her blindfold as they headed here. After she thanked him, she lapsed into silence appearing composed and looking harmless as she stared out the tinted window.

Silas knew better.

Now she took Samuel to task for his unintentional insult to Leonidas and Jacques. The Alpha had a short fuse and little tolerance for foolishness. For the time being Silas would watch, but would intercede before any lines were crossed.

Borian pulled out a tablet, tapped a few keys and a screen lowered in front of the bulletin board at the front of the room. Moments later a large map appeared.

"We take the interstate until we get to this rural road here." She pressed the button in the middle of the table to take over the cursor.

"That's south of the area," Samuel said, glancing at her and then returning to the map.

"Yeah, but it's the best way to get to the lab," Leon said, leaning back in his chair as he eyed the map.

"But if you go that way, there's not much place to hide," Borian said, gazing at the satellite view of the area.

Asia and Leon both looked at him as if he had spoken a foreign language.

"What?" Borian asked in a defensive tone.

"They'll know the moment anyone steps anywhere on that land. They've been there for decades and have avoided detection. If you think we're going to sneak up on them, that's not going to happen," Leon said.

"So we just bully our way in?" Borian asked frowning. To his credit, he wasn't being difficult, he simply didn't understand. If Silas and Jacques hadn't gone over their plan as many times as they had, he'd be confused as well.

"We go in through here." Asia pointed to an empty spot on the map.

"We cleared the trees from that area, there's nothing there," Samuel said squinting as he leaned forward.

"We'll have a diversion here," she pointed to another spot on the map as if Samuel had not spoken. "And here." She placed her finger on another spot. Tyrese and Tyrone are point and have the co-ordinates." She glanced at the twins who nodded.

"Wait… we're using explosives? In an open field?" Samuel asked as he turned to Silas.

"Yes, we are," Silas said, stopping all movement and discussion in the room. "The charges will blow within seconds of the other. Since they will know we are above ground, those areas should be clear or not. At any rate, based on the information we have, these are the best places to drop in."

"If we're so sure there is a lab down there, why not just blow the entire place up? Why enter the place at all?" Samuel asked Silas.

It was a good question if you had no firsthand knowledge of previous battles. "Because we need more information to win this war and I think there is vital information stored in that lab. We were finally able to decode some collars a few of their operatives wore when they attacked us and they were linked to this location. We damaged some of their equipment and had a small window of opportunity to get in, uploaded what we could, and got out before they blocked or traced us back to our system." He thought of the energy blast Jasmine sent to his enemy's computer through Mark which damaged their security allowing Jacques and Matt a twenty-four-hour goldmine.

Samuel nodded slowly.

"Oh, and we will blow it up when we are done," Silas added.

"Any ideas what'll be coming at my men?" Samuel asked, his gaze lighting on Silas, Tyrese, and Tyrone.

"It depends on who's there," Tyrese said, his gaze flitting from Asia to Silas. Silas saw the speculative look Rese gave Samuel and knew eventually something would be said. Both Tyrese and Tyrone were just as tall and muscular as the Alpha. When Borian glared at Asia, he received a pointed stare from Tyrese. Each sat on one of Asia's sides, their mocha brown complexions complimented Asia's much lighter one and contrasted with the other wolves in the room. His sons were handsome and deadly. Silas could not be more proud of either of them. Right now he sensed Tyrese was unhappy with Samuel and became more vigilant of listening to the discussion. Tempers could flair in an instant.

"We've seen them bulk up bigger than the Hulk, some have mechanical parts meshed with their wolves which make them harder to put down. The only way to kill those suckers is to separate their heads from their bodies," Tyrese said, eying Borian and then his Alpha as though sizing them up.

Samuel nodded but didn't say anything, although Silas sensed his surprise through their link.

Tyrese continued. "We could be going up against some of the most advanced fighters you've ever seen or a simple security team left in place as a precaution. The simple answer is we don't know what we'll face, but we have equipment that'll counter the threats we're familiar with."

Samuel rubbed the scar on his chin. "We fighting breeds or humans?"

Silas shrugged. "They have used both. If it's a wolf they've been using collars that prevent me from taking control of the wolf and accessing that person's mind."

"That sucks," Samuel said.

Silas nodded, glancing at the ring Dr. Passen gave him yesterday, which worked as an over-ride against the collars. He decided to keep that information to himself. "Yes, it does."

"Tell me about the equipment," Samuel said to Tyrese, turning to face him.

"Asia?" Tyrese said, meeting her gaze.

She stood and walked to the corner of the room, picked up a canvas bag, and returned to the table. The first items she pulled out were collars. "These are similar to the collars the mercenaries wore when they attempted to attack La Patron. She snapped one around her neck, looked around, and then spoke. "We should step outside for this."

Silas scooted back signaling everyone should do the same and followed her out the balcony door. Asia hopped over the railing and landed in a graceful crouch below. Within a few seconds, they all stood around her.

Stepping back, Silas watched as she changed into a large dark wolf standing on two feet. This version of Asia was similar to Tyrese's hybrid.

"To activate this mode, simply think bigger body and the collar will activate. Since your men haven't had any training with this body I suggest it be used as a last resort. If nothing else it might shock the enemy and buy a couple of seconds. To return to normal..." She paused as her body shrunk. "Think normal body."

"If they see these won't they know what they can do?" Borian asked, looking at the collar Tyrone had given him.

Asia bulked up without the collar. Leon, Tyrone, and Tyrese followed suit. Samuel and Borian stared up at the four of them and gawked. "No they have no idea what we can do or not," Tyrese said.

"You don't need these?" Samuel asked, holding a collar in his hand.

"No," Tyrese said without going into any other explanation. Silas put a cap on the serum that changed Tyrese and Tyrone until he knew more about long-term effects. He hadn't shared the information with his Alphas, yet.

"Can we practice with you for a few hours? I'd like to get a handle on how to move at this size," Borian asked snapping the collar around his neck. A few moments later he expanded and was similar in height to Tyrone.

"Sir?" Tyrone said, looking at Silas.

"There should be some time to practice later and first thing in the morning since we'll be leaving here around noon. But we need to go over all the equipment and plans first." Silas crouched and leaped up to the balcony. He grabbed another bag of equipment and headed to the table.

Tyrone and Leon were right behind him. Samuel and Borian were next, their entire demeanors changed, excited. Asia and Tyrese entered last and brought the last canvas bag and placed it on a chair.

"Did you have the shots with the antidotes administered to your men?" Silas asked Samuel thinking of the viruses and poisons their enemies used in the past.

"Yes, Sir. Everyone who works here and who serves me has taken all their shots.

Silas nodded. "Good, we have heavy suits to enter which will deflect heat and a needle, the downside is you cannot shift with them on. If our wolves are shot with the poisons, the antidote will dilute it to a point, and our wolf should push out the rest. We aren't sure of the side effects yet, so be alert if and when you shift."

"Yes, Sir," Samuel said, watching as Asia pulled out more devices from the bag.

"These bombs will detonate downward," she said, pointing to several seal packages. "There'll be some shaking above ground, no way to get around that, but we'll burrow down a certain distance and then place these inside."

"Is there anything I need to tell the human authorities? Will there be enough movement to warrant them coming out to investigate?" Samuel asked, turning from Asia and looking at Tyrese.

Tyrese shrugged. "Asia?"

"You may want to tell them something so that they will remain a safe distance. Plus if anyone is living down there, you don't want an audience when we bring them up," she said.

"We have equipment and a team on stand-by for a possible retraction," Borian said.

"Good. Some people were born down there and lived most of their lives below ground," Leon said drawing attention.

"Not wolves I hope," Samuel said with feeling.

"Some wolves have never left there," Leon said softly. No one spoke. The idea of a wolf being cooped up in any structure with no contact with nature was sobering.

"If they are down there, we will get them out," Borian said in a tight voice.

"Damn right we will," Leon said in a high-pitched voice, visibly vibrating as energy poured off him. His fist opened and closed as he fought to maintain control. With all the training and late nights with Jacques, the young wolf was overloaded with adrenaline. The last thing they needed was an out-of-control wolf leading an expedition.

"Go run," Silas said, looking at Leon. "Go with him Borian. Make sure he stays on your Alpha's property."

"Yes, Sir," Leon said. Borian nodded. Both men turned and ran toward the balcony and jumped, changing mid-air.

Silas glanced at Asia who stood silently between the twins watching him. "The success of this fight depends on us working together as a cohesive unit. I will not tolerate friction in the ranks. That could cause someone to hesitate when given instructions and cost them or others their lives. If there is a problem speak now so we can resolve the matter and move forward."

No one spoke.

"Why haven't you addressed Asia directly?" Tyrone asked Samuel. "It's obvious she's an integral part of our team, but you act as if she's not here."

"She reminds me of someone. Someone I trusted who betrayed me." He rubbed the scar on his chin. "But I stand with La Patron and will follow anyone he follows even if I have nothing to say to that person."

Tyrone nodded.

Silas had thought Samuel was over the incident that happened over half a decade ago, but who gets over a lover leading him to his enemies to die. It was an epic Samson and Delilah event that remains branded on your mind.

"Why are you standing with Asia?" Silas asked Tyrese through their link wondering if Jasmine had given her son's instructions as well.

"I was talking to her. She's afraid we're going to be hurt, which will hurt Mom and she'll be responsible." Tyrese chuckled. *"I don't know what Mama said to her, but everything's centering on Mom's feelings over this mission."*

Silas gazed at the calm façade Asia presented and tapped into her mind. Her terror slammed into him, its intensity surprised him. A whirlwind of emotion whipped around him. Tyrese had been right. At the center of it all was her concern for her Mistress, Jasmine. The onslaught of conflicting sensations disturbed him so he stepped out of her psyche and watched her, concerned. Had he made things worse by asking Jasmine to talk to the young bitch?

"Asia?"

She straightened. "Sir." Her demeanor and prompt response reminded him of a private responding to her superiors in the military.

"Do you have concerns you wish to discuss with us?"

Her mouth opened and closed. "No, Sir."

"I sense you are nervous about something," he said, giving her an opening.

"I am returning to hell, Sir, but I am not nervous."

He nodded, pleased to hear her honest answer since he never picked up that emotion before. "We will be following you into hell on the morrow on my orders. The safety of the team members is not your responsibility, it's mine. I approved the plan, knowing the risks and the possibility of failure. You and Leon have shared your knowledge with us and we'll take it from here, you don't have to return to the lab."

Her eyes widened. "Sir, I must go. I promised Mistress I would."

"*Mistress?*" Samuel asked Silas through their link.

"*My mate.*"

"*Thank you, Sir,*" Samuel said and fell silent.

Unsurprised by her response, Silas nodded. "We are a team. But you must promise not to take on the weight of this mission, that's my job."

She nodded slowly and he watched as the tension ebbed from her frame. "Yes, Sir. I will try."

"*You trust her? She may turn coat on us,*" Samuel said.

"*Yes, she might.*"

"*I feel we are walking into a trap.*"

"*You said earlier there was no lab beneath the ground. Now you believe there is a lab and going after it is a trap?*" Silas asked his Alpha.

Last year he hadn't spent much time in the field training or interacting with his Alphas, due to his mating and the birth of his litter, which had been an unavoidable mistake. Some of them had forgotten how to logistically think through problems to see the bigger picture. Perhaps he needed to give refresher training when this was over.

"*I apologize for the erroneous report, Sir. There is no way you would be here to lead us against an enemy if the threat wasn't real.*"

Silas nodded. The twins and Asia had moved to a corner across the room, no doubt discussing Jasmine. Even though she was thousands of miles away, her presence filled this room. As soon as this meeting was over, he'd contact her to check on things.

"*Yes, I believe we are walking into a trap,*" Samuel said.

Silas shrugged. "*You're probably right. Asia's right. They know we are here and that we are coming. If they're smart, and they are, they're prepared for us.*"

"*So…why?*"

"*Because I am losing this battle and I can no longer face my people with excuses over random bombings, or viruses that kill or manipulate our wolves. I have to send a message of intolerance to my enemies that anyone who abuses a wolf, full or half-breed, will suffer. Those days are over. This is my main lead.*"

"*But if they know we're coming, can we trust anything we find?*"

"*Maybe not. But I'm counting on something else to get us in safely.*" Silas stretched his long legs beneath the table and crossed his hands over his stomach.

"*Sir? What are you counting on?*" Samuel asked.

"*That they still want me.*"

Chapter 4

JASMINE STRODE DOWN THE hall toward Silas' office, which she would be using in his absence. She needed a break from her mom's questions and complaints. If the woman mentioned Mark's duplicity one more time, Jasmine would scream. She could still see the look of shock on her mom's face a few moments ago when she told the woman to get over herself already and give Jacques a chance. The woman's face reddened as her mouth opened and closed without speaking. Jasmine took that moment to leave the room before they got into it.

"Mistress, where would you like dinner served this evening? Hildi the head chef asked, stopping Jasmine in the hall.

"In the dining room, Rose will be joining me."

Hildi hesitated. "Is Alpha Cameron and his mate joining you for dinner?"

Frowning, Jasmine thought back to earlier in the day when Cameron came to see Silas off. Had he mentioned coming for dinner? She couldn't remember. "Not that I know of, did they say anything to you?"

"Lilly asked if I was making pot roast for dinner, she said she missed my cooking. I just wondered if that meant they would be dining with us."

Surprised Lilly asked the cook about dinner and not her, she nodded. "With La Patron leaving and all the excitement I may have missed something. It's better to be safe. Prepare enough for the Alpha and his mate." Jasmine smiled while thinking back to Silas' leaving.

"Yes, Mistress."

She nodded at Hildi and continued down the hall.

"Hey, Rose." She waved at her daughter-in-law as she entered the room.

"Hi. Everything okay?"

Jasmine nodded as she sank onto the soft leather loveseat and placed her feet over the arm-rest. "I'm taking a "mommy-break."

Rose laughed. "She still avoiding Jacques?"

"Yeah, and I think that's her problem. She's fighting the attraction so hard, she has to rehash what happened the last time she trusted a man. Problem is she's miserable and not a nice person to be around. I wish I could block her out as the kids do."

Rose's brow rose. "They block her out?"

She covered her eyes with her arm, missing Silas already and he had only been gone five hours. "Well, they don't pay her any attention when she's in the nursery. She just sits there watching them."

"Oh. She's fighting some demons. Has she seen Davian?"

Jasmine groaned, remembering the conversation she and her mom had regarding her ex-husband. Her mom had been livid the man faked his death and refused to accept her explanations. "No, not yet, but she called him on the phone and cursed him out. Some of the things she said about his dick made me close my legs and I don't have one." Her mom had been brutal.

Rose laughed.

"I couldn't believe Mama could talk like that… so dirty. I think he also tried to explain the mating thing to her, but she wasn't hearing it. She told him he was a man with no honor, then told him he was an embarrassment to the word "man." The insults went on and on until Jasmine blocked the hard-hitting words.

Rose whistled. "That had to sting. He's a proud man."

Jasmine nodded. "Yeah, well. He can't come to the compound unless Silas calls him and he never does. So her threat to cut off his penis and feed it to Matt is a moot one."

Rose coughed as her hand landed on her chest. "What?" She coughed harder while trying to inhale.

Jasmine turned slightly. "Don't choke."

"I didn't see that one coming," Rose said as she stood and went to the mini-refrigerator. "You want something to drink?"

"No thanks," Jasmine said, wondering if it was too soon to contact her mate. He said he'd be in meetings after they landed. Then he would spend time with Alpha Samuel, and left her with the promise to contact her as soon as he could. The compound was locked down and everyone settled in for the night. Her restlessness would end once she spoke with her mate.

"Good thing he took a job two counties away."

"Huh? What? Who took a job?" Jasmine asked removing her arm so she could see Rose.

"Dad. Davian. We had dinner with him and Matt last week and he told us he's been working as Head Security for Rickets department store at the main office in Benson. That's two counties away, an hour drive each way. So chances of Victoria bumping into him are slim."

Jasmine nodded slowly, ignoring the dad reference as she processed the information. The twins had come to her and Silas asking how they would feel if they spent more time with Davian and Matt. She had been surprised at their request and in hind-sight shouldn't have. Their anger at Davian had been based on how he had treated her during their long marriage. With the understanding of mates and the pull it has on a person, they finally let go of the anger. Plus, Davian had been a good dad, just a crappy husband. She and Silas agreed it was okay but reminded them that Davian was only allowed on the grounds with Silas' permission.

"How's that going to work with him taking on a teenager?" Silas never mentioned Davian working. Because of Matt's position and level of security, Davian would've discussed it with Silas and received permission first.

"What teenager?" Rose asked frowning.

"Tomas, Griggs youngest son. Silas left him with Matt and Davian until he gets back and decides what to do with him. I think he needs to be watched closely. Froggy threatened to kill him."

"That's serious. Froggy's pretty patient. I don't know how he's going to handle having a teenager underfoot. Matt's here in the labs ten to twelve hours a day and dad works three 12 hour days on three days off. Maybe they'll be back before he goes back to work."

Jasmine doubted her mate would return in three days but refrained from saying. "True. Unfortunately, I can't allow Tomas on the property for any reason. The shield I have in place does not lift until Silas returns, period. So if he escapes Davian, he needs to run in the opposite direction."

"La Patron will be pissed if Tomas runs away," Rose said in a quiet, contemplative voice.

"Yes, he will. Did Lilly mention coming to dinner tonight?"

"She said she would see me later, I suppose that's what she meant. Maybe they just want to hang out a bit since La Patron is gone. Didn't they clear it with you?"

"Not that I remember. But I didn't pay much attention." She sent a message to security alerting them that Cameron and his family would be returning to the compound for dinner and to allow them entry.

"Lilly seems to be settling in the Alpha house okay. I can't imagine living there with all that responsibility. I'm so glad Rone didn't take the job," Rose said with feeling.

"You would've done fine. You help Silas and now me with a lot of the administrative duties. I don't know how we would've made it through the children's illness if you hadn't worked overtime keeping this office going. Silas and I moved into the nursery and only left for brief periods."

Rose's face pinkened. "We're family. My little brothers and sisters were sick and we were scared… really scared that they might not make it. Rone and I couldn't sleep so we spent time here in the office working. It helped keep our minds off what was going on in the nursery. Believe me, we needed to stay busy."

Jasmine smiled as her heart thudded heavily in her chest in remembrance of the children's christening. They had been very ill. She and Silas came to blows over her family's possible involvement. Warmth filled her cheeks over her threat to leave him if he put her mom and sister out of the compound. It had been a tense time. "All the more we appreciated what you and Rone did in the office. Your help allowed us to focus on the babies and not worry over the state of affairs of the Wolf Nation."

Red-faced, Rose ducked her head and fiddled with some files.

"You're welcome," she said softly.

Glad to be off her feet and done for the day, Jasmine did a mental scan of the grounds as Silas taught her. Security was at their posts. She sensed no unusual movement on the perimeter.

"Jacques?"

"Yes, Jasmine?" He sounded winded.

"I'm doing a preliminary check of the grounds before I talk to Silas and have dinner. Is everything okay with you?" Jacques was in Silas' secure tower with access limited to her and her mom. He handled the satellite and the databases from that point. Her mate wanted no screw-ups and had long conversations with Jacques regarding how he wanted the information cataloged and stored. Scraps of data in the past caused a drain on the system and were difficult to make use of. The new software would store the information and make connections based on the words used in the sentences. Matt and Dr. Passen both agreed this might help them see and understand the bigger picture regarding the collars, and vaccinations they were working on.

"Your mother is here with me and we are fine. I will talk with you on the morrow." He closed the link before she could ask any questions. Pleased, her mom went to see Jacques, she smiled. Hopefully, tomorrow would be drama-free.

"Jasmine..."

Tingles of awareness danced up and down her spine at the sound of his voice. *Hey Wolfie. Glad you remembered me."* Teasing him, she grinned big.

Rose's brow lifted.

Jasmine turned over, away from prying eyes.

Rose chuckled. "Rone's calling me, too. I'mma head to our place so I can uh...laugh in private."

Jasmine threw her arm up in a modified wave not turning around.

Silas growled. She felt the rumbling sound like a caress. Goosebumps exploded across her flesh. *"To forget you is to forget myself. I miss my Sweet Bitch. How are my pups?"*

"Your babies are fine. Went to sleep after dinner. David was a little fussy, more clingy than usual, but he finally drifted off. How'd your meetings go?"

"Touch and go at first. Too much testosterone, but the pecking

order has been settled. Alpha Samuel and his men are practicing with the twins, Leon and Asia right now."

"Practice? What kind of practice?"

"Hybrid two-legged fighting instead of wolf four."

Remembering Tyrese's transformation, she nodded. *"You're going to fight in that form?"*

"If we have to. We will do whatever is necessary to get the answers we need. We did not start this war, but we will end it. Those bastards have preyed on my pack like parasites for decades. And for what? Money? Fame? Power?"

No answer was required so she sent waves of understanding through their link, wanting him to know she heard him and agreed.

"Fuck them. We will eradicate them from our borders or die trying. Fuckers using Pack as test animals, forget that shit."

Hearing the pain beneath his frustration she continued to send calming waves of love and understanding to him. *"I am so proud of you for taking this stand. You do whatever you need to do to make it safe for everyone."* There was a time when Silas's concern was restricted to full-blood wolves. Over the past year, her mate had been kicked into the reality of half-breeds and human breeders. Now his protection covered them all. Considering their half-breed pups, that was a good thing.

"I noticed the twins hanging close to Asia, did you say anything to them?" he asked, finished with his rant for now. She was happy to talk of more pleasant things.

"No, nothing other than I expect all of you to return. Maybe they're just looking out for her because of everything she's been through. How's she doing without the blindfold?"

He chuckled, the sound licked her skin and she shifted on the sofa to ease her ache. *"Good, Mama Bear. Like I said she's in the gym fighting with the guys. I watched for a little while before coming up here and she was holding her own. The twins were the only ones she could not take down. Leon pinned her once but she got him the other times."*

Proud, Jasmine grinned. *"She's tough. Why'd you saddle Davian with a kid? Rose says he works twelve-hour days, how's that going to work?"*

"That's up to them to make it work. I will deal with Tomas when I return. Don't get involved." His voice had hardened at the end.

Jasmine sat up. *"I'm not. But he just lost his mom; it's natural he's upset. Just because we knew her as a murderous bitch doesn't mean he didn't love her."*

"Exactly. That is why he's not allowed on the grounds for any reason. He may try something stupid in the name of love. Where are you?"

She frowned at the swift change of topics. *"Huh? What?"*

"*Are you at our place?"*

"No. I'm in your office. Rose left and I'm locking up and then going to dinner." She stood.

"*Go to my office and lock the door."* His voice dropped an octave and she shivered at the promise in it.

"*Okay, I'm going to lock the outer door first."* With a burst of speed, she ran to the entry door, locked it, and then moved quickly to his inner office, locking the door behind her. Inhaling deeply, she swallowed and spoke. *"I'm here."*

"Go to my desk, sit down and turn on the monitor."

Excited, she moved quickly to comply. Once the monitor was on she spoke. *"It's on."*

"*Type jazz."*

After she typed the letters on the keyboard, the monitor flickered and Silas' face filled the screen.

"*Ummm, Sweet Bitch,"* he purred in a sexy growl through the monitor. His emerald green eyes blazed across the screen warming her across the miles.

"Hey, Wolfie." She leaned forward placing her chin on top of clasped hands. *"So we're camming now?"*

"I just needed to see you. The separation is harder now and this eases me and my beast." His long, jet black hair brushed against his shoulder and framed his square-shaped face. Lips that made her scream in pleasure tilted in a small smile. He looked positively yummy sitting in the chair shirtless with pointy nipples on his broad, muscular chest.

"You are one good-looking wolf, and all mine," she said dragging her gaze from his nipples to his mouth. "Is Samuel mated?" she asked to take her mind off sexing this man ten ways and then some.

His eyes narrowed slightly. "No. Not yet."

"Is he interested in Asia?" She thought of her mom's behavior while denying her mate and wondered if that might be the reason for the Alpha's behavior.

Silas chuckled. "If he was, it died when she beat his beta in the ring. Samuel didn't fight her. Tyrone trained with him."

Jasmine laughed, pleased Asia held her own.

"Do that again," he said in a low voice filled with longing.

Surprised she stopped and stared at him. "What?"

"Laugh. I want to take that sound with me. I love hearing you laugh, it fills me with light. Laugh for me."

Touched, she smiled as her heart expanded with love for this complicated man. She racked her mind for something humorous. Earlier in the nursery, Adam tossed his ball to Renee interrupting her drawing. He ran, laughing and looking over his shoulder, when she threw it back and hit him in the back, making him fall. It had been funny. She and her mom laughed then, just as she laughed now.

The more she remembered Adam running on his chubby legs and Renee's tongue hanging out as she took her time to aim, the harder she laughed. When she could talk she shared the incident with Silas through their link. He chuckled as he leaned back in the chair with his hands crossed over his stomach.

"I love you," he said when their laughter died down.

Her breath caught at the vibrancy of his blue-green-colored eyes. Pleased he was calm and she'd done that for him, she pursed her lips and sent a kiss through their link. "Love you too," she whispered.

"You're the light of my day. I cannot imagine life without you, Jasmine."

She gasped at the caress accompanying her name. He rarely used her given name and she treasured his declaration all the more because he did. "I love you so much, Silas. I cannot imagine spending my days without you either." She shook her head. "Life before you…I was existing. Now I feel as if I am alive for the first time." She met his intense gaze. "Does that make sense?" She had met him when she was 36 with two adult sons. For most, that's the time to wind down and learn those hobbies put aside in place of sports and recreation for your kids. But for her, she had found love.

"It makes all the sense in the world to me. I have waited 300 years for you, Sweetness, and will never let you go. I am yours until the Goddess removes us from this plane and ushers us to the next. You have my word on that."

Damn, the man made her toes curl and core throb when he talked commitment to her like that. Most women wanted a man who openly declared to the world she was the only woman he wanted in his life. "I don't want you to let me go and I don't want to leave. You know that baby." She licked her lips and sent him a kiss loving the sultry look in his eyes. If he were in the room right now she would have him on his back riding him like a cowgirl. The vision made her cream her thong.

"I would like more pups."

Her head snapped up. The lusty vision disappeared like smoke. "What? Pups?" What the hell? He couldn't have said what she thought he said.

He nodded, looking relaxed as if he hadn't known she was thinking about riding his dick. "I've been thinking about it. We've got six; why not make it an even dozen?"

She gasped at the inclusion of her older sons. That was low to include them with his outrageous request, but it made her heart melt a tiny bit. Thankfully her mind was unaffected. With a slight narrowing of her eyes, she met his gaze while thinking of an appropriate reply. "Only if..." She placed her forefinger on her puckered lips.

He leaned forward eagerly. "If what?"

"You carry them. I'm not having any more kids. Six is a good number. One day I'll have grandbabies to spoil and that's good enough for me. That's how it's done, Silas. We need to be available for our kids as they grow older." The idea of going through another pregnancy killed her mood and she pushed away from the desk, ready to sign off for the night.

He raised his hands in a placating gesture. "Okay, I can see this is not a good time for this discussion. Maybe later when I return. Everything settled for the night?"

She crossed her arms over her chest glaring at him. "Yes."

He stared at her for a few moments and then released a long sigh. "I should not have asked that question, not now. I apologize. Don't be angry. I am leaving in a few hours and I do not want there to be problems between us."

She eyed him and then released her arms. The man was a manipulative rascal. "You did that on purpose."

"What?" he laughed, half-covering his mouth with his hand. "I... well I thought that was the best time to put it out there."

Yep, he was her rascal and there was one way to deal with him. "There will be no discussion later. I've given you my answer. I love you Silas Knight but at times you're an ass. I'm tired. Do we have a monitor in our room?" She stood and turned away from him.

"Not yet. But I like the idea of being able to watch you sleep. I'll take care of that when I ...what?"

"Hmmm?" she looked over her shoulder as her pants followed her blouse to the floor. Clad in her see-through bra and thong, she turned to face him. "What, what?" she said in the same tone he had used when he asked for more children.

His eyes blazed emerald green as he shifted in his chair. The sound of his zipper being yanked down filtered through the monitor. "Sweet Bitch, you're killing me," he growled low.

"Really? I thought I was giving you something to take with you, but if this is hurting you, I'll stop." Turning, she bent, giving him an eyeful of her ass while she picked up her clothes.

"No." His shout took on a gravelly quality. "This is what I need. No clothes, Jasmine. Take everything off... please."

Now that she started this game she wasn't sure how to proceed. She had only meant to teach him a lesson but the feral gleam in his eyes told a different tale. Her lover was turned on and his wolf as well. Going on instinct, she pulled off her bra slowly and then peeled her panties down her legs.

"You are so beautiful." The awe in his voice set off sparks in her.

She looked at her body and saw the few extra pounds from her last pregnancy. Her breasts were larger than she'd like, and in her mind, her hips were too big. But when he looked at her, like a man starved and she was the meal he craved, she felt sexy, gorgeous.

"Dance for me."

In the next moment, soft music played in the background from his room. She closed her eyes to pick up the beat and moved her hips in time with the rhythm. A few seconds later she opened her eyes and gasped at the ferocity of his gaze. Blatant hunger was stamped across his face. His need flowed fast and hard through their link. She rolled her hips and lifted her breasts toward him in time with the music.

His harsh breathing spurred her on. She mimicked sexy moves she'd done in bed with him loving the sounds of his growls and panting.

"I'm so hard... I need you," he panted.

Feeling his need through their link she was conflicted and glanced at him. They had a rule; neither was allowed to come without the other. She wasn't as turned on as him but maybe she could do something, although she had no idea what. He had thrown away all of her vibrators and sex toys. "Do you want to ... make yourself come?"

He shook his head. "No. Not without you. This is the sweetest torture and I brought it on myself. Should have remembered women do not fight fair and there is no way to win against your weapons."

He raked his hand through his hair and yanked hard. His eyes were a brilliant emerald as he took in gulps of air. Fascinated, she watched him struggle to bring his body down. After several deep breaths, he closed his eyes for a few as if seeing her hurt.

She slipped on her pants and top and stuffed her thong and bra into her pocket. Dinner would be a little late, she needed to change.

A long raggedy sigh whistled through his lips. He opened his eyes and they were a dark green. She exhaled, feeling better seeing him in control.

"I have to take a shower to calm down." He stood and it was her turn to burn at the sight of his naked glory. The veins on his hard penis pulsed. She wet her lips at the sight of his wasted pre-cum. A heavy throb settled between her legs as she hungrily watched him walk off. She almost missed his last words.

"Good night, Sweet Bitch, you don't fight fair."

Chapter 5

AT FIVE O'CLOCK THE next evening, three teams of three stepped onto the area above the lab. Traffic had been a bitch and they had arrived from Northern Pennsylvania later than originally planned. Wearing heavy haze mat equipment, they moved quickly to their targeted area and placed the small heavy equipment on the ground. Within moments the soft whirring of the drills filled the air. The twins and Leon separated from their teams and with deft precision assembled the bombs.

The rest of the group stood on the perimeter of the woods waiting. Asia gazed around the area. Tendrils of apprehension raced down her spine. They were not alone out here. Tilting her head slightly, she inhaled and caught an old, yet familiar scent.

Damn. They sent Mikko. The two of them had been competitors in the field for years. Although he never said, she knew he resented her high ranking and would take her out in a second if he could. By sending Mikko, her former owners sought to even the playing field. Which meant there was something below they did not want to lose.

Her mind raced as she developed and discarded a course of action. It seemed each time she was close to her goal something, in this case, someone, stood in her path. She glanced at the seemingly relaxed pose of La Patron and made a decision.

"*Sir?*" she said through their link.

He glanced at her.

"*We are not alone.*"

"*I know.*"

She nodded and tried to relax. If she had not told him he may have become suspicious, maybe even accused her of ulterior motives. Blanking her mind and emotions had been the most valuable lesson she had learned through the years. La Patron must never know of her deep-rooted rage and hatred of those who turned her into a mutilated animal. Or her anger at him. They all lied to her. Wanted to use her. La Patron dangled freedom in front of her like a carrot and then sent his mate who snatched it away when she branded Asia that last time in the lab. She rubbed her right forearm where Mistress Jasmine's fingerprints formed a tattoo, linking them together.

"*He is part wolf as you but his wolf is sick. He does not embrace that part of him.*"

She had no idea what Mikko did or didn't do. They never talked. But she'd heard stories of his brutality over the years.

"*Do you know him? Can you call him closer? I would like to meet him.*"

"*He is Mikko. A highly trained assassin. His kill count is almost as high as mine, for him to be here is troubling. He may not come if I call, we are not friends.*"

She heard La Patron's sigh. "*So they sent the big guns for me. I should be flattered. Is he the only one here?*"

"*Although I cannot sense any others, I believe there are more. He is good but you are La Patron. They know he cannot win against you alone. They must have a new masking gadget that we were not aware of. We are probably surrounded.*"

"*But they offered him up, nice bunch. Step forward.*"

She moved forward along with the others. A cool swish of air touched her back and then a blast of blue fire streaked backward from the invisible circle she was now enclosed in. The trees and grass remained intact. Human screams of agony filled the air confirming her suspicions that a new tool had been created in her absence. The pain-filled sounds chilled her soul. She thanked the Goddess she had chosen to speak up.

Another round of fire spread further back and more screams

were heard. She swallowed hard reworking her escape plan. This small show of his power proved La Patron was not one to play with. Maybe she should wait until after the mission. Things would be more relaxed. She eyed La Patron again as he raised his hands.

The air inside the bubble became heavy and dark. Within seconds, outlines of those who were not a part of their team became visible. One second they were standing, the next they lay writhing on the ground, holding their heads. The Alpha's men who stood near her ran forward and secured them. Dr. Passen had provided tools to remove and lock collars. Moments later the men lay prone, fully visible.

The next moment they were wolves.

"Bastards would use my own against me," La Patron murmured as he strode forward.

Frozen by equal measures of fear and determination, she watched as he stooped down to examine each wolf, touching a few and stroking others. Mentally she took a step back from the sight and focused. She needed to get inside the lab by any means necessary. Her one link to her past was hidden in the stone work of the janitor's closet.

Last night when La Patron pulled her from the assignment, she wanted to scream. She'd worked so hard, given them as much information as she could, done everything within her power to return to this lab. To fulfill her vow to the Mistress she needed the contents of that box.

She sensed movement behind her and jumped, spinning in the air. More wolves trotted forward, their gazes locked on La Patron. Moving out of their way, she took a step backward, and then another, each time hoping no one noticed. Mikko was still out there, wounded no doubt, but healing at an accelerated rate as her kind often did. Soon he'd be up again and deadly as ever. She needed to get to him and remove the passkey that would allow her to enter the lab through the tree. Exhaling she sent a quick message to La Patron praying he was too distracted with the wolves to pay her much attention.

"Mikko is up, I'm going to take him out." She spun and took off in the direction of her former associate. Within a few feet, she stopped. He had been closer than they realized and had taken a major hit from the fire.

"Freeze bitch," he growled, pointing a Primp, a powerful,

modified weapon they used in the field, at her. She knew better than anyone the damage it could do. "Umph," he groaned as chunks of charred flesh and skin were pushed aside as new skin emerged. Although he was in excruciating pain, his hand never wavered.

"There's…a bount…bounty on your head." He pulled his leg upright and she saw the gleam of metal covered in blood before the repair process began. Sweat beaded on his upper lip and forehead. His eyes were feverishly bright.

"Really? How much?" She held her hands up, wondering how much time she had before someone came after her.

He snorted and then wheezed. "Not… not worth this." He coughed and spit bloody saliva. "What the…hell… did you do to… piss them off?"

She stared at him in surprise. He was asking questions instead of shooting her or taking her in, which would save her time now that she thought about it. "I was captured during my last assignment dealing with La Patron and have been in a cell until yesterday. So *you* tell me what I did."

He coughed again while gazing up at her. "There's…got to be…more to it. They've gone to a lot…lot of trouble to get you. Called a lot of us from the field for this hunt."

She froze, not caring for that news. "What? Why?" She wanted to stamp her foot in frustration. Was this going to be her lot in life? Close like Moses had been in the bible, but not close enough to experience living free. Now she had no choice. She needed to get the information from the lab and seek out her past. La Patron would kill her slowly if any of those assassins came within a mile of his compound. And she knew Logan and Meary would never stop until they killed her. Those two held grudges like super glue.

"I don't know why, I just asked you." She glanced at his legs. Except for his pinkish and red skin, they appeared perfectly healthy and whole. He stretched one and then the other before standing slowly on the newly regenerated appendages.

"Who else is looking for me?"

"Logan, Meary, and a few others. I was told to come here, didn't know you'd be with La Patron. By the time I realized it was him, it was too late. He'd fried my ass." He rotated his shoulder and then his neck without lowering or releasing the primp.

She sensed Tyrese nearby. "What are you doing here? Did they send you for La Patron?" She raised her voice, sounding irritated.

He frowned. "What?"

"What do they have in the lab? Who's down there?" She hissed knowing Tyrese could hear every word.

"I don't know who's in the lab. It's been –"

"You're lying. How did they know we were coming? How many of you were in the woods? How long have you been here?"

"You are a crazy bitch and should be put down like the dog you are. No wonder they want you dead or alive, you've flipped." He raised the weapon and before she could blink, Tyrese slammed into him.

"Sir, Tyrese and Mikko are fighting." She took a step back edging toward Mikko's small backpack.

"I thought you were going to take care of it," Silas said.

Unsure which way his mood swung, she opted for the truth, just in case he'd heard Mikko earlier. *"He drew a weapon that would stop a sixteen-wheeler and told me there is a large bounty on my head, dead or alive."* She went on to tell him everything else Mikko said for good measure. Now was not the time to have La Patron doubting her.

"Wait until they are done and return with Tyrese."

She released a breath and turned her attention to the fight. La Patron's certainty that Tyrese would win this battle was well placed. Even wounded Mikko put up a good battle. Tyrese punched him in the face so hard she was sure Mikko was broken. He spun, hit the ground, and sprung up with a kick to Tyrese's chest. He followed it with a roundhouse to Tyrese's head, which spun the larger man. When Mikko picked up Tyrese and body-slammed him on the ground she was impressed.

Tyrese jumped up, grabbed Mikko by the neck, lifted and shook him like a rag doll. Seconds later Tyrese's fingernails lengthened into claws piercing Mikko's neck. The look of surprise on his face would forever be embedded in her memory. He knew he had lost the fight and that there was no way to recover from the blood pouring from his neck. A ghost of a smile appeared on his face and she thought he looked peaceful. Tyrese bulked up, ripped Mikko's head from his body, and tossed it aside before looking in her direction.

Taking another step back, she eyed the weapon Mikko held and glanced at Tyrese. He was morphing back to his normal size, which was still much larger than her.

"You okay?"

She wanted to dance at the concern in his voice. "Yeah." She picked up the palm-sized device and showed it to him. "This is a primp. It's modified...not a gun, but similar to a gun. One-shot will stop a bull and the one behind him."

Tyrese stepped closer and looked. "Really? That's what he was pointing at you?" He looked at her. "I wondered why you were just standing there."

"He was regenerating and was about to collect the bounty money on my head when you showed up. Good thing because I promised Mistress I would return to the compound when we're done." She looked at him with a wry smile. "Thanks."

He nodded and stooped to look inside Mikko's small backpack. She tried to see the contents from over his shoulder. "What's this?" He held up a black pen that sent a thrill of excitement through her.

Once again, years of masking her true feelings served her well. "I'm not sure, let me see? A pen?" She said after flipping it over a couple of times deactivating the timer. She handed it to him and he waved it off while pulling out what looked like a calculator. After placing the pen in one of her pockets, she stared silently as he tapped on the calculator. It was new. But if Mikko had it, it was something she wanted to know more about.

"Maybe we should let Matt or Passen have a look at these things," she said preferring the deadly items be put away for now.

He nodded, then put everything back into the bag and closed it. "Good idea." They returned to the circle where La Patron held court. She was shocked at the number of wolves trying to get close to him. There had to be over thirty.

"Damn," Tyrese said handing her the backpack. He waded through the wolves and stationed himself in front of La Patron. Tyrone and Leon followed suit and pretty soon the wolves appeared to be more organized. Without opening the bag she squeezed the supple leather searching for an oval stone. The newer assassins didn't use the tree, but she and a few others still did.

"*Sir, by now they know our entry points and are prepared,*" she said to see if he understood what was happening. They had released the wolves from below, or at least some of them. As stalling tactic went, it was a good one.

"I am aware of that. Do you have an alternative plan?" he snapped. She sensed his frustration through their link.

"Not at the moment, Sir. Other than kicking in the front door, we need to rethink this." She paused. *"These wolves weren't burned. I wonder where they came from. How far away? Also who was burned?"*

"I don't need questions. I need answers. I am sending these wolves to the infirmary, some are in bad shape. Come and look, do you recognize any?"

The last thing she wanted to do was look into the face of wolves who had suffered alongside her for years. The guilt and impotent rage at not being able to help those much weaker ate at her until she built a wall so high she no longer saw or felt much of anything.

She moved toward the group of wolves and inhaled. None of them smelled familiar, but she had been gone for a while and that might be the reason. Still…there should be something familiar. Curious, she walked among them, soothing, touching, and inhaling their scents.

"Leon?" she called him over.

"Yeah?" he said sidling closer.

"What do they smell like?"

Leon inhaled and frowned. "Something's off." He leaned forward and inhaled again. "Sir, there is something wrong with their smell." He walked to their bundle of supplies and searched until he pulled out a metal box.

She stiffened when he returned with the bomb detector and ran it over each wolf. No one moved until he was done. When he turned toward La Patron with a grin she exhaled. Sending in this many wolves with bombs would have been overkill, not to mention it would be on every news station in the country.

"Glad it wasn't that," he said smiling. Tyrone slapped him upside the head. Everyone was nervous.

She turned toward Silas and spoke through their link. *"Sir, I am sorry, but there is something wrong with these wolves, they've done something to them. I would advise against you sending them with anyone. They should be taken up into the mountains and left there."*

The wolves whined and instead of howling, they made mewling sounds. Silas waved Samuel over and they spoke for a few moments. Alpha Samuel waved Borian over and the three of them talked a few moments longer.

With each passing second, Asia tensed, expecting either an assassin to come at her back or lab security to come at them with additional force. Thankfully the shield was up again.

When two men from the Alpha's team shifted and tried to lead the wolves toward the woods the wolves sat down around La Patron's foot. Leon and the twins tried to get the wolves to move. But to no avail.

La Patron stood in the midst of the circle of wolves, with the twins at his side watching. The Pennsylvania Alpha and some of his men stood a short distance away talking. An uneasy feeling crept up her spine. Something was wrong; security should have been here by now. She looked over her shoulder and wondered who was in the woods. Should she take her chances and leave with the excuse of scouting around. La Patron would never let her go alone, if at all. Just as she opened her link to ask what he wanted her to do, a loud clap filled the air. The ground fell from beneath her feet. Air whooshed beside her as she looked up toward the sky.

Her last sight was of La Patron and the twins in the air while everyone else fell below. So much for being a team.

Chapter 6

HER FIRST FULL DAY on the job and Jasmine wanted to scream. The next person who questioned her instructions would feel her wrath. She headed toward the nursery to calm down from her latest discussion with Hank, the head of security. Of course, he waited until Silas left to question the reasonableness of her order to lock down the compound. After she stated calmly that she wanted no strangers in and no one already approved to leave, she thought that would be the end of it. But he continued with examples of why she was wrong in her decision. Fed up, she told him to contact Silas and if her mate told them to change her instructions, she would. Seeing the color leech from his skin would have been satisfying if she had not been so pissed.

When she entered the nursery she realized the delay with Hank cost her missing her baby's meal time. They were all asleep. Their nurses moved about quietly straightening the area in the dimmed, quiet room.

"I missed them," she said to no one in particular while gazing at the peaceful faces of her children.

"Yes, Mistress. They just dropped off to sleep," one of the nurses said softly. Nodding, she sat in one of the rocking chairs to take a break before returning to Silas' office. The soothing motion of the rocker, the baby powder scent, and the sweet sounds of her innocent one's breathing almost lulled her to sleep.

"Mistress?" Rose said softly from the doorway. Jasmine opened one eye and then the other as she took in her daughter-in-law's nervous posture. Rose wore a cream-colored wrap-around dress that highlighted her curvy figure, long neck, and tanned complexion. She wore her thick jet black hair swept back from her face and hanging down her back. Swallowing back a sigh, Jasmine stood and walked toward the door.

"Yes? What happened?" she took Rose's hand and led her into the much brighter hallway, closing the door behind her.

Rose cleared her throat and looked at the floor for a moment.

Jasmine knew it wasn't Tyrone, she would know if it was. "What?"

"Lilly and Cameron are back and want to enter the compound," she said in a rush. "Hank told them you had to grant permission even though Cameron is the state Alpha."

Jasmine's heart sank. Last night at dinner she told her guest she would be locking down the compound after they left and they seemed okay with it. She and Cameron were cordial but never developed a close relationship. When she talked to Silas about it, he shrugged it off and told her not to worry. She should have pushed to find a solution before now. If she allowed them in, she would break her own order. But if she refused it would be disrespecting one of Silas' Alphas.

"He never mentioned he was returning when he was here last night."

"No, Lilly didn't either. She asked me if I wanted to stay with them until Rone came back. I told her no, I had to work. Plus, my home is here."

Jasmine nodded as she weighed her options. Although the compound was not under Cameron's authority, a lot of the workers lived off-site and did fall under his jurisdiction. As a new Alpha, she needed to show him the same respect she showed all the others.

"Hank, allow Alpha Cameron and his mate to enter the compound." She hoped he did not make a snide comment.

"Yes, Mistress."

"When they arrive, bring them to the office. I have to finish going over some papers for Silas."

Once the decision was made to go after the lab and take it down, her mate insisted she spend a few hours a day in his chair, learning and sharing his responsibilities. It was a daunting task. She had no idea he approved funding grants for schools and businesses all over the country. All types of correspondence crossed his desk and although Rose answered most on his behalf, he still glanced over them before they left his office. Last week she started weeding through grant applications and whittled the stack in half. She intended to have responses sent to all of the applicants before Silas returned. To do that, she needed quiet.

"Hello, Mistress Jasmine," Lilly said from the door.

Smiling, Jasmine placed her pen on the desk and stood to hug the young woman. "Hi, I didn't know you guys were coming back today." She leaned back and met Lilly's smile.

"Cameron had to go out of town to check out a tip regarding Griggs followers. He took Thorne and asked if I wanted to hang over here with Rose while he was gone. I hope it's okay. We forgot about the compound being locked down until we got here."

Jasmine met Rose's worried gaze. "It's okay this time, but I'm not going to open it again after you leave today. It works better for me to keep everything locked."

Lilly nodded. "That way you don't have to worry about anything sneaking in like before causing problems. I don't blame you; thanks for letting me hang today."

Jasmine nodded. The sneaking in comment didn't sit too well, but she didn't comment.

"You need help with anything? I help Cameron with his paperwork and can help you if you need me to," Lilly said taking a seat against the wall instead of leaving the office.

"No, I have to go through these personally, but Rose may have some things you can help her with." Jasmine didn't think Rose had time to visit since they both wanted their desks cleared so they could have time off to spend with their mates when they returned.

"She said she was busy....seems like I came at a bad time. I should've called first."

Jasmine smiled but didn't answer as she returned to her desk to work on the grants.

"Thorne wanted to meet Tomas," Lilly said into the quiet.

"Really?" Jasmine said picking up her pen to initial a page.

"Yes. They're close in age. I thought it might be a good idea, what do you think?"

The application for a grant to study the impact feline tails had on the length of a wolf's tail made little sense to Jasmine despite the arguments made in the narrative. The author of the proposal had no foundation for his ridiculous claims, which caused her to snort as she placed it in the reject pile.

"I'm sorry? You don't think it's a good idea?"

"What?" Jasmine asked frowning looking up from her work.

"Thorne befriending Tomas."

"No. Tomas just lost his mother and is grieving." Jasmine didn't want to get into the particulars of Corrina Griggs with Lilly.

"That's why I thought it would be a good idea. Both teens lost their mothers at an early age. I discussed it with Cameron and he agreed with me. Part of being a good Alpha is to meet the emotional needs as well as the physical needs of the Pack."

Jasmine froze and looked at Lilly. "Are you… are you telling me how to run a Pack?" Jasmine leaned back in her chair. Lilly's relaxed posture made it seem as if they were having tea and discussing kingdom policies. Did the young bitch think they were on the same level?

"No. Well, I was asking your opinion –"

"And I told you no. It is not going to happen." Jasmine crossed her arms and met Lilly's stare.

"Can you tell me why it is not going to happen?" Lilly asked pushing boundaries.

"No."

Lilly frowned. "No?"

Jasmine nodded. "No. I'm not going to explain it to you."

"Oh. You'll tell Cameron why?"

"No. I'm not explaining anything to you or Cameron. I am telling you Tomas and Thorne are not and will not be getting together anytime soon. It will not be happening." Jasmine met the unamused gaze of the young bitch.

Lilly sat forward and crossed her legs at the knee. "Okay. I'm sure you have your reasons, and that they are good ones. Especially since those two have a lot in common… you know."

Jasmine shrugged becoming irritated at the intrusion in her work space and the attitude of the new Alpha Bitch.

"I'm sorry I didn't mean to piss you off. I just thought since we were both, you know, First Ladies, we could talk about stuff." Lilly smoothed down her pant leg and missed Jasmine's wide-eyed stare.

"Lilly, I am not pissed. If I were you would feel it. I don't appreciate you assuming I would discuss things with you that do not concern you. When I said no… that should've been the end of the matter. But you kept pressing. I am not a First Lady. I am First Bitch of the Wolf Nation. My mate is La Patron, he has no equal, and neither do I."

Red-faced, Lilly scrambled to stand. "I…I am sorry. I didn't mean to sound like… like I'm…You're…I apologize, Mistress. You're right, I was out of line. I am the Alpha Bitch of West Virginia. While you're… you're the First Bitch of everything," she whispered the last and bowed from her waist.

Feeling slightly sorry for the young woman, Jasmine eased up. "We both know who we are and more importantly you're family. Some lines cannot be crossed and information that will never be shared, but if I can help you settle more in your role as Alpha Bitch let me know."

"You just did, Mistress. That was a gracious set down."

Jasmine nodded with a slight smile.

Cameron strode into the office and wrapped his arm around Lilly's waist. "What's funny?"

If he had been in the outer office, Jasmine suspected he heard everything that went down already. First, he came uninvited to dinner last night, and then today he dropped off his mate without asking which caused her to change security instructions again. Granted, he was Silas' godson but he had crossed the line and she needed to stop it now.

"Nothing, Mistress and I were just talking. How'd it go?" Lilly asked looking up at him.

"It was a bust. They were passing through the State and were able to prove it. I gave them a warning and had them escorted to the State line."

Lilly nodded.

Jasmine watched and refrained from speaking. He had not greeted her yet and that was a breakdown of protocol. Inwardly she sighed. Silas told her she would need to train the Pack how she expected to be treated. She was not a wolf and the normal fighting methods did not apply.

"Why can't Tomas and Thorne meet?" Cameron asked turning to her.

With a whisper of energy, Jasmine closed the door behind her uninvited guests. Lilly looked at the door and then at her. Cameron continued staring at her as if she had to answer him.

"We don't want them to meet," she said in a tight voice as anger churned in her gut.

Releasing his mate, he stepped forward. "Lilly told me that, I want to know why."

Jasmine's energy whipped out, lifted him from the floor, and slammed him in the chair his mate occupied earlier. She watched as he tried to disentangle himself and failed.

After a few moments, he glared at her. "What's this about? I asked a question and you pin me to the chair? Is that how you're running things while La Patron is away?"

"Cam, stop," Lilly shouted. Her hair lifted and moved in the breeze of Jasmine's energy.

A warmth cloaked Jasmine as she realized she had her anger under control and it was a glorious feeling. "Yes. This is how *I* am running things." She emphasized the word I as she lifted him from the chair and held him high in the air by one arm leaving his feet dangling. "I am going to ask you one question and your answer will govern where you sleep tonight. So think before you speak."

"What? Govern where I –"

"Shut up, Cam. Listen, please. She's not playing," Lilly said standing nearby rubbing her arms as tendrils of energy moved the fabric of her blouse and pants. Jasmine knew Cameron was just as uncomfortable.

"If Silas had been in this room when you entered, would you have greeted him?"

Cameron stopped moving.

Lilly's eyes widened as she looked first at her mate and then at Jasmine.

"Yes, I would have greeted him," Cameron said slowly. "I apologize for not greeting you... Mistress. Please forgive me."

Jasmine smelled the insincerity of his response, but let it go. They would probably never be close friends and that was okay. But he would respect her position. If the state Alpha disrespected her, it would set a precedent and ultimately Silas would step in. Her mate left the ball in her court to teach them how she wanted to be treated and she intended to play hard ball.

"I forgive you for that, but there is one thing you need to understand," she said dialing down her energy.

"And that is?"

"I don't explain anything to you. Not one thing. You are not privy to everything that goes on in this office or the reasons for the decisions we make. Do not ever demand an explanation from me again." She sent a light energy smack against him.

"Umph," he groaned as his back arched in pain.

Lilly's eyes flicked from her mate to Jasmine to her mate again as if willing him to say the right thing, which in this instance was yes.

"Yes, Mistress. Again, I apologize for over-stepping my bounds in your office. I will not do so again."

Jasmine eyed him critically, assessing the sincerity of his words.

"*Mistress?*" Hank contacted her through their link.

"*Yes?*" Leaning forward, she rubbed her brow with her fingertips, wondering what he needed now.

"*Security on the front gate just contacted me to say they were returning to their posts after completing a circle around the west wing. I did not authorize them to leave their posts, did you?*"

"*No, I have not changed any instructions other than the one I gave you earlier. But I think I know what happened, stand by.*"

Exhaling, Jasmine cleared her throat, glanced at the clock, and then exhaled again. It wasn't even noon. Lilly glanced at her and then up at her mate again. No doubt asking him what was going on.

"Cameron, did you give instructions to my compound security?" Jasmine added a note of incredulity in her voice. Being an Alpha had truly gone to his mind.

He cleared his throat. "I instructed the men to complete a level one security scan."

"On what authority did you do that?" Jasmine asked in a low voice, tapping the desk with her fingernail.

"I...well...I assumed as Alpha I should offer assistance."

"And did you offer me assistance?"

"Yes, by having the men complete the scan."

"No, that is not assisting me and you know that. That is

overstepping me and giving instructions to staff not under your control. Tell me, did La Patron tell you to come here in his absence? Or to order security scans?"

"No, he did not."

"So for all you know, you just caused a few men to violate an order Silas put in place."

"No, Mistress. If La Patron told them to do something, they would never have moved when I gave them instructions. They would've told me they couldn't violate his orders."

Lilly covered her face with her palm in the sudden silence of the room.

"Hank?"

"Yes, Mistress."

"Alpha Cameron sent the men to do a first level scan. Each man who left their post will be docked a day's pay and scrub all three floors of the gym tonight before seeking their rest."

"Yes, Mistress." She heard the note of respect in his voice and smiled.

"Tell them the next time anyone disregards an order from me, I will pin them to the wall in the gallery for everyone to see."

"Yes, Mistress, I will be sure to pass that along."

"I apologize again, Mistress," Cameron said. No doubt Lilly had lit into him like fire after his insulting response. "I had no right to give instructions to your staff without your permission. I am still learning my role as Alpha. Plus, your role is new to me as well and I am accustoming myself to the fact La Patron is mated with a den. I hope you will accept my apologies and I accept any punishment you deem worthy of my offense."

Jasmine glanced at the stack on her desk and knew she would be working later than she planned. "Join the guards who left their posts to follow your instructions in the gym after they finish their shifts. Help scrub the floors on all three levels."

Lilly's mouth opened and then snapped shut before turning to the side with a small grin.

"Yes Mistress," Cameron said in a resigned tone.

"I made an exception for you last night and today and allowed you in the compound. You knew it was locked down."

"I didn't realize that included us. You mean we cannot come back and forth while La Patron is away?"

"No one, not even my mother, is leaving or returning to this compound while Silas is away. Believe me, it is better for everyone. I don't have the same level of control that he does and if something goes wrong I could bring down the mountains or something." She tried to inject some levity into a serious situation.

"I understand. I wanted to be close and available in case you needed me. I hoped to show La Patron he can trust me in his absence," Cameron said in a quiet tone.

"If he didn't trust you, you wouldn't be Alpha," Jasmine countered.

Cameron scoffed. "I'm Alpha because Tyrone didn't want the job and everyone knows that. He would've won the challenge and that's probably the real reason the full-blood backed down."

"Well then, do your job," Jasmine said disliking the whine in his voice. "You have the entire state of West Virginia to clean up. Go meet your pack, introduce your bitch, tell them what plans you have to take this state and them into the next century. Be a good leader to the Pack in his absence and that will send the right message, not issuing orders in his compound. That won't gain you any points with anyone."

"Yes, Mistress. Once again, I apologize and will remember my place. May I be excused?"

Tired of the delay, Jasmine released him. He fell to the ground with a thud. Standing slowly, he turned to face her and bowed from the waist. Lilly came to stand next to him and bowed as well.

"You are both dismissed," she said into the quiet.

"Yes, Mistress," they said as one.

Chapter 7

THEY HAD BEEN AT the drill site for three hours, darkness settled with a swiftness. The extra lighting had been late in arriving slowing them down. Just as Silas decided to drag the wolves away, he heard a soft click and reacted without thought. Jumping up, he pulled the twins with him and within seconds placed an energy shield around them. Looking down he gazed at the swinging arms and legs of Alpha Samuel and the wolves. Turning slightly, he met Asia's sad and resigned gaze. Seeing the defeated look in her eyes ripped through him. He had failed them all. If the ring he wore from Dr. Passen hadn't neutralized whatever hold his enemy had on those wolves, he wouldn't have been distracted. But they had responded when he pulled the wolves of the invisible ones who infiltrated the circle. Even now he was amazed at how many brethren the enemy compromised. His heart ached at the sight of so many weak and sickly wolves.

"Son of a bitch blew the lab," Tyrone said in awe as Silas lowered them to the ground.

"Can you reach Leon?" Tyrese asked testing the ground with his foot as he peered through the dust and rubble toward the large, gaping hole.

Silas didn't answer, instead, he sent waves of inquiry through the debris, searching for his Alpha, and Asia. It troubled him when there were no replies. Inhaling, he clenched and unclenched his fist and did a search again.

"*Samuel? Asia?*" he waited for a sign that they had survived the fall. In his peripheral vision, he saw a group of Samuel's men come closer to the crater-like hole.

"Sir, may we begin a search below?" One of the men asked. When Silas turned, he noticed it was Borian.

"Scan for more bombs first," he said even though Leon's detector had not picked up anything below ground.

Borian nodded. "Yes, Sir. Then we may proceed with the extraction?"

"How will you get down?"

"This part of the ground appears stable." He tapped the ground with his foot. "We'll bring in the cranes and lower a few men down at a time. We had two nearby in case we needed to lift out prisoners."

"What if there are more bombs we can't pick up?" Silas asked.

"Then we all die. But leaving my Alpha below is not an option…Sir."

Silas nodded, glad for Samuel's foresight on having the cranes nearby. It made things easier and they could move quickly. "Okay, sounds good." Besides, he didn't have a better idea or plan. "There is a lot of concrete and steel in the way, you'll have to move some of that as well. Set up the lights so you can see better. Get a couple of dump trucks up here so we don't leave a mess for the humans. Also, get more men up here to help."

Borian nodded, opened his mouth, and then closed it. "Sir?"

"Yes?" Silas looked at the Beta fairly sure he knew what was bothering the man.

"I've been trying to reach my Alpha, but he nor his wolf is answering."

"I know. We'll see what we see when we get down there. First, we have to clear out a path through steel and concrete, so let's get started." He clapped Borian on the shoulder and stepped to the side. *They blew the lab*…that possibility never occurred to him or Jacques. Although it should have. If there was something of value that they couldn't move, it was simpler to destroy it. Silas had to re-evaluate his enemies.

"They're bringing in the cranes," Tyrese said coming to stand next to him. "I'd like permission to go below on the first crane to assess the damage and organize a search team."

Silas gazed around the woods. Tyrese vibrated from the force of his fury which clouded his judgment. "Inhale."

Tyrese's head snapped up from staring at the hole in the ground. Frowning, he took a deep breath, froze, and then turned slowly to his right.

Silas nodded. "We may have a fight up here. I am sending Samuel's men down. You and Rone stand sentry near the cranes, keep them safe."

"Yes, Sir."

"I will be here to assist if necessary." He inhaled again picking up a different scent. A full-blood wolf, but different. This wolf had been in the woods the entire time watching. Silas intended to be free in case the wolf grew tired of sitting on the sidelines.

Rescuing those from below was a slow process. The heavy cranes crashed through the trees and remained a good distance from the fall site. It was a testament to how well Samuel ran this state that no police or news trucks showed up. Once the equipment was in place each crane lowered two men who were packed with first aid equipment and collapsible stretchers. The idea was to have first aid available in case they came across anyone who needed it before they began excavating. The next few drops were filled with laborers to strap the concrete and steel for removal. Two large dump trucks pulled up on the opposite side of the hole just as the first load of concrete was pulled up. Over the next few hours, the laborious process of clearing a path to search for survivors crawled at a tortoise pace. Tempers flared and Silas or one of the twins acted as referee.

"Samuel?"

"Sir?"

Silas exhaled with a sigh of relief. *"Your men are on their way to get you and the others. Start talking to them through your link."*

"Yes...Sir."

"Asia?" Silas called and grew more concerned when there was no response. Not only was there no response, there was nothing from her wolf either.

"I contacted Leon, he's okay. He's looking around. Gotta love technology that keeps a wolf going after a fall like that," Tyrone said walking up to him.

"I'm not getting anything from Asia and she's got more technology than any of them." Silas gazed at the hole wondering if she was hurt or worse. Jasmine would be very upset if Asia died out here.

"Give her some time, she may be in a place where nothing can get in or out," Tyrone said. He turned sideways to Silas and spoke through their link. "*There's five modified breeds in the woods. But there's a strange full blood out there too, just sitting, watching. It's like the breeds don't see him. You think they're together?*"

"No." Silas wasn't sure how he knew that, he just did. The full blood watching them was different from any wolf he had met before and that made things interesting.

"What do the breeds want?"

"I don't know, should I ask them?" Silas asked smiling.

"*Well, that would be nice.*"

Silas slapped him on the shoulder. "*No, it's not time to play yet. We need to get our people out of the ground. If by some miracle there is anything of value left below, we need to excavate it as well.*"

Tyrone nodded and walked off swinging his arms in a circular motion. They were all keyed up and a battle or run through the woods would be just the thing. Unfortunately, they could do neither right now. Silas walked the circumference of the hole still amazed at their tactic. What were they trying to do?

Kill him? Falling twenty, fifty, or hundred feet would not have accomplished that. Stop him from accessing the lab below? What was down there? Equipment? People? He had no idea.

The news that the wolves who had surrounded him just before the explosion were dead hit hard, although he had known that was a strong possibility. Samuel's men who wore the collars were alive and picking their way through the debris while waiting for help to arrive.

"*Silas?*"

He closed his eyes briefly as her voice eased him. "*Sweet Bitch.*"

"*What's wrong?*"

He released a long sigh and told her what happened.

"*Have you scanned for more bombs?*"

"*Yes.*"

"*The twins?*"

"*They're fine, spoiling for a fight, but okay.*" They would've been okay even if they had fallen, but saving them had been a natural reflex. Family. Bit by bit he was becoming more and more a family man.

"Asia?"

He exhaled. *"I have not heard from her or been able to reach her. Tyrone thinks she may have fallen into an area where she cannot receive or send messages."*

"Does that make sense? I mean are there places like that?"

"Well, yes –"

"What if they caught her again and slipped one of the collars on her? She could be lost in plain sight and you wouldn't pick up her signal. Someone needs to go and look for her."

"We are looking for her. We have cranes and are sending teams down right now."

"Yes, I heard that. But...are they looking for her. You said there was some friction in the ranks, they might not care to search for her."

"That's not how it works. She's wolf. We don't leave ours behind. We'll find her."

"Okay. I'm trusting you on this, Silas."

He scanned the horizon, noticed the full blood hadn't moved, and spoke. *"I know. I know. We got our hands full here with the rescue. A few people have been pulled up and sent to the hospital, but it will be a long night. I'll talk to you later when I know more."*

"Okay, I... I love you. Stop beating yourself over this. There's only so much you can do. Jacques and mom are together upstairs, do you need him?"

Silas thought about it for a moment and decided to allow his friend some time alone with his mate. *"Not right now, I'll call him later."*

Turning slightly to his left he disconnected and compelled the breed who was within a hundred feet of the site. Moments later a tall, muscular, blond-haired male was dragged into the clearing fighting every step Silas forced his wolf to take until he came within a few feet. Silas pushed the male to his knees and then looked around the work site.

"Back to work," he said in a raised voice looking at everyone. "We need to start pulling our pack out." He waited until the workers resumed their activity and ordered the twins to be more vigilant in case the breed on his knees had partners.

The male on the ground glared up at him, showing fang. Silas laughed at the pathetic attempt to intimidate him. "What are you doing here?"

The male growled.

Silas searched his limited store of patience and found it was all gone. Within a blink of an eye, he lifted the stupid breed by the neck and tossed him to the other side of the clearing. By the time the fool landed with a loud oomph, Silas stood above him with his foot on his neck. Silas ripped through the Breed's meager mental barriers and searched for clues.

"You're looking for Asia?" he murmured surprised. He had forgotten what she'd told him about the other one Tyrese disposed of. The male nodded through gasps of air.

"Why?" He breached the lowered barriers and found nothing. He lifted the male and shook him. "I asked a question." His incisors lengthened.

The male's eyes widened and he struggled to break free in earnest. "I don't know. I'm just trying to collect the bounty."

"Bounty?" Silas spoke slowly around his crowded teeth.

"Yes. Five million, dead or alive, plus freedom from the Liege."

"Liege?" Silas hadn't heard that name before.

The male bit his lip, holding them tight together. Silas rummaged through his mind, the Liege came up frequently. By the time Silas had taken all the information he needed and uploaded it to Jacques, the male whose name was T-Rex, bled from his nose and ears. Silas crushed his throat, and then ripped his head off before tossing his remains into the dump truck.

"*Jacques?*" he called to make sure everything he had just retrieved from Rex had been received. With the new information on Liege, they had names to target. When he received no response he called again. "*Jacques?*"

Irritated at the delay, Silas called to his mate. *"Jasmine, I called Jacques and he didn't answer. I don't have time for this bullshit. I sent information that needs to be verified and cataloged, now. We're making plans on the run and he's MIA."*

"Everything okay?" Tyrese asked walking up to him, glancing at the dump truck.

"He was here for Asia, there's a large bounty on her head plus freedom."

Tyrese whistled. "How much?"

"Five million, dead or alive. But I think being free from this group is the driving force. Check the woods. I no longer sense the others. There's probably another way inside and they're down below looking for her. His jaw clenched as he called her again. *"Asia. Damn it, you better answer me. They upped the ante on that bounty. Five million, dead or alive... plus freedom from the Liege, whoever that is. Those who were in the woods have left and I think are in the lab looking for you."* He paused and inhaled. *"You do not need to fight this alone, let us help you."*

"She'll never be free, huh?" Tyrese asked quietly. "Like you said, it's not even the money, it's being free that'll keep them coming."

Silas nodded, knowing the cost to keep her safe would be high but he would pay it. "Get down there, find her and watch her back. She's alive, maybe dazed or banged up. Make sure she gets whatever she needs to help her shake these bastards. For some reason, they want her bad enough to wipe out their elites. Make sure they do not get what they want."

Tyrese's eyes glowed briefly as he bulked, turned, and ran toward the hole, and jumped without hesitation.

"*Rese?*" Tyrone asked from across the clearing watching his brother disappear. Silas told him about the bounty as he scanned for more assassins. There were none. The full-blooded wolf remained in the same spot, watching.

Mentally Silas pushed at the wolf. The brush of a large paw hit his chest. Surprised at the strength behind the swipe, Silas gazed into the forest in the direction of the wolf wanting a meeting more than ever.

"Sir," Borian called. "We're pulling up more men, did you want to see them before we send them to the infirmary?"

Normally, Alpha Samuel would commend each wolf harmed in service to the Pack before they left. Now that job fell to Silas. "Yes, I'm coming." He turned in the direction of the full blood and spoke. *"I'll be back."*

"I'll be waiting," the low growling voice said through a new link, surprising Silas further.

Chapter 8

AFTER WORK JASMINE HAD taken a quick stroll through the gym to see the wolves hard at work scrubbing not only the floors but the walls as well. Each stopped and knelt with their forehead on the ground begging her forgiveness. She acknowledged them with a nod and continued her inspection. The gym was the length and width of a professional football field, and this one had three floors. Tired from a long day of reading grants, she left the gym and headed for her wing.

Sensing her mate's distress and his subsequent explanation of the explosion shook her. She linked with him to monitor his stress levels and to be available if he needed her. Silas's demand to deal with Jacques came just after she left the nursery and sat soaking in their Jacuzzi tub. Leaving the warm swirling water to deal with Jacques pissed her off.

When Silas was out on a mission, everyone inside the compound was on call and supposed to be available in case he needed them. Jacques knew this and still hadn't answered Silas's summons. Fuming, she punched in the code to the private elevator at the end of the hall in their wing and rode up in silence.

When the door opened onto Silas' private command center she exhaled to calm her nerves before tapping in another code to gain access.

"One moment Jasmine Knight," the computer said informing her Jacques had put a short delay on the door before it opened. Arms crossed she tapped her foot as she waited. When the door opened, she spoke without walking inside.

"I hope you have a good reason why you didn't answer Silas, Jacques. He's in the field, fighting for all of us, his life and my son's lives are in danger and you aren't responding to his call." She exhaled again fighting fatigue and control of her anger. The last thing she wanted was to shoot unbridled energy into the room with all the computers.

"He had a good reason, dear. Not that it's your business what my mate and I do behind closed doors. But we…my mate and I were… mating," her mom said glibly from the other side of the door.

"What?" Jasmine pushed open the door, not caring that is slammed against the wall. "You waited until now? Now? When Jacques has to be laser-focused on this mission to mate?"

Her mom's brow rose. "I didn't know there was a prescribed time. Tonight seemed right so we did it. What's wrong? You're the one who told me I needed to just go ahead and mate with him. So now you're angry that we did?" She waved Jasmine down. "We were working on it before you knocked.

"Jacques… get out here," Jasmine growled as irritated energy sifted through her.

Her mom jumped up. "Oh hell no he won't. I'm his mate and he's tired. Whatever you want with him will wait until tomorrow. You need to leave." Her mom pointed to the door as if Jasmine had any intention of obeying her.

Instead of snapping at her mom as she wanted, she strove for calm. "I am not dealing with him as your daughter. I am dealing with him as the mate of La Patron. Don't interfere, Mom or I will call his wolf and have him wagging his damn tail in a few minutes."

Victoria narrowed her eyes and stepped closer. "I don't give a damn who you are, that is my mate and I say he stays in bed."

Jasmine bristled as she felt her mom's energy brush against her. What the hell? "Right now my mate and all six of my kids are on the damn line. That trumps you and your damn mate. Test me if you want, but he is coming out here and he *will* do what Silas needs him to do." With that, energy whipped around the room pinning her mom against the wall.

"Jacques come here, now." A few seconds a dark brown wolf the size of a miniature pony trotted toward her, whining and yipping as he looked back at her mom. "She's fine and you know she is." She released her hold on his wolf and watched him morph into a man again.

"My precious," he said going toward Victoria. "Release her," he growled.

Pent-up anger from her day lashed through her at his attitude. First Hank, then Cameron, and now Jacques, oh hell no, she was too tired for this shit.

Jasmine compelled his wolf again and made him crawl forward. "You have forgotten something. I am Silas' mate, equally in charge, equally respected," she snarled. Tired of being disrespected, she leaned forward. "You don't growl at me, ever. As a reminder, I am pulling your voice. From now on, until Silas returns, you will speak in a whisper. Make sure you explain to him why I took your voice when you ask him to return it because that is the only way you'll ever speak normally again."

Jacques lowered his massive head to his paws and whimpered.

"Jasmine, that's…you're allowing this power to go to your head. He didn't mean anything, he was just concerned for me, that's all," her mom said from the back wall.

Without turning, Jasmine raised her finger behind her. "He never would've done that had Silas been here, no matter what. And he knows it. Just so you know, if he messed up this mission by being unavailable for any reason, I will fuck him up worse. You can take that to the bank."

"Jasmine –"

"All due respect, Mom," Jasmine said turning to face the woman with her hand on her hips. "I'll tell you like I told Lilly earlier. There is one Head Bitch in this compound and it's me. People seem to forget that. You don't run anything here, you're my guest. Now you're mated to one of Silas' closest friends and that'll buy you some leverage. But don't ever attempt to tell me how to run my mate's business again. Don't throw your energy at me like that again either. I am working on controlling this power I share with Silas, but I'm not very good yet. I could hurt you. So you need to respect my position or stay out of my way."

Her mom stared at her for a few moments and then nodded. "I can't move. Jacques can't move or shift. He says you are as strong as Silas and that I should listen to you. He is afraid I'll anger you. My own kid, he's afraid my daughter will hurt me." She shook her head. "Okay, you're the Head Bitch. I was out of line and I apologize. My mate tells me he'll teach me protocol and all that stuff before Silas returns. He is afraid your mate will hurt him for growling at you." She eyed Jasmine as if she couldn't believe it.

"Chances are Silas will beat him within an inch of his life. Jacques knows better, and he knows how Silas is."

Her mom's mouth opened and closed.

"Jacques, have you contacted Silas?" Jasmine asked, ignoring her mom's sputtering. Asia was lost. Tyrese was in a jungle of concrete and steel searching for her before the assassins found her. Silas had to stand in for the missing Alpha. And she had to be alert for all the challenges of running this compound tomorrow and her mom wanted to discuss her mate's punishment...now was not the time.

His large head lifted as their gazes connected. "Yes, Mistress. If you permit I would check the computer for his transmission."

She nodded and allowed him to shift.

"Thank you, Mistress and I humbly apologize for my outburst," he whispered. "You are correct. I know better and deserve any punishment La Patron delivers." He bent from the waist and headed toward the bank of computers.

"Can you release me?" her mom asked as Jasmine followed Jacques.

"Yes."

Her mom stepped away from the wall and sat on the nearby chair. "When you said you and Silas were mated, I don't think I fully understood this transference of energy thing. Are all mates like that?"

"We can talk about that later. I need to make sure all of Silas' notes are here." She sat in front of a monitor next to Jacques. "Are you getting anything?" she asked him.

"Not yet, Mistress," he whispered in a raspy voice that would definitely get on her nerves.

"Can't he just send it again?" her mom asked from across the room.

Jasmine glared at Jacques.

"No precious, the source of his information is...gone. He sent it straight from that source," Jacques said softly without looking at Victoria.

"Well, there is not much you can do, is there?"

Jasmine gritted her teeth at her mom's questions.

"Please, Mistress," Jacques whispered. "We are newly mated and feeling the pull. That is all. Let me respond to her."

Remembering the time she and Silas remained locked together during their mating, she nodded. The timing was terrible, but there was nothing to be gained by wishing otherwise.

"I am trying a few more avenues to get the download, shouldn't be much longer, sweetheart."

Jasmine rolled her eyes at their sugary talk. Squinting, she pointed at some scrolling text across the monitor. "Is that it?" Excitement laced her voice. Silas had been certain this information would help their cause and she intended to make sure it reached them uncorrupted.

"Yes, Mistress. I need to run it through a few programs for verification and then bugs, should take another ten to fifteen minutes... I can call you when it's uploaded."

She looked up at his hope-filled expression and then at her mom half sitting on the sofa with a silly grin. She prayed for patience. "Let me ask Silas if I need to verify this tonight or if it can wait till morning."

"Yes. Thank you." The raspiness in his tone scraped against her nerves. She was tempted to restore his voice, but refrained.

"Silas?"

"Busy here, Sweetness."

She exhaled and asked him about the transmission.

"Verify it tonight."

"Why? Can it be fixed tonight if there is a problem?"

There was silence for a few seconds. *"Why did you ask if you have no intention of doing as I requested? I am busy dealing with over thirty dead wolves, I need you to handle that for me and find out as much as possible about the group. Can you do that?"* The bite in his voice pissed her off.

Closing her eyes, she counted to five; reminding herself he was under stress and that although she had the challenges of running the compound, dealing with four active babies and her mom all day, her life had not been in any real danger.

"*Yes, Silas. I will do that. Be careful, love,*" she said softly, sending waves of love through their link.

"*Good.*" He disconnected.

Exhaling at his abruptness, she stared at the monitor for a few minutes. "Is this the only place I can verify the upload?" she asked knowing the answer. Silas had been fanatical regarding security for the computer system.

"Yes, Mistress," Jacques whispered sounding resigned. She didn't doubt Silas had given him a blistering earful as well.

"Mom, we have to finish this, shouldn't be long. Can you get us something to drink?" She asked without looking at either her mom or Jacques. The situation couldn't be helped. Whatever Silas sent to them took precedence over everything, including getting her rest.

"Sure. What do you want?"

Pleased her mom didn't sound angry she relaxed in her chair, watching the monitor. "A bottle of water please."

"Me too, love," Jacques said while tapping the keys and watching the monitor.

Ten minutes later Jasmine and Jacques watched in amazement as information from several assassinations and bombings filled the screen.

"*Who or What's the Liege?*" she asked through Silas' link to Jacques.

He shook his head. "*I do not know. Never saw this before. Asia nor Leon had the name in their memories.*"

She looked at the pieces of information impressed with how quickly Jacques made sense of some of the disjointed comments. "Hell, our dance card is full of enemies trying to annihilate us, thank you very much," she huffed at the idea that someone new gunned for them.

Jacques smiled. "Not necessarily. Remember both of their last missions involved coming close to La Patron. It's possible certain memories were scrubbed before they were allowed to leave their base. It's what I would have done with the equipment they have."

She nodded, frowning. "But a Liege is an old-time Lord or something, right?"

"Yes, but remember this has been going on a long time."

"You think there's one person behind this and he's older than

Silas?" The idea of old men running around ruling the world sent chills down her back.

"Could be, Mistress. I honestly don't know. But I will begin researching the information immediately. La Patron was correct in insisting we jump on this right away, some of it is fresh and may lead us to whoever is pulling the strings."

"Liege?" she asked, turning the name over on her tongue.

"Perhaps."

Chapter 9

STRUGGLING TO BREATHE, ASIA lay entombed beneath the dirt, concrete, and twisted steel. She had no idea of her injuries, all feelings were suspended. Lightheaded, she felt as if she were floating on a steady sea moving forward into nothingness. Death appeared peaceful and restful even. For the first time in years, her mind quieted. Her wolf whined softly and then joined her in their rest. Darkness loomed before her and she welcomed it. Light brought pain and disillusionment; perhaps the dark had the answers to her questions. She blinked a few times until all thought stopped and the darkness was complete.

Asia's eyes flew open as a sharp, slow grinding pain wracked her body from head to foot. How long she'd been trapped below the mound of rubble she had no idea, but the liquid fire coursing through her frame squelched her former thoughts of death. Unfortunately, she was painfully still among the living. Shudders ripped through her repeatedly. Silent screams echoed in her head as unspeakable shards of pain pierced her mind, causing her to run into the dark for solace.

Drifting in and out of sleep, Asia heard voices. Nearby scraping sounds woke her. How long had she been out?

"The last transmission they received was somewhere down here and then it whisked out. They want us to dig her out to be sure she's dead," a male voice said.

Asia tried to focus as parts of a conversation filtered through to her. She tried to swallow and couldn't. The mind-bending pain tapered off to a dull throb which she could handle. Help was near and she needed assistance. As more of the conversation filtered down, she realized they were not the help she needed in her weakened condition.

"I thought that meant death. When we no longer transmit that's how they know we're dead, right?" A different voice, female spoke this time.

How many were up there? Asia wondered, listening carefully.

"That's what we've always been told, but they want proof she's dead, and for five mill and the chance to be free to live a life, I'll dig her ass out and put it on a platter," the male said and then made a rude sound, like a snort.

"Yeah, good point. There's not much room around here to move stuff around, we're going to have to stack the concrete over there and just move the steel to the side."

"There's more dirt here than anything. She can't breathe if she's in there anyway."

"Freedom and five million says prove it," the female said laughing. Asia tried to place the voice and could not identify it.

"*Tyrese?*"

"*Sir?*" she called La Patron through their link. Nothing. No static. No sounds. No response.

Panic welled inside as she called Dr. Passen, Jacques, and then Matt. Her links were broken. She was truly alone and as much as she had always dreamed of it, right now with hunters digging her out, it sucked.

"*Mistress I am so sorry I failed you...*" she sighed as thoughts of her last conversation with Jasmine filtered through her mind.

"*Asia, oh my God. I was so worried. Silas and Rese are searching everywhere for you. Where are you? First, how are you? Are you hurt? Do you need medical help? Thank you, God, for answering my prayers.*"

"*Mistress?*" she asked, afraid she had entered the land of delusions. They had never spoken through a link before that she recalled. She held her breath waiting for confirmation that she had indeed spoken to the one person who might grieve her passing.

"Yes, this is Jasmine. Are you hurt? Is that why you haven't answered Silas or Rese?"

"Oh Mistress," she cried, overwhelmed to hear her voice. "My links are broken. I called out to La Patron and everyone else. No one answered. Thank you for speaking to me."

"I heard that silly apology you made. You didn't fail me or anyone by the way. Those assholes blew a section of the lab and you fell below. Are you buried?"

"Yes. I thought I had died, but the Goddess has other plans it seems."

"I am very happy she does."

The genuine gratitude in the Mistress' voice brought water to her eyes. "Thank you, I needed to hear that."

"We all care deeply for you, Asia. As my mate says, you're Pack which means you're family. No one is leaving that area without you. So tell me anything and I'll relate to Silas and we'll get you out of there."

Inside, her entire being warmed as if she were reborn at this moment. Pack. That word had never meant much to her before, but when you slide into death and walk out on the other side it takes on a new meaning.

Shame welled up over her previous plans to run away. She confessed. "I am... was...angry at La Patron for promising me freedom and then snatching it away. I asked myself how is he any different than the others. I planned to grab a box from here with the only clues of my previous life and leave. My return to the compound would have been delayed."

After a short silence, Jasmine spoke. "What did you plan to do once you had the box?"

"There are some locations I wanted to check to see if there were scraps of information that would help me discover more about my past. And lay on the beach for a few hours drinking a margarita. That is something I always wanted to do."

"Sounds like a good plan to me. You said was, what happened and how did Silas snatch away your freedom?"

The scraping sound continued above but sounded distant. More importantly, she needed Mistress to see her clearly, to know her true motives. This time she would prove her gratitude in more than empty words, she would be open and above board.

"You bonded me to you and you have saved me repeatedly. In my desire to be free I failed to see the gift I was given. In what is truly my darkest moment you are the light, the link to life. Earlier I welcomed death with open arms. It was better than being buried alive."

"No. No, stop talking like that."

Asia chuckled, feeling curiously lighter as the truth rose from the murky depths of despair. *"It seems I have mechanisms that defy the odds."*

"Good... when did I bond with you?"

It never occurred to Asia that the bonding was accidental. Her shame intensified. *"The last time we talked."*

"I don't remember any bonding, I remember being upset over the way you discounted your life...but... nothing like a bonding."

"You grabbed my arm tight and made me promise to return. You said I could die, but not cease to live," she said slowly as the words clicked into place. She had died. Had her vow caused her body to regenerate?

"That's bonding?"

Asia shook her head wondering what all of this meant. *"Your fingerprints became a tattoo on my arm. The vow I made to you became my focus, trumping plans I had been making for years and I hated that. I wanted to be free, but..."*

"Asia I am so sorry. I didn't mean to do that to you. I want you to be free. To fall in love and have babies I can bounce on my knee. Whatever happened to bond us wasn't Silas, it was me. I'm still trying to gain control over this power. I will reverse it and free you, don't worry."

"No." She smiled as the reality of what happened flowed through her.

"No?"

"You are the only person I can communicate with."

"Yes, but I'm sure we can fix that."

"You don't understand. I'm doing a bad job explaining. One second let me think."

"Do you have time? I mean you've been under there for a while."

"Yes...yes I have. I heard two voices earlier. I think they're bounty hunters trying to dig me out."

"What? Why didn't you... hold on. I need to tell Silas. I am going to be pissed if they pull you out and start some bullshit after everything you've been through."

Asia smiled at Jasmine's rant...she tasted her Mistress's name on her tongue. It felt right to call her that in her private thoughts. Something major happened and she needed to understand a semblance of what it was so she could explain.

One thing she knew with certainty was that she died, which must have broken all of her links minus the one that she made a vow to live. The bounty hunters said something about a transmission winking out which signified death.

Euphoria bubbled from within her. Somehow death had destroyed her former employer's final link to her. Idly she wondered what it was, the metal they used in her arm and legs? Possibly. She wiggled both her toes and fingers, happy to feel the dirt beneath them.

"Okay, Tyrese is looking for two people digging, when he clears the way, we'll figure out a way for you to direct him where you are."

"Okay."

"Continue," Jasmine said.

Asia thought hard over what she was about to say, it sounded weird and given her career or body chemistry that was saying a lot. *"I died which canceled everything, including the last link they had to me."*

"Oh my God, thank you, thank you. Not that you had to die, but in this case dying worked in your favor. I'm just happy you're free from those bitches."

Asia laughed. It hurt. Her mouth could only move a few inches, but the genuine joy in Jasmine's voice over her good fortune made the discomfort worth it.

"Yes. I am. They are digging me out to prove I am dead, from what I gather that is not the norm. I am supposed to be dead." She paused. *"But I'm not."* Maybe it was more than her vow to Jasmine. Had they done more experiments on her during that last surgery? She had no idea.

"Hmmm... sounds like they knew there was a chance this might happen, that's why they want your body. Silas said you're the prototype for a lot of their inventions."

"Yes. They will never stop looking for me until they have my body." Life on the run, looking over her shoulder loomed big on the horizon.

"I don't mean to sound spooky, but you've been buried underground for five hours with no water or air. You should be dead or close to it. Not alert and rethinking your life. Whatever they did to you is cutting edge and worth billions. It's no wonder they want your body so they can replicate or even jump-start you again."

Stunned, Asia realized Jasmine was right. Remembering the excruciating pain earlier, she shuddered. Had her body regenerated on its own after she entered the darkness? Was that even possible? Had she actually died, died? Or did her body go into some kind of mechanical stasis?

"You are probably right. Although I have no real idea what happened, it is a mystery to me and something I never want to repeat. The good news is they cannot locate me like before. All ties to their money maker have been broken by a flaw in their design. I can move freely, see, hear and think without them in my mind. It was a glorious death, Mistress," she said with feeling.

Jasmine laughed.

Asia stiffened as she heard the sounds of footsteps. *"Someone is here."*

"Okay," Jasmine said.

"Who are you?" the male voice asked. His voice sounded further away this time.

"Are you new?" the female voice asked.

"I'm the one who's going to stop you from digging." Asia closed her eyes at the certainty in Tyrese's voice. He had never been diplomatic and in this instance she was glad.

"Tyrese is here."

"Good, I'll let him know you are still buried so he'll hurry up."

Lying still, Asia wished she could see what was happening. There was a slight tingling in her forehead. Seconds later her vision darkened and then she saw outlines of three people, not clearly. But the shape standing alone was Tyrese. She hoped he remembered her warning about the primp, although the tight quarters made firing the weapon unlikely.

"Really? Stop us from digging, why?" the male asked, stepping to the side while the female moved a few steps in the other direction. If Tyrese hadn't spent hours tag team fighting with his twin she might be worried he didn't recognize the common maneuver. They planned to jump him.

The images sharpened a bit. She could not make out features, but the body outlines had more depth now kind of like night vision goggles. Excited by this new development she wondered what other changes occurred when her body re-booted. Her hearing was sharper. She moved slightly to the right. Debris fell as her movement unsettled the mound on top of her. She had just alerted her enemies that she was alive.

She sighed at her stupidity when she noticed all three heads turn in her direction. Chances are she could free herself now but she didn't want anyone to see her new form whatever that was. She was counting on Tyrese winning this fight so she could escape undetected. A weak groan escaped her throat. Every area of the lab had cameras; if the janitor's closet was still standing, the cameras would pick her up as she went inside.

Sounds of body-slamming grabbed her attention. The fight heated up. Tyrese hadn't bulked yet, but he was a shadowy blur in a small space. The two hunters were good, but no match for his speed. After slamming the male into a far wall with a loud crunch, the female picked up a primp and tried to aim it at Tyrese.

Asia could not believe how fast he moved. The female pulled the trigger and hit her partner. Blood and body mass mixed with debris flew everywhere. The loud clap ricocheted and before the sound stopped reverberating, Tyrese had decapitated the female and tossed her body to the side. After taking two steps he bent from the waist, breathing. She hoped he wasn't hurt.

Just as she thought to test her theory of escaping her grave, he stood and walked toward the mound. "Mom says you can hear. You shook the ground a minute ago. Give me an idea where to dig and I'll have you out in a few minutes."

Sweeter words had never been spoken. Moving to the left and then right, she hoped he could get an idea where she was located as the dirt moved.

"Okay, you're in the far corner. Assholes were digging over here." He strode to an area she assumed was near her. She moved again for good measure.

"I got it. Lots of concrete and some steel. Give me a sec." The ground pressed in a bit as he bulked up and she wanted to tell him to move back. But a few seconds later the weight on her legs and stomach lessened as he tossed blocks of cement off her like a plastic ball. Sounds of running feet chilled her. Had more assassins been alerted? Clenching her fist she prepared to break through the debris and join Tyrese in the fight this time.

"You found anything?" Tyrese asked in a gravelly voice that he rarely used in this form.

"Yes, some equipment. It looks old," Alpha Samuel said. "You found her?"

"Yes, she's buried here." He continued removing rubble.

"The whole time? I mean is she… alive?"

"Yes. Did you have your men disable all the cameras and do a sweep for more?" Tyrese asked as the weight from the debris lightened considerably from her upper body.

Pleased that Tyrese remembered their enemies used cameras extensively, she sighed in relief.

"Yes, we disabled and pulled out a couple from the walls we found using your equipment. There are a handful of people, wolves, who were born and raised here. They don't know anything else and are afraid to leave. La Patron said we can leave them here if they don't want to go."

"You don't agree?" Tyrese asked stopping. Because of her interest in the Alpha's answer, she didn't mind the delay.

"On the one hand, I feel I've done enough damage through sheer ignorance and should leave them alone. On the other I want them to learn what Pack means, to experience the warmth and love of a den. They have no idea what being a wolf means. It's not something to be embarrassed about but they're ashamed and that hurts on a level I cannot explain. They're wolves, ours to protect. They were born here during my time as Alpha and I failed them. I had no idea this place operated in my backyard. It's a damn breeding farm where they experimented for years on my pack. They violated my den and stole pack members."

"You can't undo the past, Samuel," Tyrese said in a somber tone.

"I know, I just want a chance to make up for it. I want to make their futures better in some way, you know what I mean?"

"Yes," she whispered.

"Yeah, I do," Tyrese said and then resumed removing the debris from on top of her.

"Need help?" Samuel asked.

"Nah, bout done. Everyone out?"

"We took care of two hunters and Leon handled one. I'd only sensed five before, but heard La Patron took one out so maybe there were six."

"All your men accounted for?"

"Those who made it. I lost two. They didn't have collars and were crushed."

"Sorry man."

"I'm going to talk to the residents again, see if I can change their minds."

"Have Rone talk to them. No telling what they've seen over the years. Might be insightful."

"Tyrone?"

"He has a magic tongue when it comes to talking with people. He's the only one La Patron uses for interrogation." Tyrese chuckled and Asia agreed. Tyrone had a gift for making you feel comfortable and spilling secrets before you could blink.

"Really? I might do that." Samuel paused. "What does he use you for?"

"Exterminations," Tyrese said succinctly.

Asia agreed as she heard the footsteps leave.

Tyrese stepped back. "You can come out now."

Anxious over her new body, she didn't bother to wonder how he knew she could get out. She threw both hands up and pushed. It moved some. She thought of bench pressing and pushed harder this time. A grinding sound and then a loud swoosh accompanied the falling rubble. Clouds of dust floated above her head, filling her nostrils. She sneezed as she pushed herself up.

"Give me your hand." She saw his arm through the haze and latched on.

"You gain weight or something? Hold on I need to get a little more bulk."

Tyrese had no tact.

She felt the same as she had before regenerating and refused to be embarrassed by his outburst. Looking down, she tried to see her body clearly but couldn't. Dirt clung to her in places she knew would itch later, which meant she was half-naked.

"Okay now." His arm seemed wider when she latched on. This time he pulled her up with ease and helped her off the rocky mound that had been her temporary burial ground.

When he released her, she stumbled. He grabbed her again but remained silent as she took a few steps on shaky legs. As her legs strengthened, instinctively she leaned forward and picked up a large boulder in each hand and completed bicep curls until she no longer felt the weight of the stones. Tossing them aside, she picked up a large slab of concrete with embedded twisted metal. It took a few tries, but eventually, her body could handle the weight and stress.

When she finished, she turned to find him leaning against a far wall watching her. "What?" she asked, embarrassed by him seeing her in a weakened condition.

"Nothing, just watched as your body morphed into a sexy, lean, lethal woman."

Confused, she placed her hand on her hip. "What are you talking about?"

"When I pulled you out, you weren't shaped. Well, not like now. I've never seen anyone's body change so quickly as if there was an internal mold. Has this happened before? You went right into shaping up."

She frowned looking down. "I don't know. Could have. I didn't think I just acted. Now that you mention it, not many people step from their graves and start lifting concrete instead of weights."

He nodded. "Your face was larger, your body lacked that kind of definition, and your hair well, it's still all over the place."

Her hand flew up touching the thick, wiry ringlets of her natural hair. She looked down at her form. There was a little more meat on her body, but that didn't faze her. Her muscular body wasn't over the top.

"Okay...so what are you saying?" She asked as she looked around for something to put on and saw the female hunter on the ground with her neck at an odd angle. Spying a larger backpack near the corner, Asia dug into it and pulled out a beige jumpsuit and soft-soled canvas slip-ons. She put them on and turned to face him again, feeling more in control.

"You changed. What happened while you were buried?" he crossed his arms staring at her. There was something in the tone of his voice that alerted her she needed to be straight with him. They were cool, but if he thought for one moment she was a threat to his pack, he would attempt to terminate her immediately and deal with the fallout later.

"I died."

His eyes widened as he stood straighter. "You did? Is that what happened to our link?"

She nodded, telling him an edited version of what she told his mother while searching through both backpacks. Each had those calculators, this time she put one in a pocket as well as the ink pen and a few other items she recognized.

"So who are you now?"

"I'm Asia. Just free of my oppressors and linked to one person who has my total allegiance." She stood to face him wondering what he would think of her declaration. Jasmine didn't want anyone tethered to her in that way. And she did not particularly want to be connected to anyone at such a deep level, but this was her new reality. Thank the Goddess it could have been worse.

He stared at her for a few moments and then grinned. "I wonder if she told Silas yet? We have all been worried over her obsession with you. Are you like my sister now or something?"

Asia relaxed a bit. "Sister? No. I hope not. But we have more in common now. We have to help Mistress control her energy as she steps fully into her role as La Patroness." She stopped at Tyrese's surprised expression.

"Can I be in the room when you call her that?" Tyrese asked as they stepped into the hall.

"Call her what?" Asia asked stepping aside and then heading in the direction of the janitor's closet.

"La Patroness."

Chapter 10

SILAS WATCHED THE LAST EMT truck leave the clearing beneath the bright spotlights that were hauled in to assist in the recovery and exhaled. The cost of this battle had been high. He needed to run…or fight. Gazing in the direction of the woods, he sensed the black wolf remained in the same spot he had been hours ago.

Tyrone and Samuel were below with the residents. Silas hoped they agreed to leave with Samuel but he did not have it in him to compel their wolves or force them to leave. If they chose to die here, he would honor their decision. The dump trucks filled in the hole with soil and leveled the land as much as possible. Soon a tree would be planted in honor of the Pack members who lost their lives today.

When Jasmine contacted him over Asia's situation he had been both surprised and pleased. Somehow this Liege group tapped into technology that regenerated body parts. Cheating death was a definite game-changer. Small countries could flex their muscles if they had the funds to outfit half an army. Asia was a walking advertisement that the mechanisms worked.

He would have Jacques check on the legality of Asia's situation. But when there was enough money on the table human authorities had no problems looking the other way, especially when the test subjects were full-blood wolves with little interaction with human doctors or hospitals. The injection Tyrese received that altered his body chemistry must have been the tip of the iceberg in their research. The collars that saved the lives of many wolves today altered their body chemistry temporarily, but gave similar results as the vaccine Tyrese received. An army would have more control over their troops with the collars than the shots. Silas shook his head at the scope of what his enemies had done.

"I need to sit down for a bit, heading to the woods, be back in a few," Silas told the twins through their link.

"Yes Sir, have fun," Tyrone said. *"Not much here, their memories have been wiped."* He spoke of the residents.

"Okay. Help Samuel any way you can." He disconnected from Tyrone and contacted Tyrese.

"Yes, Sir," Tyrese answered a few moments later. *"We're heading to a different section of the lab, this part wasn't damaged. I had to get the scanning equipment before we go any further. I'll keep you informed."*

"Do that, Rese."

Silas stepped in the direction of the forest and waved back a small security detail. "I need a few minutes alone. I'll be back in a bit."

The two men looked doubtful as they looked at the darkened woods and then back at him. "Yes, Sir," one spoke as they both returned to the perimeter of the hole.

Like a homing pigeon, Silas headed straight toward the pony-sized black wolf. The moment he entered the small area where the wolf had sat all day, the wolf moved with lightning speed slamming into him and knocking the air from his lungs.

Silas slid a few feet on the ground before he jumped up changing mid-air into his wolf and landed on the back of his attacker. The black wolf shook him off, but not before Silas nipped his ear. Adrenaline pumped through him like a drug. Teeth bared Silas attacked his opponent with blinding ferocity. He slammed into the large wolf knocking him back a few feet and then leaped again. The wolf pivoted and Silas slid past his challenger. Both recovered fast and charged each other again.

Anger over everything that had happened since he discovered

half-breeds in his backyard surged through him. On hind legs, the two combatants twisted and turned their bodies searching for an opening that would destroy the other. Silas pushed his adversary back a few steps. The black wolf moved a few inches before snapping foot-long fangs at Silas' neck.

Silas ducked and pushed his nemesis, tripping him. Springing forward to pin the wolf, the challenger hulked into their hybrid fighting mode and swung his massive paw at Silas knocking him back a few feet. Before the dust cleared, Silas had morphed as well, leaping toward the wolf catching him in the chest, and digging his teeth deep. A loud howl echoed through the trees and then blow after blow from the huge paw and claws hit his head sending rivulets of blood down his face.

Silas dug his claws into the softer underbelly of his opponent. Determined to win the challenge, but not kill his opponent, he dug his teeth in deeper. Razor-sharp claws pierced his back and his side trying to dislodge him. After a few minutes, the blows to his head seemed lighter, or either he was becoming lightheaded, he was not sure which. But he refused to let go.

As his world dimmed, a stream of energy flowed through him. He exhaled as every cell in his body reenergized, pumping him up. *Goddess, I love my mate.* He pulled out one hand from his opponent's body ripping out muscle, tissue, and skin.

"Argh…" his opponent yelled as Silas drew back and punched the bloody area. His fangs remained locked in the upper chest of his enemy while he dug his claws into the sides and drug them forward tearing through skin and flesh. When his opponent pushed at his shoulders, Silas shook him off.

"It's good. We're done. You are who I suspected, but I needed to be sure. Let me go so we can talk." The wolf spoke through the same link he had earlier, once again surprising Silas. The voice held confidence, the connection tight.

More animal than human, Silas didn't immediately understand what was said. Locked into his enemy Silas refused to give way.

"Stop damn it. You cannot kill me, just as I cannot kill you. I am healing already except where your teeth are lodged in my chest." He paused and spoke slowly in a gruff tone. *"Just as your head has healed. Stop this, I have waited all day to talk to you."*

The cessation of movement allowed his wolf to ease down long enough for Silas to weigh the words. After a quick mental assessment, he realized he was no longer bleeding. He exhaled and eyed his opponent's upraised hands. Pissed, he snatched back in a zig-zag motion ripping flesh and skin.

"Owww, asshole. That hurts. *You did not need to take an extra pound of flesh, you already did that.*" His opponent stepped back and returned to his wolf.

Silas wondered if his challenger ever shifted to human. "You attacked me for no reason other than it is night-time and I'm the asshole?" He flowed from his hybrid form to his wolf. Allowed his body to completely heal and a few moments later returned to human.

"You kept me waiting and I needed to be sure you were worthy as pack leader."

Silas hackles rose at the nonchalant tone. "Fuck you." When you lost pack members it was not a good day for bullshit.

"No thanks... you're mated. And to a strong bitch, I sensed her earlier when she surged through you, that's also good."

"Who the fuck are you and what do you know about me or my mate?" Silas stepped toward the black wolf as his anger spiked.

"I have been called many things, but my name is Angus. And that was a compliment regarding your bitch. Most of us never find our mate during our lifetime. May your den always be full of healthy pups."

Silas weighed the words for their sincerity, sensing there was no guile he nodded. "Why did you say I cannot kill you? What is special about you?"

"I also said I cannot kill you. For some reason, we cannot exterminate one another; it has always been that way. There are times when it is inconvenient and other times, like now, I am happy it is a reality. I am not ready to meet the Goddess on the final plane and I suspect you would send me to the other side in a heartbeat."

Silas agreed silently. "You have been waiting for me, I'm here. What do you want?"

"I am a full-blooded black wolf just as you. There is only a handful of us left scattered about the world. I wanted to meet you. Word of your wisdom and exploits traveled on the wings of the wind and I was sent to see the truth of the matter for myself."

"So you were lying when you said you had to see if I were worthy?"

"Not lying, I needed to test you for myself." The wolf lay his head on his paws as if resting.

Silas ground his teeth forcing calm and then crossed his arms over his chest. Jasmine taunted him often for taking an hour to say a minute's worth of information. First chance he got, he would apologize and work like hell to rid himself of the irritating habit. "Someone sent you to sit in the woods and watch my pack die?" he asked deliberately twisting words to make a point.

"Yes. To watch, observe and not interfere. We wanted to see how you reacted in any type of catastrophe and today certainly qualified."

Ignoring the pity in the voice, Silas searched the woods for more strangers. "We? Who are we?"

"Your pack is under attack, which means all wolves are under attack. We do not understand why they chose you. You are formidable in your own right. Over two hundred years ago you fought and built order out of chaos in this raw new world. You developed an intricate Pack structure. That was no easy feat. Fifty personally trained Alphas leading each state with several highly trained betas to back them up. Your wolves own thriving businesses, live in healthy communities with the best schools and a few private colleges."

"We have had our problems, not all wolves want to live civilized."

"There will always be rebels. It is the nature of the living. What you have accomplished in this country is quite impressive."

Unsurprised that he had been investigated, Silas peered at the intruder wondering when he would get to the point of this impromptu visit. The rest of the stuff Angus tossed out was bullshit fertilizer. "My pack is under attack…so far you have not said anything I don't know. I hope you did not travel from… where are you from? You never said who sent you, or where they are?"

"I'm from Plias. You don't know where it is since it is the original title of a place that man has changed its name many times. We are on the African continent. And we are the clan of Black Wolf. I thought that would be obvious… perhaps I should reassess the wisdom comment," he murmured.

Unprepared for the answer he received, Silas parried. "Wolves don't have clans."

"Clan, family, tribe. The labels change, but they all mean the same thing. A group with common interests and goals who are related by blood. Before other names arrived, we called ourselves clan and still do."

Silas had no logical rebuttal and refrained from commenting further. "You are here... why?" He turned to face the pony-sized wolf and met an emerald green gaze similar to his own. During the first one hundred years of his life, he searched for a Pack resembling him and never met any. A few times through the centuries, he thought he caught flashes of one but was never certain. Once the Goddess chose him to lead the new emerging nation his focus changed. He had been commanded to create a large Pack for the country. It was a daunting task and he never gave them much thought again.

"To get an idea the way the wind of this war is flowing. It has not touched down on the main continent yet, but if it is successful here it is only a matter of time before it does."

"So you came to see if I was getting my ass kicked." Silas chuckled and opened his link so Jasmine could listen in on the conversation directly. The manner she added her strength to his earlier said she was concerned, not worried. But weariness weighed on him and it would be easier for her to hear everything now than a lengthy re-cap later.

"Not precisely. We also wished to see the warrior bitch in action. There is a lot of talk about her in some circles."

Anger and concern over Asia's future ripped through him, followed by a jolt of awareness from Jasmine. "She is Pack. A highly regarded member of my pack."

"She has been altered, is no longer wolf."

Silas bristled. "She is wolf and she is Pack." He sensed his mate's agreement.

"To create one as special as she, they must start with a wolf and add to their limbs. But not just any wolf. Hundreds of our brethren have died in their experiments. But not her." He paused.

"Is she of our breed?"

Asia was a dark-skinned female just as his mate, but that did not mean either of them had a black wolf in their family tree. The coat of a wolf had little to do with race.

"I don't know. I don't care. She is Pack and that is enough for me. No one touches her without her permission." Pointing at his unwanted guest, he snarled the last of it to drive home his point.

Angus appeared unmoved. "There is a reason she was chosen. Something about her is special. I would talk with her."

Silas had no real control over who Asia talked to. If Angus dangled tidbits of "I might know something of your history, she would run across the clearing to hear whatever he had to say. "I will tell her that. But it is her choice." He thought for a moment. "And do not compel her wolf, either."

The wolf's mouth opened wide and then snapped close a few times. "I have manners and that is rude. I have a few questions to ask and would appreciate any time she allowed." He paused. "The collars around the necks of the wolves, what are they? Were they the reason some were injured instead of dying in that fall?"

Silas simply stared. "What makes you think I am going to tell you anything? Because your wolf is the same color as mine?" he scoffed and turned to leave. He had spent enough time talking and getting the runaround. He would go below and join the search.

"Yes. That and you know we are kin. Or have you walked so long amongst humans your wolf no longer recognizes Pack? Blood pack?"

"My pack has been with me for the past two hundred years, my wolf recognizes them just fine." He kept walking.

"So you do not want to know who you are? Where you came from? Your heritage that you will pass to your pups one day? You are not interested in anything I have to say?"

Silas stopped and looked over his shoulder as a thought occurred to him. "Did you rape a twelve-year-old girl in Virginia when the colonies were new?"

"What?"

Silas turned and crossed his arms. "I do not remember the name of the town or the girl's name, but her friend saw a black wolf with green eyes. She said he raped her best friend. It was not me. I was not on the eastern shore during that time. Were you here?"

"I have never raped a child. If I had sex with her, she was mature." He sounded offended.

"Meaning she was old enough to have a child. I think the young girl was pregnant and died," Silas said trying to remember the particulars.

"During the formation of this country we roamed more frequently until our Alpha was murdered. Understand this; Alpha was an unbeatable fighter who had destroyed every challenger during his one hundred years as our leader. He was respected and feared everywhere. We enjoyed a time of peace with no threats against our border. So when he was murdered no one could explain his death. It was a mystery that set things in a motion that are still spinning." The cautious manner in which he spoke arrested Silas' attention. An icy chill raced down his spine.

"*Ask him about the breeders,*" Jasmine said.

"What kind of things?" Silas asked.

"We can share information," Angus said raising his large head from his paws as he stared at Silas. "Everything I tell you will be the truth as I know it. I expect the same from you."

"*Silas we need to know more about your past. It might have something to do with what is going on now,*" his mate urged when he hesitated.

"Okay, I'll share information and speak truthfully." Silas returned to the small area and sat on the ground near the wolf. "What kinds of things?" he asked again leaning against a tree trunk.

"There are many theories why our Alpha went into the small village that night. Some say he was obsessed with a young girl there. Others say a witch bespelled him. The speculation goes on and on. The truth of his motives died with him that night. The next day two women saw him lying on the side of the road and thought he was a mere human. They took him home to nurse him to health."

Silas's head snapped up. "Nurse a dead man?"

"Yes. Supposedly they did not know he was dead. Remember this was during a time where they believed a body could still be raised within three days."

Silas nodded. The first settlers had been religious zealots. He could see them telling the dead Alpha to take his bed and walk.

"They worked on him for two days and the third day his body was missing."

"Missing?" He asked to be sure he heard correctly.

"Yes. And one of the women gave birth nine months later to a son. Supposedly she had been a virgin. Sound familiar?" Angus asked.

"Oh hell." Silas chuckled.

Jasmine laughed.

"Chances are she had a lover and used our Alpha as an excuse to cover her condition. The story goes she told everyone Alpha had married her and the other woman served as a witness. That way she was not stoned or made an outcast for fornication. For the next three years, she gave birth to a son almost to the birth date of the first son."

Silas frowned at the added complication. "That changes things, takes it from a prank to reality. Someone had to make her pregnant."

"Yes, that's true. After the first son, the town's people were leery. But when she was pregnant with the second child they accused her of immoral behavior and threatened to run her out of town. When the second son was born, he looked exactly the same as the first. Since the hypocrites had already accepted the first son, they would not refuse his twin."

Silas remembered those dark times with little affection. It had been hard for him and anyone with a dual nature. Even though the early settlers came to the new world to escape religious persecution, they were intolerant of anything different.

"When her second son was one month, they made her move in a cottage that was in the middle of the square so they could watch her closely. Each day someone from the village stayed in her home under the guise of assisting with the babes. One night the woman from the village woke and met a handsome man inside the home sitting on the floor playing with the babes. The mother was asleep. Nine months later, both women gave birth to sons and were ran out of town."

"That sounds like a fairy tale," Jasmine said.

"Okay, so the Alpha was a ghost who impregnated women, and that started things in motion?" Silas asked not understanding where the story was going.

"Alpha impregnated human women."

Silas stilled as the ramifications slammed into him.

"Oh shit," Jasmine whispered.

"They say he came back once a year to talk to his sons and procreate with any female he could. It was always the same night, in the same area. It did not matter if the female was willing or not. If she was old enough to breed, she was a candidate."

"That's terrible and twisted," Jasmine said.

"It's a possible explanation how this got started. What surprises me is that it was going on during the same time period I have Jacques researching."

"And it came through your line."

"What?" He did not want to think of the ramifications of that.

"This whole human breeding thing started from the Black Wolf clan. Your original clan. Your roots. Your—"

"Okay, okay, I get it. But to believe that you have to believe the Alpha rose from the dead."

"Says the man who is a walking, talking wolf. Talk about weird stuff." She chuckled.

Silas was not amused.

"Hey, you believe in spiritual things like the Goddess, how much of a jump is this? Then again, maybe he wasn't fully dead," she said.

"Then why did he appear once a year?" He countered.

"Menopausal? Weird? Polygamist? I don't know. But the time is about right, according to Griggs anyway."

"What happened to his sons?" Silas asked instead of talking to his mate. He did not appreciate her humor of a possible connection to his origins and human breeders. That was not something he wanted to think about right now.

"As far as I know they never acknowledged their dual nature until the cycle was broken."

Silas frowned. "What cycle?"

"I bet you're thinking of all the mean things you said about breeders right now knowing we could all be related..." Jasmine said laughing.

He ignored her.

"One of the women had a daughter, twins I think. After the girls were born, Alpha did not appear for three years. By then he had a large clan of mixed breeds. His sons followed in his footsteps, traveling all over the country, planting their seeds. Most of them were hanged for crimes and did not live past a hundred."

"The daughters?"

"One died as a young child. We are still tracking the other's lineage. But she was the cream of his litter. Even mixed, her pups were closer to our pack than any of the son's litters."

"We could be cousins or something, huh?" Jasmine asked with a chuckle in her voice.

"You think Asia is from her line?" Silas said wishing his mate would muzzle herself.

"She could be. So could your bitch. She is very strong and it is not all from you."

"Really? Damn you Black Wolves sure have made serious inroads on the half-breeds of the world." Jasmine said.

He frowned at her poor humor. She had no idea what all she was capable of yet. They needed to take this information seriously.

"If Asia is a descendant of the Alpha, you think that is the reason she has been targeted?"

"No. We believe that is the reason she has been successful. There is a difference. Recently we discovered an ongoing intensive background study on her. Someone even came to the continent poking their noses where it did not belong. It caused quite a stir, we had no idea."

"No one will believe a dead Alpha impregnated those women," Silas scoffed.

"Unless they are the same ones who know wolves and men can be one. It goes back to what I asked before. Why her? Why does her body have the ability to be altered and not others? They are seeking more of our kind."

"Are there many others?"

"Pure black wolves? No. Less than a hundred around the world. But most are strong and have large Packs. Not as large as yours…"

Silas waved down the comment, it was irrelevant at the moment. "Are there many from his son's line still living?"

"We have someone tracking that information as well. It is more difficult because many sons mated with many women who birthed a lot of children. We may never know all of the offspring because of the time period's poor record-keeping."

"That's true," Silas said thinking how most people could not read or write let alone record a birth in those times. "So it is easier to track the daughter's line. She was his only living female child, right?"

"As far as we know. Alpha rarely appears anymore. I have heard stories that he visits his seed, grandchildren in dreams, and speaks of their heritage. But I cannot confirm if that is true or not."

"So where do we or Asia play in all of this?" Silas asked glad his mate had stopped with the teasing.

"We are not exactly sure… but suspect Asia will be a solid leader in this war. A force of nature as she comes into her own. Do you know if she is mated? Or has had a mate?"

Silas shrugged, refusing to share anything personal regarding Asia. She would share whatever she wanted Angus to know. "You will need to ask her."

"Of course." Angus paused. "There are others, your sons, for example. We have researched their line. Bennetts has been known far and wide as a fierce fighting clan for generations. But the twins are better, faster, and meaner than their relatives. Their ability to adapt quickly to change has been noted. They may be descendants as well. They exhibit the mental and physical agility of the black wolf as well as an innate loyalty to Pack. Those are core traits of our clan."

Silas always thought there was something different, special about how quickly Tyrone and Tyrese learned new skills. When he met Tyrone in the hospital, he picked up a different scent, but could not identify it at the time. With everything happening rapidly, moving from the hospital, Jasmine going into heat, his wolf fighting the attraction and their mating, he had forgotten the small difference, until now. They certainly carried the traits Angus mentioned and more. Before he trained them, they fought on the same level as his Alphas. Now they were an unbeatable tag team. He trusted the twins not only with his life but the lives of his mate and pups. There was no one else on the planet that he trusted to that degree.

"What do you mean?" he asked wanting Jasmine to hear the pronouncement clearly.

"We believe your mate is a descendant of the daughter of our Alpha."

Chapter 11

THE FURTHER THEY MOVED from the area of the explosion, the more the lab resembled the area Asia was intimately familiar with. They passed the corridor leading to the larger apartments. Inwardly she chuckled. Her cell at the compound was larger than those apartments. But when all you know is what you are told and what you see, you believe. Her heart ached for the elderly residents who had been left behind like unwanted garbage. They had worked and lived here all their lives without compensation. Now, older and they had nothing to fall back on to survive. No one would be providing food for them to eat or clothes to wear. This facility would be torn apart and never utilized again. La Patron had made that very clear.

Looking ahead in the dim corridor, she exhaled. "We're close, at the hallway make a left." The inability to share a link with Tyrese mystified her. She had always been able to link with anyone she chose. They spent a few moments earlier trying without success to relink.

He nodded and continued walking slowly waving his scanner from side to side. Large, outdated black and white safety posters appeared on the walls in no specific order. Her captors never missed a trick to keep them clueless to the real world. There were no televisions or radios for entertainment. If she hadn't gone on assignments, stayed in hotels, been given the appropriate wardrobes, and taught several languages, she would be just as clueless as the residents talking with Alpha Samuel.

They stopped short of the hallway they needed to travel. Tyrese pointed to a pair of steel double doors. Swallowing hard, fighting memories she wished died when she did earlier, she whispered. "Surgery areas. I am not going in there."

"No. No, of course not." He turned and wrapped a comforting arm around her. She tensed for a moment. Uncertainty rocked her. Should she take the offered embrace or not? Accepting his care would make the horrors all the more real. She glanced over his shoulder and saw the doors again. Closing her eyes, she held tight and breathed in his scent to free her nostrils of the stench of remembered surgeries.

"They do unspeakable things in there," she whispered as the horrors of her confinement slipped from the vault in her mind and replayed in living color.

His large palm stroked her hair. She squeezed her eyes tight to keep out the visions, but they continued on a loop. Too many times, they wheeled her down this long hall into that room on a gurney, drugged, and prepped for experimental surgery. Behind those doors, they turned her into a monster with metal parts. They played with her mind, stole her memories and identity.

Her body shook until she lay limp in his arms, terrified because she could not stop the shudders running through her body. Or the tears that overflowed from her eyes and ran down her cheeks.

"It's over now, Asia. It's over. They can't trace you anymore. You still have your skills, in time your memory will be better than ever. Shhhh, they can't hurt you anymore. We won't let them. Plus, you don't know my mama, she don't play when it comes to hers. And she considers you one of hers. So don't worry, we have your back." He continued rubbing her until she pulled it together and wiped her face with her palm.

Ducking her head, she forced herself to step away even though she wished she could linger in the shelter of his arms. They were on the clock and needed to get Leon and the others over here to go through the rooms to search for anything of value.

"Thanks, sorry about that. The concrete floors, block walls, even the smell takes me back to a place I swore I would never return." She wiped her hand on the jumpsuit. "I am nobody's victim, Rese. Never again." Certainty rose in her chest, she refused to allow anyone to use her again. For some reason the Goddess gave her a fresh start, she would make it count this time.

He wiped her tear with his thumb and stared into her eyes. "Never again, Asia," he whispered.

She nodded, pleased that he got it. He got *her*. They were similar in temperament and would make a good team. Unfortunately, he believed her mate was someone important, somewhere on the horizon. She remembered the day he told her that tidbit. If he hadn't wanted her to smell something she would have laughed him out of her small cell. It wasn't until she realized he had stopped coming to see her as often that she realized he was serious. Tyrese was no lightweight. If he believed her mate was nearby, then she had to take the possibility seriously. But not now. Not when she needed to focus on the job of clearing the path for the team and retrieving her legacy.

"Ready?" he whispered.

"Yeah." Inhaling, her gaze flicked over the doors that warped her past and then looked toward the opening to the hall where pieces of her future were stored.

Asia and Tyrese turned the corner to the wing where she stowed her box in the janitor's closet. She wondered if Jan was okay? Was he one of the residents in the room with Samuel? She hoped the kind, older man could finally take time off from work and just chill.

Tyrese led the way with his scanning device. Tapping his back lightly, she pointed to the small alcove where the door was located.

He nodded and continued scanning past the doorway and across the hall. Her heart raced in her chest with each step he took. This section of the lab was further away from the fall site and in good condition. That information made her pause and look around carefully. A thick ledge sat on top of the wall. All the years she lived here, she never noticed how much thicker the walls were in this area.

Dread skittered down her back as she continued to stare up at the thick wall. "Tyrese, we need to leave," she whispered backing away from the closet door.

"What's wrong?"

"Everything." She turned and glanced behind him. The eerie silence made goosebumps rise across her flesh.

His head swiveled, looking behind and then in front of him before taking her hand. Seconds later they moved in the direction they had come. "I called for backup, Rone and Leon are on their way."

The hairs rose on her back. Her leg struggled to move, one in front of the other. Biting her lip, she tried to tell him it was too late. Her enemies were in the corridor with them. Pinpricks of awareness rose on her arm and legs. The bastards had found her. Instead of speaking her thoughts, she screamed as excruciating pain from the metal in her leg ripped through her, snatching her breath.

One moment she held Tyrese's hand, the next she flew backward seeing his startled gaze as the wall behind them opened, gobbled her, and slammed close. A bulked Tyrese running after her was the last thing she saw.

Her back hit a soft wall, as she started sliding down her arms were jerked upward. Cold metal surrounded her wrists. Seconds later her ankles were bound as well. Fear robbed her of reason as she bucked and writhed on the padded surface trying to break free.

How had they found her?

She continued fighting to be free until her wolf whined, telling her to stop and pay attention. From the first time they put her under the microscope to now, every action and reaction was recorded. She could not believe how quickly she fell back into the old habit of fighting for release. Somewhere, someone watched with a timer and recorded how long she struggled. More importantly, she had not broken free of her restraints. Damn it. She had just given them information they did not need to have.

Never again. The refrain continued rolling through her mind, strengthening her. Closing her eyes, Asia focused on the building. She would tell Mistress anything that would expedite her freedom.

There was nothing. No sounds. That couldn't be right. Someone watched nearby, she knew that as well as she knew her name. Focusing harder, she sent her senses further, through the thick walls. Pushing, she saw the grainy concrete that proved how thick the wall was before finally seeing the floor and wall on the other side. Elated that her powers were intact, she searched for her captors. She inhaled. Two scents were familiar, but she could not immediately place names. There was another, but it was so different she was not sure if he was human or wolf or other.

"Why did she stop?" A female voice asked in the distance.

Asia turned, searching for the person who spoke. The voice was unfamiliar. Floating downward, she noticed four outlined bodies. One shape was a bit shorter than her and appeared to have a slim muscular build, but his scent was strange, almost appealing. She strained to make out his facial features but could see nothing more than the grainy outline. The male stood next to a feminine shape, tall and slender with a long ponytail.

"*Asia?*" Jasmine called.

"*Yes, Mistress?*" She expected to hear from Mistress earlier and wondered what took so long.

"*Are you okay?*"

She understood her Mistress did not know what else to ask, but that question was…lame. Most who are abducted are not okay. *I am stuck on a padded wall somewhere in the lab.*"

"We don't know," another masculine voice replied.

She turned to see the outline of a familiar voice and scent. Deets. He was one of the first doctors, pervert in disguise, who had worked on her. She hadn't seen him in over 15 years and wondered why he was here.

"*Can you tell me anything that will help us find you?*" Jasmine asked sounding worried.

"*Not yet Mistress. But there are three men and a woman discussing me, I am listening without them knowing it.*"

"*Four? Are you still in the lab?*"

"Are you sure she regenerated? Perhaps this is her old form?" the odd man asked.

Asia wondered why the stranger made Deets uneasy, fear wafted off him in waves. She did not pick up malice or anything of that nature from the stranger. What were he and the woman doing there?

"Everything inside her shut down. Her heart, her mind, everything. There was no signal that she was alive. That is the only thing we are sure of. If Bruce hadn't suggested we wait to see if she came for her box we would never have caught her," Deets said.

"Good job…sorry your name again?" the male stranger asked.

"Bruce, Sir."

"You work here?"

"Yes, Sir. I'm the janitor. No one pays attention to the cleaning staff. We see a lot that goes on."

Asia gasped at the voice of the janitor she had thought of as a friend over the years. She recognized his scent, but didn't know his name was Bruce, she had called him Jan, short for janitor. The older man had been a hallmark in the lab for as longs as she remembered. She couldn't count the times they had talked about meaningless things or he held her hand offering comfort when someone they knew passed. It took a moment to grasp that he had been the one who sold her out.

"I... think so, Mistress. They have my box, they used it as bait."

"I am sorry, Asia. We will still find your past, you can count on that. The boys are tearing the place apart searching for you. I told them four people were holding you."

Asia smiled. Only a mother would call Tyrone and Tyrese boys.

"We've been using him for years as an extra pair of eyes and ears around here. He's given us invaluable information, a great source. Her hiding her box in his closet is just one thing. Go get my equipment, Bruce," Deets said.

With a heavy heart, she watched the man who had once consoled her leave the room. His betrayal cut deep. Few people in the world knew her abhorrence to unnecessary violence and brutal acts. He had been a caregiver of those secrets. From the first time he had found her lying next to the toilet after emptying her stomach when she returned from an assignment, he had made himself available whenever she returned. Most times he shut down the area for cleaning so she would have privacy and wait with her until she was done. Sometimes he held her head, others he simply handed her a cloth to wipe her mouth. They never talked during those times. He was just there in case she needed anything.

"What was in the box?" the woman asked.

"Newspaper clippings, an old bracelet, a picture. Just bits and pieces she collected over the years. Would you like to see them, Sir?" Deets asked.

Asia snapped to attention and almost lost her focus. Newspaper clippings? Bracelet? What picture?

"Yes. I'm interested in seeing what was important enough that she would stay down here when she was free. It must be important. Are you preparing for the tests?" the woman answered in a low cultured voice. Asia tried to place the accent, but couldn't.

"Yes, Ma'am. Now that she has worn herself out, it won't be as difficult to install another tracking implant. I've been working on upgrading the implementation and data tracking on these and feel confident you'll be pleased," Deets said with a touch of pride in his voice.

"The new one?" The male stranger asked.

"Yes, Sir. This one has better termination capabilities and cannot be overridden. We will be able to track La Patron and enter his compound at will with this one. Once I inject it into her system, it will travel through her bloodstream and eventually burrow itself into her brain. From that point on, she is ours to control." Deets' eagerness sickened her.

"Good. The last one had too many complications. Either she works for us, or we want her exterminated. If you can make that happen good, otherwise, take her to Newport and have her incinerated there," the woman said.

"Mistress?"

"Asia?"

"They plan to put another chip inside me." She told Jasmine what she had just heard. *"Kill me, please."*

"What? Kill...no I can't do that. Let's talk about this."

"I am not going to live as their puppet, Mistress. Death is better. Release me from my vow or kill me. I don't care which."

"Stop it," Jasmine yelled and tendrils of power shot through the link.

Asia shuddered as waves of calming energy enveloped her, canceling her anxiety. *"Yes, Ma'am."*

"What is it with you and death? You always act as if it is the only other option, it's not. Now tell me again exactly what they said, not what you think they said or what you think they meant."

"Yes, Ma'am." She repeated the conversation to that point. There was a brief period of silence.

"Silas agrees with me."

Asia was surprised at how calm and confident her Mistress sounded. *"Ma'am?"*

"We are not going to allow them to put anything inside or on you ever again. We are in agreement. Are you ready?"

Hesitating, Asia thought about the timing. *"Ma'am... is there a way to delay him from inserting the implant? I think La Patron needs to find the strange man and stop him. I think he is the one in charge of all of this. They plan to leave soon and I will be with them. But if La Patron stops them at the boat, that will buy us time."*

"You think he is the Liege?"

"Who?"

"Nothing. Silas heard everything you said and they are working on all that. I am staying with you. Anything that asshole tries to put inside you dies. I have been practicing controlling my energy."

Asia grimaced, remembering the last time her Mistress became angry. Mark, Victoria's fiancée had burned from the inside out and his mind turned to mush. *"Thank you, Mistress."*

"Don't fail, Deets. We are too close to reaching our goal to have a loose experiment running around. Billions of dollars are on the line. Our clients don't need to know the flaws in our products. No one wants a soldier they cannot control," the male stranger said, causing the smell of Deets's fear to rise higher.

"Yes, Sir."

"I need to get the rest of the boxes and store them. Meet you below," the woman said and left the room without a backward glance.

The male stranger turned to Deets and spoke. "How soon before we can leave here, La Patron and Angus are above, that is too close."

"Mistress who is Angus? The odd-smelling man knows La Patron and Angus are nearby. He is afraid of them."

"He is a full-blood black wolf who has been watching everything. I wonder how they know him. One sec, let me talk to Silas."

Asia thought over Jasmine's words. La Patron was the only Black wolf she had ever seen, other than the one in her bizarre dream. In her dream, there were wolves of all colors frolicking in what appeared to be a large meadow. At the top, seated on a large stone sat a huge black wolf. He never did much, other than watch. Her dream never varied. Whenever she woke from her rest she always seemed stronger. She thought it was La Patron watching over them. Maybe she was wrong. One of the byproducts of her implants was the loss of restful sleep and dreams. It had been years since she thought of it.

Deets spoke. "I sent Bruce for my equipment. I need to sedate her so that she does not emit signals that they can pick up through the links. Otherwise, they will sense her when we leave this alcove. Afterward, I will inject the tracking chip and then bring her down to the tunnel so we can leave."

"Good. I am going below to oversee the loading of the last shipment and then I will give the order to blow the entire lab. Make sure you are done and on the boat, I would hate to lose another doctor."

"Yes, Sir."

"Mistress the odd man will blow up the lab after he loads his boat, he will leave with or without me. Please tell La Patron to hurry. I have changed my mind, I prefer to live."

"Of course you do. I'll tell Silas, but they are moving like the wind already. There is a lot of ground to cover. I think you and I need to form a plan just in case."

Asia could not imagine what kind of plan the two of them could hatch, but found comfort in the fact she was not alone. *"Yes, Mistress."* Thinking fast, she tried to calculate the potential damage. How many people lived in the area? Not only would the bomb change the direction of the Susquehanna River, but the highway and surrounding towns would suffer as well. No telling how many lives would be lost with that one selfish act. Hopefully, the mountains were far away enough not to be impacted, otherwise, the results would be catastrophic.

A soft swooshing sound met her ears. Asia watched as the janitor returned pushing a cart into the room. "Anyone see you? Ask any questions?" Deets asked as he moved aside.

"No, Sir, I have a lot of practice of walking unseen. They are searching for her though."

"Won't be long. I just have to flood the room with this to knock her out and then insert the chip," Deets said as he reached into a jar on top of the cart and pulled out a small vial.

"Yes, Sir." Bruce looked around the small space and stopped. If she had been standing in the room their gazes would have met. He remained in that position a moment longer and slid his gaze to the opposite side of the room.

Was it possible that he sensed her? No. Maybe. She had no idea.

"You need to go and join the group leaving for the Alpha's compound before we blow the lab. Get as far away as you can, the river is going to flood this area once the bomb goes off. I don't want you to get hurt. We need accurate information on how the Alpha operates and what his weaknesses are. Maybe you can offer to clean his den," Deets said as he inserted the syringe filled with the contents from the vial into a round circle on the wall.

"Yes, Sir. I'll do that. Good luck to you, Sir." He left the room. Asia watched as he walked to a wall, tapped it a couple of times. It slid open and then closed after he crossed over.

Asia heard the hiss in her small prison as the air became tainted with the contents from the vial. Inhaling, she recognized the potent brew. Fear latched on with a tenacious grip as she tasted the poison that would leave her in an unconscious state.

"Mistress, they are filling the room with gas so they can insert the implant. Do you have a plan?"

"Don't breathe it."

"What?" What kind of plan was that?

"You didn't breathe before when you were underground, don't breathe now."

Asia thought about it for a moment, realized Mistress was right, and told her body not to breathe in the poisonous air. She lay motionless, waiting. Nothing happened. Air particles loaded with chemicals floated above and around her head. Instead of inhaling, she counted them.

"Mistress, he will come in the room soon, shall I kill him?"

"No. Not yet anyway. Silas would like to see the chip."

Asia's heart dropped and she was tempted to inhale the poisoned air. *"He wants me to carry the chip inside?"*

"What? Hell no. What's wrong with you? I told you we agreed nothing goes inside you, period. Based on what you've said, he would like to have Passen and Matt look over the chip. Maybe put it in one of their people and send them back to the fold, that kind of thing. But no chips in you. Got that?"

It took everything within her to hide the smile that filled her belly. Knowing she was closely observed she remained still. *"Yes, Mistress. I wish we could shoot the implant up Deets ass. Problem is I don't know how to channel the transmissions so he will answer to La Patron. Plus, he probably already has an implant. They don't trust anybody."* Which meant their options to save lives were limited. Deets had to carry out his mission or the area would be destroyed with all of them inside. There would be no one to warn the authorities of the pending disaster or to disarm the explosives. She made a decision. There was only one way to win this battle.

"You're probably right. Silas said the doctor with Merriweather killed himself before he could question him. So we need to focus on getting the implant and getting you out of there. Seems like Deets is our key for both."

"Yes, Ma'am. But I am sure he is being monitored." Now that she knew that she would not be offered as cannon fodder, she set her mind to the task of beating her captors at their own game. *"I will take the shot, but I need you to catch the implant before it attaches."*

"No shots, Asia. We agreed."

Asia knew she had to make Jasmine understand otherwise they could all die. *"If Deets fails to do his job, the odd man will leave him and blow up the lab. Deets has to believe he completed his task to take me with him for us to get close enough to the odd man. Otherwise, Deets will self-destruct. The explosion will impact the river and the mountains. No telling how many people will die."*

"What? Wait. Silas planned to blow up the lab."

"Yes, Mistress. But we were only blowing it up so that it could not be used again. They are blowing it up to obliterate heavy equipment which—"

"Which means more explosives. I get it. So we have to stop them, but you have to play possum long enough to get close to stop them from detonating the lab. Does that sum it up?"

Asia sighed as the door, creaked open. *"Yes, Ma'am. Whatever we're going to do we need to decide now, Deets just entered the room with a mask."*

"A mask? The gas right...hmmm, okay we'll try this your way. I don't like it, but I can't think of anything else."

Beneath lowered lids, Asia watched as he placed the small tray with a syringe and a small vial on a nearby table and bit back a groan. Once a perv, always a perv. He pulled off one of his rubber gloves, placed it on the tray, and stepped closer. His hand hovered over her thigh and moved slowly up toward her breast. After ordering her body to remain still, she counted to a hundred thinking of ways she would like to kill the bastard.

"I have missed you, Asia. None of the others fought as wild as you. Soon, I will have you again. I am now in charge of monitoring the implants and am required to handle all of the debriefings when you return from every assignment."

The tips of her claws slid out quickly before she caught herself. For the moment, she needed this windbag. Mistress and La Patron were formulating alternate plans to save as many as they could. She had lived through his mauling before and would survive again. Regulating her breathing, she did not flinch when he pulled the zipper down the front of her jumpsuit. When his cold palm rested on her breast she thought of sitting on the beach with two margaritas.

"No bra… did you lose it when you regenerated? I wish I could've seen that." He squeezed the tips of her nipples hard and if she had not sent her body into a semi-comatose state she would've screamed.

"Maybe next time, huh?" His thin hand moved down across her belly. When he leaned forward and placed a kiss on her nipple, she wanted to slap him.

"Mistress…" she called in desperation.

"Asia, what's wrong?"

"He's … he's sucking on my breast, not as a lover might. But as babes do…I am going to be sick." She had been prepared for his fingers penetrating her between her legs or in her ass. He had been doing that for years. For the most part, it was impersonal and, because he was a quick shooter, over within a few minutes. But this… she was not prepared for him to spend this much time sucking and cooing and making baby sounds.

"I am so sorry." Jasmine entered her mind bringing light and colors and tinkling sounds that took her mind off what was happening in the room. Moments later, her stomach settled.

"You are so sweet, I wish I could keep you with me," he said softly. "You would like that, wouldn't you? I think you always enjoyed the fun we had in debriefing." When he moved away, she thanked the Goddess for the favor.

"He is done and preparing the shot."

"Okay. As soon as it enters you, I will destroy it. Do you know how you're supposed to act?"

"Supposedly I am still drugged."

"Are you sure we need to take it this far? I promised you no shots."

Asia bit back a sigh at Jasmine's hesitancy. As repulsive as the idea of an implant entering her body, she knew this part of the plan was the most important. *"Yes. If he does not take me down below, a lot of people are going to die. I am trusting you to grab the implant. Save it if you can. Destroy it if you cannot. Just don't allow it to get to my brain."*

"Okay." Warmth filled her from the top of her head to the tips of her toes. In the background, the telltale sound of a syringe being filled

and the dropping of the container to the tray hit the airwaves.

Asia strengthened her resolve to remain still and more importantly to trust. The first was easier than the second. When the needlepoint pierced her chest, her body bowed. It was a visceral response and out of her control. She counted to ten as he slowly injected the fluid and implant into her chest. When he pulled it out, fire leapt in her breast.

Struggling to breathe, perspiration poured from her forehead. Her lips went numb and her fingertips tingled.

"*Got it.*"

"*Thank you.*" Asia lay still as Deets stood over her watching as tremors wracked her body.

He touched her arm for a few moments. "Good. Let's get out of here before this place blows."

What she had thought was a padded wall was a small gurney turned sideways. Deets released the wheels and rolled her through the door. Eyes closed, she concentrated so that she could find this area again, it needed to be researched before it was destroyed. A cool breeze brushed across her face and then the sound of something heavy sliding across the concrete. They remained still until the sound stopped.

After a series of beeps, they moved again. The temperature changed and she could not make out anything other than Deets. Wherever he was taking her was at the end of a long, dark walkway.

"*Mistress he is taking me somewhere. I do not know this area of the lab. Can you lock on me?*"

"*Lock on you?*"

"*Yes. Can you determine my exact location and tell La Patron?*"

"*I...I don't know. Let me ask Silas.*"

She picked up sounds as the air grew cooler. Inhaling she picked up scents. Humans, for the most part, two breeds. The odd-smelling man's scent was a distance away.

"Stop, she has to be scanned," someone said in a commanding voice. They stopped as a human ran a handheld device around her. "That the implant?"

"Yes, it will move through her system and lodge into her brain," Deets said in a haughty tone.

"How long?" the man asked.

"She's drugged, that slows everything down. But within twenty-four hours."

"Will those restraints hold if she wakes before then?"

"Yes."

"Okay, we'll load her in the storage area."

The human rolled her toward the longboat. Her stomach grew queasy. She would help in any way she could, except on water. The closer she moved to the brackish-smelling water, the more her stomach rebelled.

"Mistress...help!"

Chapter 12

THE MOMENT SILAS RECEIVED Tyrese's call for assistance, he jumped up and ran toward the clearing. Everything had been filled except the opening for the men below to exit. "What happened?" he asked Tyrese as he reached below.

"They took Asia. Snatched her out of my hands, damn it." Silas heard the self-disgust in Tyrese's voice. "If they took her, it was because they were still able to connect to her in some way. Perhaps the metal in her body or something. Where are you looking?" He sensed Angus trotting behind him as he moved through the damaged areas.

"All the halls, the corridors. Nothing. The wall opened up and she disappeared. I can't find anything, can't smell anything."

"Jasmine, Asia has been taken. Contact her for clues so we can find her."

"What? Never mind."

He knew what that meant; his mate was upset and wanted answers. *"Your mom is contacting her and will tell us something soon."*

"I didn't think to contact mom, she is going to kill me," Tyrese said.

Silas did not respond to that remark because Tyrese should have contacted Jasmine. She was the only one who could link with Asia. "Continue your search." He dismissed Tyrese as he strode down the hall and turned into the room where the residents were congregated. Samuel sat on a bench talking to one of the older women.

"*They have been abused,*" Angus said coming to stand next to him. The top of the black wolf's head reached his elbow. Wide-eyed, the residents stared at them.

"*Yes, their wolves sense me, but are confused.*" Silas hated what had been done to these wolves and was determined to put an end to this butchery.

"*She is in a room somewhere in the lab. Three men are holding her.*" Jasmine's voice changed and he sensed her anger through their link. "*She is in that damn lab somewhere, Silas. Find her.*"

He bristled at her command. "*We are looking for her. Did she give you any clues where she is?*"

"*No. How the hell is she supposed to do that? They have her chained to a damn wall like a fucking animal. You promised –*"

"*Stop. Do not yell at me as if I am sitting on my ass. We are searching everywhere for her. Now get us some damn clues to help.*" He exhaled as she cut the connection. His bitch had a temper and he wouldn't have her any other way, but there were times he wished she didn't direct it at him.

"*What will you do with these... the ones who are lost?* Angus asked.

"*It is up to their Alpha. I support his decision.*"

"*They require special care, I sense their desperation.*"

Silas glanced at the huge, dark as midnight animal standing next to him. "*Perhaps they are desperate to be out of reach of such a hungry-looking wolf.*"

"*Possibly.*"

Samuel stood and walked toward him. "La Patron." He bowed and glanced at Angus.

"Alpha Samuel, this is Angus. Angus, Alpha Samuel."

Samuel nodded and returned his attention to Silas. "They are considering returning with me to my den. But they do not wish to shift. They despise their wolves." His gaze slid to Angus. "May I introduce you to them, Sir?"

"*Silas, they plan to place another chip inside her. She wants to* die. *I said we said no way. Now tell me how to stop this? How do I fix this, damn it?"* Jasmine asked speaking fast, her energy flew wild through their link. She was too close to the edge.

He held up his finger to Samuel and turned around. *"You're right no more chips...although it would help if we had one that hadn't been used. Passen and Matt could replicate it in the lab and we could turn the tables on them."*

"Nothing goes inside her, I promised."

"I understand, think of a way to grab the technology without her being hurt. That is the main reason we are here."

"I don't care about your mission right now," she snapped. A stream of unbridled energy grazed his jaw. *"I just want her life saved. I won't forgive myself if she is enslaved again because she thinks she is serving me. I am not going to allow that."*

He sighed, knowing she wouldn't be swayed. *"I agree, no shots."*

"Listen in as she repeats what she heard the men said so we can make a plan to get her out of there."

Seconds later he listened as Asia told all she knew. It wasn't much, but it was more than he knew. He sent brief messages to Leon and the twins telling them to return to him. They needed to make plans for the fallout.

"Okay. They are going to blow up the lab and Asia says it will be worse than what you planned to do," Jasmine said sounding winded.

He brought her current on what he knew. *"We don't have much time. Keep me informed of your plans; I need to get the residents out of here."*

"Oh yeah, the janitor, Bruce, he gave them her box and turned her in. Kick his ass for me."

Silas shook his head. *"Bloodthirsty bitch."*

"Stop flirting and find those bastards."

He turned to find Samuel and Angus watching him. "They have taken Asia and plan to blow the lab. It will affect the river, the highway, and all the surrounding towns."

Samuel's eyes widened. "I need to prepare my pack."

Silas nodded. "I'll introduce myself to the residents, staying is no longer an option for them. Make arrangements for them to leave at once."

"Yes, Sir." Samuel left the room heading to the opening with his cell phone in hand.

"*Silas the stranger knows Angus, Asia says he is afraid of the two of you. I hope you can use that against him.*"

"Thanks... you okay?" She had been practicing controlling her energy but was nowhere as good as she needed to be to enter a person and leave them whole. He hoped the connection she shared with Asia helped to keep her focused otherwise Asia might die and his mate would be forever changed, loaded with guilt.

"*Yeah, I'm fine,*" she said too glibly. She had shuttered their link so he could not fully gauge her feelings. Perhaps that was for the best. She needed to do this on her own.

"Good, I'm proud of you. Let me know if you find out anything else."

"*Gotta go, the disgusting man is preparing to give her the shot.*"

He wanted to offer assistance but refrained. She hadn't asked. Instead, he walked further into the room just as a door in the back of the room opened. The residents perked up, smiled, nodded as the man dressed in a gray jumpsuit walked in and took a seat.

Pleased that they had a pack mentality, even if they did not shift, Silas crossed his arms and stared at the older man. "Bruce?"

The older man nodded. "La Patron?"

Silas nodded, pleased when the man bowed in respect. He wasn't sure if they understood Pack protocol.

Smiling, Bruce ran his hand across his face. "She saw me, then? I wasn't sure, but I hoped."

Taken aback, Silas' brow rose. "You knew Asia was there?"

"You saw her?" someone asked.

"She is safe?" another asked.

Bruce nodded slowly. Silas wasn't sure whose questions the man answered until he spoke. "I sensed her wolf. Deets couldn't pick up anything and I know very little of the other two. Neither the man or woman have been here before, at least I have never seen them. As for her safety? It depends on what she does next."

Silas sensed the man knew more than what he was saying. He ran a scan over Bruce searching for technology as well as the odor of deceit. "Tell me what you know and make it quick, they will blow up the lab."

Bruce nodded. "Yes. I know. First off, they do not have her box.

We have preserved it for her." He waved and one of the women walked toward Silas and pulled something from beneath her dress. She placed a small metal box at his feet.

"That is the box she returned for. We have no idea what is in it and ask that you respect her privacy as well. The young bitch has suffered more than most and deserves her freedom," Bruce said.

"Jasmine, I have Asia's box."

"Okay, I'll tell her later. He is moving her down somewhere. I will show my ass Silas if someone doesn't stop this soon."

"Where are they taking her?" Silas asked Bruce, sensing he was the pack leader.

"To another lab or the incinerator. At least that is what they said in front of me. I don't trust those two. Especially the male, he did not smell right."

Another lab? Silas hadn't thought this was the only location, but he had hoped. "Do you know where the other lab is located?"

"No, Sir. I have never left here, and they never discussed particulars of other locations," Bruce said.

Asia also said the stranger had an odd smell. "Describe the stranger to me," Silas said. When Bruce finished the brief description the male could be any average height white male with brown hair walking the planet. There was nothing distinguishable about him.

"Take us where they are taking her now." Silas sensed his mate's growing anger and sought to soothe her before she detonated.

"Yes, Sir. But first, we would give you these things in case we do not survive." Bruce waved and each person stood, shed their clothes, and removed bagged disks, or chips, or flash drives that were taped to their bodies. One by one they quickly dropped the bounty at Silas' feet.

Excited over what he received, Silas needed Bruce to confirm what was on the disks. He raised his brow at the man.

Bruce gazed at the small pile on the floor as he spoke. "It did not take us long to realize what they were doing here was wrong. Others saw the abuse, fought back, and died. We decided the best way to beat our oppressors was to become invisible while gathering information. Information that could be used against them one day. They thought we stayed because we feared the outside. We stayed to see that one day they would be destroyed. We were not sure how or who to give this to until we heard your name, La Patron. They were envious of your control over our brethren, and partnered with others over the years to slow you down, keep you unaware."

"No one pays attention to the cook and what she sees or hears," a woman said as she returned to her seat.

"Or the seamstress who makes their clothes," another said.

Silas stood in wonder at what they had done.

Bruce waved toward the residents. "We have silently copied everything we could over the years and stored it in various ways as you can see. This tyranny on our people must end." He paused and looked at Silas who still had not spoken.

"One of the reasons Asia must leave here with them is so that she can see the enemy in his camp. We have never had a stranger come here before. The way Deets responded to him suggests he is a high-ranking member of the group or has access to higher-ups."

Impressed by the windfall at his feet and how well Bruce spoke, Silas nodded. "We are working on a plan with Asia. And one day I would like to sit and discuss things with you, with all of you." No need to tell anyone about his mate and the likelihood that Asia would not be going to the enemy's camp today.

Leon, Tyrone, and Tyrese stepped inside the room as Silas gazed at all the data and returned his gaze to Bruce. "Thank you, this will help us tremendously."

"Hello Leon," Bruce said.

"Hey, Jan. Good to see you." Leon walked to the back and hugged the man while Silas told the twins what was on the floor.

"Do you have a box or bag that I can put this in and take up," Tyrone asked?

"Yes." One of the men stood and pulled a large garbage bag from his pocket.

"Thanks," Tyrone said as he took the bag and carefully placed the various forms of data inside. "This will make Matt and Passen's week. Jacques will be doing flips as well."

Silas nodded and spoke to the twins through their link. "Your mother is with Asia in the tunnel. If we do not break up the party soon she has promised to set things ablaze."

Tyrese nodded.

Tyrone shook his head and handed the bag to Samuel as he walked in. "Please lock this up, we will pick it up after we grab Asia."

"Where is she?"

"Bruce is taking us down. Take the residents with you. Leave now," Silas said turning to follow the janitor who had stood.

"Yes, Sir." Samuel waved to the residents who remained sitting. "Come with me, we have to leave. By the time we reach the top, transportation will be waiting."

The residents did not move.

Tired of the delay, Silas looked at Bruce. "Either you tell them to leave or I will compel their wolves and have Alpha drag them upstairs. You have three seconds to make a decision. One…"

Bruce's gaze slid across his and then he nodded. The residents stood and filed out the room looking back at them as they went. The janitor turned, opened the door, and took them through.

"He was kinda like their Alpha, huh?" Tyrone asked Silas but included Tyrese in their conversation as they moved slowly down the steep steps.

"Yeah, that was weird," Tyrese said.

"Having a pack mentality will help them later." Silas glanced behind at Angus, surprised the wolf hadn't said much. *"Any thoughts on who the stranger might be? Asia said he knew you and I were above ground, called you by name."*

"If you are implying that he is with me, or that I am acquainted with anyone remotely responsible for this outrageous operation, I take offense. If that is not your implication the answer is the same as what I suppose yours must be. I do not know who he is, but I want to find out."

"I changed the implant," Bruce whispered over his shoulder.

"What?" Silas asked as they moved single file down the concrete steps.

"Deets sent me to get his supplies. I exchanged the chip implant with one of the first ones they made. What he inserted in Asia is harmless and will dissolve within five days. That's one of the reasons they ditched them. Left them lying around for me to clean up." He chuckled.

Silas wanted to howl, his relief was that profound. Not that he did not trust his mate, he did implicitly, but he knew she was not ready to take on the emotional weight of holding a life in her hand. "You have the chip he planned to install?"

"Yes, Sir. I will give it to you when we clear the stairs."

"Asia is nearing the end of a dark tunnel. Most of the people are

human, two breeds. Tell me you are close, Silas."

"I am close Sweet Bitch. You are doing a great job easing Asia's distress and keeping her calm. The Goddess showed her wisdom when she joined the two of—"

"Stop the bullshit and get the hell in here, I am not allowing them to take her, Silas. I don't give a damn about your quest."

"I understand, sweetness. I am close." No need to tell her about the bogus chip or that he had hit the mother lode with all the data that had been taken over the years. She was too close to the edge and needed to remain focused.

"Once we get to the bottom, they will know we are here. Be prepared for gunfire and all hell to break loose," Bruce said. "I will go first and draw their fire, that will give you time to get out."

"No," Silas said as he released energy creating a shield. It was obvious Bruce had no real idea how wolves or Silas' wolves fought. They did not need the janitor to give his life as a safeguard. "Return upstairs and leave this place. Find your pack and work alongside Alpha Samuel to get them settled into his den. You have served our Nation well today. I will find and repay you."

"Yes…Yes, Sir," Bruce said as they neared the bottom. "Here and no repayment is necessary." He placed the chip in Silas's hand and then pointed to the door. "I need to place my palm print on the door for it to open."

"No. I am sure that has been changed and will only give them more time to prepare for our attack. I will open the door," Silas said waving the older wolf toward the stairs. "Go and thank you again."

Inhaling, Silas smelled the humans and the mutated breeds on the opposite side of the door and was sure everyone else had as well.

"Yes, Sir." Bruce ran back up the stairs. Silas sent Samuel a message that the janitor was on his way and to take him along with the rest of the residents.

"You are going to leave this cramped space, I hope," Angus said in a dry tone.

"You are going to do more than observe this time, I hope," Silas said mimicking him.

"Of course."

Silas focused on the door and exhaled. The heavy metal door flew backward, knocking whoever was in its path on their ass. Immediately gunfire erupted. Encased in a protective shield, Silas and the others stepped out the doorway and onto the landing. Leon, Tyrone, and Tyrese bulked and spun out taking on anyone in their path.

"*I'm here sweet bitch, where are you?*"

"*Trying to keep Asia from getting seasick. They are taking her to the boat.*"

Silas saw two boats further up and headed toward them, Angus was on his heels. All around them gunfire broke out. After the twins and Leon took out the breeds the sounds lessened to muffled screams.

"Shit," Angus growled and changed directions running full tilt away from the boats toward a nondescript male who met Bruce's description, a distance away.

"*Angus,*" Silas called watching the wolf bound across the long walkway. There was no response. When no fight broke out between Angus and the stranger, Silas ground his teeth wishing he had time to deal with what appeared to be a heated discussion.

"*You don't know him, huh?*" Silas shot through the link.

"*I will deal with him while you get Asia,*" Angus said.

"*Fuck you. I will deal with him after I get my pack member. And you as well,*" Silas said pissed as he headed toward the gangplank. A human stepped forward with a small weapon aimed at him.

"Step back," the man said.

Silas's anger over being duped by Angus was a tangible thing. He stepped back and sent a whirlwind to disable and remove the man. Once lifted and thrown to the far end of the cave, Silas stepped on board the first boat and inhaled. He smelled her, but it was distant. Exhaling, he retraced his steps to the dock and headed to the next boat. Her scent was stronger but still distant. Glancing over his shoulder, he watched as the head of one of the breeds flew into the water. Tyrese jumped down from a high ledge holding two men under his arm. The unnatural angles of the heads told the story of their condition as he threw them on a growing pile of bodies.

"Asia?" Silas called out as he walked on board.

"*I am on board the boat, where is she?*"

"*Go down one level.*"

Silas searched for the door. "How do I get down there? I don't see a door."

"*I cannot do everything. My hands are full keeping her stomach settled and holding onto the implant.*"

Guilt swamped him. *"According to the janitor, the implant is a fake. He switched them and gave me the real one."* He continued looking for a way below.

"You believed him?"

"Yes. He smelled as if he were telling the truth."

"So did Mark."

He frowned at the reminder of his recent failure to detect a spy who stayed in the compound several days. It was only when Jasmine saw him attack Asia that she realized his duplicity and killed him. *"Was that necessary?"*

"Just reminding you that sometimes we get tricked. I'll just hold onto this until I can get it to pass through her system."

"Or you can bring it through her skin. The hole will heal quickly." He eyed what could be an entry and pressed along the side. Moments later a panel opened. Inhaling, he smiled. *"I found her."*

"Thank goodness. Get her out of there so I can get out of her mind. I have seen more than I care to know. She is terrified of being on the water and passed out."

Silas looked around at the stacked boxes, wondering at the contents. Stooping, he unsheathed a sharp nail and opened a box. It was filled with debris. He opened another box and found the same. Curious, he shook a few more boxes, and based on the sound, he suspected they contained the same.

"Silas? Can I release her now?"

"Yes, but I still don't see her, are you sure she is on the boat?" He searched the area for doors and compartments. Nothing. *"Her scent is faint, so she was here, but I am not sure she's here now. Can she tell you anything?"*

"No. She passed out once they took her on the ship. I have no idea where she is. She's close by I'm sure. Now might be a good time to pull out the chip..."

"Not until we have her back. If they do not see a chip, they will put another one inside her. I need you to safeguard her a little longer while I search for her."

"Okay, will do."

With one last look at the boxes, he intensified his search, pulling up anything that looked like it might have been an access point for hiding someone. After tearing the place apart, he still came up empty. Frustrated, he stormed off the boat and headed to the first one. Her scent was absent from this vessel so he left the deck and looked around.

"Where could she be?" Outside, he searched for Angus and the stranger down the ramp. Seeing them standing together angered him. He sent a whipcord of energy to show his disapproval.

"That was not necessary, La Patron," Angus said. "It is not what you think."

"You have no idea what I think. Where is Asia? What the fuck is going on? Who is your friend? Why is he on my land? Near my pack?"

"I will explain... Asia?"

"She is missing, ask your friend if he knows where she is." Silas snapped while scanning the area.

"He is upset that she is missing. He has been outside the entire time and has not seen her. I offer my services to join the search," Angus said.

Silas snorted. *"I asked you if you knew him."*

"I did not know who was here at the time you asked."

"So you do know him, you are working with him." Silas' energy boiled on behalf of his pack and formed in the atmosphere as it neared Angus. The need to destroy the threat overwhelmed him.

"No. It is complicated. It is not what you think. Oh shit." Angus said as he and the stranger were encased in a heavy cage of energy.

"I will ask again, where is Asia?"

"I do not know. I would tell you if I did, her safety is paramount to me and our nation," Angus said.

"Mélange must have taken her."

Silas spun toward the stranger. "Who are you?"

"Brix," Angus said.

"I wasn't talking to you," Silas snapped at Angus while watching Brix. "Who is Mélange and why would he take Asia, and where?"

"Mélange is a woman and there is a large bounty on Asia's head as well as bonuses. I guess she could not resist the allure," he said in a low tone, but Silas heard the anger beneath.

"How do I find her and where would she take Asia for the reward?"

"I don't sense her presence or Asia's here any longer. To collect the bounty she has to take Asia to one of the main labs. There are two in the states. One within three or four hours of here. I would guess that is where she is headed."

Silas ran his hand through his hair, glaring at Angus.

"Why are the two of you here?" Silas ground out.

"We cannot destroy one another, you know that. There are things you do not understand."

Silas laughed and it lacked all humor. "You think I need to be the one to destroy you? You trespassed on my land, in my country. As you know, I have over fifty well-trained Alphas with no black clan connection, any or all of them will gun for your traitorous ass. I can pull energy from every wolf in this god-damn country to fry you and your partner without ever touching you. There are things you do not understand."

"I see your point, Silas. And you are correct. I should have sought your permission before crossing into your territory. If you would calm for a moment I would explain the matter to you. But this cage is removing air and I am having trouble breathing."

"I do not care. My people have been under attack, used, and abused for decades. And you stand with their abuser. I will bundle you both up and deliver you to the council of Alphas as an appetizer."

Angus sighed. *"What I tell you, must be kept in the strictest confidence."*

"Fuck off," Silas said not wanting to hear anymore. He would have his hands full dealing with his irate mate in a few moments. Jasmine would be pissed Asia had been taken beneath his nose. That made two of them.

"He has infiltrated a terrorist group on our behalf. His identity is a carefully guarded secret, we are close to discovering the head of the snake."

"What is the name of this group?" Silas asked watching the fighting died down in the distance. They needed to regroup and go after Asia. He hated being in this position.

"Liege. They call themselves Liege and have been around for centuries. Their fingers are at the pulse of the global economy and world governments. It has taken decades to penetrate their organization."

Silas stilled at the name he had heard twice in a few hours and thought of the boxes he had found in the boat. Someone went through a lot of trouble to make it look like they had contraband when they did not. "Tell me another story," he said aloud, including Brix in the conversation.

"It is the truth. Although it seems as if we will lose him."

"I am not apologizing for anything. You should have told me what was going when we met in the forest or once we came down here."

"I am not at liberty to discuss his situation. There are only two people who are aware of what he is doing. He was not supposed to be here, I thought he was in the middle east."

"Middle East? How many labs does this group have?" He sent a message to Samuel to order his plane and have it ready to meet them within the hour.

"I have been sharing information with you and yet you are suffocating my wolf."

Silas allowed the air to permeate the cage.

"Thank you. As for the number of labs, I am not sure. At least fifteen, including smaller satellite ones. This lab is one of the older ones. Most are cutting edge facilities."

"Hmm. How many in the States?"

"Five I believe. Two large ones and three smaller ones. Are you preparing to go after Asia?"

"Why do you care?" Silas snapped.

"She is critical to our survival, an ultimate force who can change the tides of this war."

"We take care of Pack, she is not your concern," Silas said and walked off. They needed to make plans to go after Asia.

Tyrese walked over to Silas and stopped. Inhaling, he looked around. "Where is Asia?"

"I don't know. Somehow they were able to take her out of here." He waved toward Angus and Brix. "He thinks she took Asia for the reward money to one of the labs. Claims it is about two hours from here."

"Should I order the plane?" Tyrese said glancing at his watch.

"I had Samuel take care of that. Asia passed out, and Jasmine cannot talk to her to get any information that will help us track her."

"What did mom say? Is she pissed?"

Silas stretched before answering. "I have not told her Asia is missing yet. She has me muted and hasn't picked up anything."

Tyrese whistled. "She may blow. Will Asia be okay if Mom does?"

"It's not Asia we need to worry about. My mate will make all of our lives miserable if we do not save Asia quickly. I am concerned, she will do something that may damage the young bitch. Jasmine does not have the best control over her powers yet."

"True. I'll start clean up, then so we can leave," Tyrese said moving away.

"Did you find the doctor?"

"Self-terminated when he saw Leon. Didn't stop the big guy from stomping all over the man though." He shrugged. "There is something... someone. Do you sense it?" Tyrese asked looking around.

Silas inhaled. The only unfamiliar scent was the stranger with Angus. And then he heard it. Damn. If he never heard the sound of a ticking bomb again, he would dance naked beneath the stars in gratitude.

"Sir," Samuel called. *"The moment the door blew the clock on the explosives started. I must alert the human authorities so they can send in a team to dismantle it and clear the area. If humans die behind this I will lose my standing in the state."*

Silas looked around at the dead bodies and knew they needed more time for a cleaning crew before anyone could come below. *"We need cleaners for the human remains first. How much time on the clock?"*

"It was set so they had enough time to clear the area. There are fifty minutes left and I am not sure this is the only set of bombs."

"None of your wolves can scent explosives?" Silas asked surprised.

"Yes, but they were injured in the first explosion."

"You have Bruce?"

"Yes, Sir. He was the one who showed me a likely place where the explosives might be. He said the explosives are not far from where Asia was held. They intend to blow up the load-bearing walls, which will take down everything else like dominoes. And, Sir... this lab is more extensive than we knew. There are wings beneath the river and the mountains. An explosion of this magnitude will impact the entire region."

Silas cursed.

"Something wrong?" Angus asked as Silas and Tyrese headed back toward the doorway.

Silas snorted. *"You tell me. I don't have time right now to deal with you or your friend, but I will be back as soon as I take care of this."*

"What? What has happened now?" Angus asked, sounding harassed.

Silas ignored him while stepping aside as three of Samuel's wolves came through the door with equipment and began cleaning the area.

Chapter 13

JASMINE LAY EXHAUSTED ON the extra-long sofa in her living room, gazing at her hands. They still shook. Curling her fingers into a ball, she held them close to her chest and exhaled. It had taken every bit of bravado she owned to sound confident while talking to Asia. Inside, she had been a petrified ball of goo, scared shitless of making a wrong move entering the woman's body and then holding onto the implant. When Silas suggested she let it go, she wanted to release the tiny device but fear held her immobile. She was afraid her exit would leave scorch marks. Now Asia was on her way back to her tormentors. Jasmine inhaled and exhaled to calm her nerves. As Silas told her what happened, she heard his frustration and limited her comments. They needed to work together as a team; slinging insults or hurling accusations wasted energy. She would save it for the bitch who took Asia.

The plane was on its way. As soon as the bomb threat was neutralized, Silas and the boys would go after her. His suggestion that she rest while Asia was knocked out was a good one. She glanced at the clock. It was after midnight, she started her day at eight this morning. Until Silas told her the bomb scare was over, she couldn't rest. Bombs… again. Why couldn't they come up with something less common?

She never calculated or understood any of this would be part of her new life when she mated Silas. Living on the edge didn't agree with her. Placing her palm on her chest, she breathed deeply and focused on an imaginary waterfall to slow her heartbeat.

Earlier, when Asia reached out, she left Jacques to head for her wing. Even though she had no idea how to help, she wanted to be in a place with no distractions. Hours passed. At some point, Rose came and left a sandwich tray on the table. Stomach growling, Jasmine rolled over, picked up half of the club sandwich, and devoured it without thinking.

While calming and distracting Asia from the lecherous Doctor, Jasmine inadvertently tapped into Asia's memories and had been blindsided by recurring episodes of the young woman's life. Unprepared to see this violent side of Asia, Jasmine offered bright lights and tinkling music while gasping in shock at Asia's past. The young bitch had been cold and cunning with deadly precision that would make James Bond envious. As one assignment rolled into the next, Jasmine noticed Asia on the assignments was not the same person who called out to her a few moments earlier. There was no hesitation; no apparent weaknesses or vulnerabilities as Asia destroyed lives while carrying out her missions. Like an emotionless robot in a dreary colored world, Asia functioned like a machine, doing what was expected of her.

Being inside Asia's mind had been a harrowing experience, totally different than when she linked with Silas. Her mate rarely thought in the gray areas. For the most part, it was either one way or the other for him. The only time he dabbled in the gray was when he dealt with human issues. But Asia's thoughts were centered on her environment, like a chameleon. When she was on assignment, she became one with the culture and flowed flawlessly. Jasmine sensed there was some emotional fallout afterward on some of the jobs but wasn't sure. No wonder Asia didn't trust anyone. There was no color, no sunshine, no real reason to live, at least not in the manner of her old life.

"Why is she connected to me?" Jasmine murmured. The two of them were like oil and water. She certainly hadn't meant to mark or link to the young bitch. Asia's vow the day before she left made Jasmine uncomfortable. Silas was the only person Jasmine wanted to serve her. "And what am I supposed to do with her? I can't keep going through days like today, my heart won't take it," she murmured while peeking up at the ceiling hoping the Goddess would appear.

She did not.

Rolling onto her side, she went over the conversation with Angus and thought of the BlackWolf clan with a chuckle. Her mate hadn't appreciated her teasing him regarding the beginning of the half-breeds into his world. He had been so hateful at the beginning of their relationship, she simply had to rub it in. Most fairy tales were grounded with an element of truth so they couldn't discount the entire old wives tale.

After clearing the table and placing the dishes in the sink, she left to check on her babies. Too much information raced around her mind for her to sleep, plus Silas might need her.

When she entered the nursery, she stopped short seeing her mom sitting in the rocking chair. Jacques must still be working. "Mama."

Her mom nodded. "Can't sleep either?"

"No. I got a lot on my mind." She took the rocking chair next to her mother and listened to the sounds of her children sleeping. Every once in a while one of them would snort, or make some sound. It was comforting. Her mind strayed to Silas and the situation he faced. She wanted to talk to him but knew he needed to focus. The lives of his team and those who lived in that area depended on his clear thinking. Over a few months, she had grown to consider Leon and Asia as family. She prayed they all returned safely.

"You ever wish you could go back in time and change some things you've done. Kind of like making right the things you did wrong?"

Jasmine looked up at the ceiling not wanting to hear about Mark, the fiancé who went bad, again. But, she had pinned her mom to the wall earlier and sought to make amends. "Probably...most people wish they could."

"True. I wonder sometimes. What if I had met Jacques first...before I met your dad? I mean, if he is my mate now, he was my mate, then, right?" Her mom whispered.

Sensing this conversation might get deep in a hurry, Jasmine touched her mom's arm. When her mother looked at her with troubled eyes Jasmine knew they needed to find a comfortable, secure place to chat. "Let's go to my place and talk in private." She glanced to the area where the nurses slept.

Her mom caught on and nodded. Together, they walked arm in arm down the hall and entered Jasmine's suite. "You want something to drink?" she asked as she headed to the refrigerator to grab a glass of wine. It was late. She had heard, seen, and done things today that required she take the edge off.

"No, I'm good." Her mom sat on the sofa where Jasmine had lain earlier.

She brought her wine and cheese puffs in a bowl, placed them on the end table next to her chair. "The way I understand it, Jacques was always your mate." Jasmine eased them back into the conversation.

Her mom stretched out on the sofa and leaned her head against the armrest. "I wish I had met him… before. But life doesn't always work out the way we expect does it?" Her mom looked at her. "Look at you…a few years ago you were miserable and now… you're different. It's in your eyes. You glow. And it's because you're mated."

Not fully understanding where her mom was headed, but willing to go along for the ride, she nodded. "I never knew love like this before. Silas…he is my everything."

"I've always longed for that in my relationships, always wanted more. Your father… he was a good man. George loved me, I knew he did… but I wanted, I guess what you have now."

Jasmine didn't know what to say. Her dad had been a good man, and a good father. When he died, his absence left a hole in her life.

"If I had been more…content. Certain things never would've happened. I would never have gone out that night with my friends after work. Never would've drunk more than I should've or flirted with that jerk."

Frozen in place by her mom's confession, Jasmine blinked and then gulped her wine. What jerk? She wondered. Should she ask? Were they having a woman-to-woman talk or was her mom just blowing off steam while waiting for Jacques to finish his assignments.

"He was handsome, though," her mom said in a wistful tone that made Jasmine stare at her.

"Who?"

Her mom scooted down the sofa and covered her eyes with her arm. The silence drew out so long Jasmine took another sip of her drink and popped a couple of cheese puffs in her mouth.

"The man in the bar that night, can't remember his name now

and I swore I'd never forget. I shouldn't have gone, it was a weeknight and Renee was crawling. But I wanted to hang out just a bit with the girls, you know what I mean?"

Jasmine had no idea. Mother of twins and married to a career military man at a young age, she had never done that. "Yeah."

"We get there, the place isn't that crowded, but people are coming in from work, eating and drinking, unwinding. Back then food was free during happy hour. So we grab a table and start talking, pretty soon guys are sending us drinks from all over the place. It felt good...too good. Your dad had stopped that."

"What?"

"Looking at me with appreciation. Like Silas looks at you every time he sees you. The first time I met Jacques he looked at me that way too. It does something to a woman. At least to me. And this guy knew how to play the game. He hung onto my every word, paid for everything."

She sighed, a long whistling sound. "I was stupid, gullible, and needy of male attention. He had me at hello, beautiful. My single friends were jealous because he was rich and handsome and he only wanted me."

Was her mom telling her about an affair? Or a booty call? Jasmine took another gulp of her drink and wondered if she could listen to her mom talk about this.

"Within an hour I was wasted. Truth is I was proud this fine sexy man had chosen me, so when he offered to walk me to my car later, it never occurred to me to say no or that I might be in any kind of danger."

Needing more reinforcements, Jasmine jumped up and walked quickly to the bar in the corner and pulled out the bottle of rum to go with the can of coke she pulled from the mini-fridge. If her mom was going where she thought she was going, Jasmine needed to be numb so she didn't react.

"Danger?" Jasmine said in what she hoped was a calm tone as she mixed her drink. Her mom told her and Renee she had been raped... was this what happened?

"Yeah. I was dumb and drunk. He was a bigot and wanted to taste a black chick, his words afterward, not mine. I was too ashamed to tell anyone that he...he had taken me against my will. Not after the way I had been all over him inside..."

After taking a sip of her drink Jasmine looked at her mother lying on the sofa. "My sperm donor raped you?"

Her mom uncovered her eyes and met Jasmine's gaze. For a long moment neither spoke. "Yes, he did."

Jasmine nodded and took another sip to douse the anger boiling inside. "You know his name?" she asked without looking at her mom.

"No. Not his real name. But I recognized him in the paper a year later. Some man killed him, cut off his head with a machete. He raped the man's daughter. At the time it was big news because the father got away with it, killing the guy that is. When I saw his picture in the paper, I recognized him and thanked God for karma. You know what I mean?"

Jasmine nodded thinking of the story Angus told them regarding the Alpha's seed and wondered at the coincidence. "Karma is a bitch."

Her mom turned on her side and met her gaze. "I used to wonder what my life would've been like if I hadn't gone to that bar that day. For a long time after that night, I kept seeing his face, the anger, the disdain he had for me. The filthy words he spoke as he… well you know. I couldn't be with my husband for a long time. When I found out I was pregnant, I wanted to die."

"I'm glad you didn't."

Her mom smiled. "Me too. I think your father suspected, but he never said. I made a vow to be happy at home and never hung out with the girls again… but now, meeting Jacques, I can't help but wonder what my life would have been like if I met him years ago."

Jasmine sat her drink down and placed her hands behind her head. "Well, your life would suck big time, because I wouldn't be in it. Just think of all the arguments you would've missed. The fallouts we had over clothes and curfews. Plus you wouldn't have had grandsons at a ridiculously young age. Or the headaches that accompanied a teen pregnancy." Laughing with her mom, she shrugged. "I'm the product of a mistake you made. But I know a few people who are damn skippy that you went to that club that night. Life is weird. Sometimes we have to roll with the punches. I would love to read that news article about when the rapist died if you can remember anything about it."

Jasmine intended to have the male researched to complete her family tree and see if there were any BlackWolves. Karma would truly be Silas' bitch if they discovered Angus was right and the crux of the breed problem started from his line.

"Of course I won't ever forget, I'll write what I remember down for you." She paused. "Thank you for that. I've wanted to tell you about it for a long time but was too embarrassed. It was the main reason I couldn't get overly upset when you got pregnant. If Davian's relatives weren't such dicks, I never would've allowed you to marry him so young. But he wanted to take care of you and the boys. Plus you said you loved him."

Jasmine shrugged at the faded memory. "I did not know what love was until Silas, Mom. The thing with Davian…I wouldn't change the beginning because I got Rone and Rese. But the rest of it, yeah, we should've cut it short by at least five or ten years."

"I hear you. You and me both."

Chapter 14

LEON LED THE WAY up the stairs, followed by Silas and the twins. Once they reached the upper level, Bruce was there to meet them in the hall.

He nodded and stepped to the side. "Over here," he called over his shoulder as he led the way down the hall before turning the corner. When they caught up with him, he placed his palm against what appeared to be a solid wall. After a series of beeps and a click, it opened.

"Nice trick," Leon said as he followed the janitor down the dim hall. A musky odor wafted toward them.

Samuel hung back. "Do I call the humans now Sir or wait?"

Silas glanced back as the others filed past. "Give us a few minutes to see if we can clean up this mess. If we can't then you can call them. I know it's cutting it close, but you don't want the media all over this right now. There's stuff on those boats that need to be sorted or destroyed." He placed his hand on Samuel's shoulder. "Clear your pack from the area just in case."

Samuel nodded. "Yes, Sir, and thank you." He turned and jogged in the direction they had just left. Silas stepped through the dimly lit passage and went to join his team.

"What is going on? I can help if you just tell me what's going on?" Angus said.

Silas shook his head as he continued forward without responding. When he reached the others, Tyrese had a look on his face that spelled trouble. Tyrone stood with one hand on the top of his head, looking down at Leon and Bruce, who surrounded a large cardboard box with a lot of brown shiny tape.

Damn.

"How bad is it?" Silas asked picking up the vibes in the small space.

"Very bad, Sir," Leon said. "The way this is set up, if it is moved at all it'll blow. So even if I could deactivate it, I'd have to move something to get to the main part—"

"Which will activate it," Silas said, pissed.

"You promised to share information with me...so far you have not kept your end of the bargain," Angus said.

"There are boxes of rocks on the boat. That's information I bet you didn't know," Silas sneered.

"What? No...I didn't know that."

"Any ideas? We are running out of time," Silas said into the silence.

"Alpha Samuel read the time wrong. There's an hour and forty-five minutes on the timer," Leon said slowly, moving aside so Tyrese and then Tyrone could see.

Tyrese exhaled. "He's right. We have a little more time. I should check on clean-up before the bomb squad arrives. Then we can leave, I contacted the pilot and have him picking us up nearby. He said he would be here in thirty to forty minutes."

Silas nodded. "Rone, you and Leon go check those boats, I want to know what they were planning to move out of here."

"Yes, Sir," Leon said as he and Tyrone followed Tyrese.

Silas crossed his arms and looked down at Bruce. "Can you explain how Samuel made such an error? It's not like him and his fear that we are running out of time was genuine. You were with him, Bruce."

Bruce stood.

"I was with him, Sir, but I did not look at the bomb then as I did now. He came in here alone while I continued searching other possible locations for explosives. When he left the room, he told me the timer had fifty-five minutes left. I said it may have started the moment the door blew. I have no idea how he made that mistake."

Silas made a mental note to discuss the situation later with Samuel. That was a huge mistake and may have caused Silas to handle the matter differently than he would have with more time. "Did you find other locations?"

"Yes, Sir. But no explosives. Just this one. But this one is all they need," Bruce said looking at the box on the floor.

"Silas I see your men out here, what is going on?" Angus said sounding pissed.

"We are searching for the end of the rainbow, have you seen it?"

Silas turned and waved him out of the room. When they were outside, he looked at Bruce. "Lock it up for now. We will leave it open for the local bomb squad before we leave."

"Yes, Sir." Bruce closed the doorway.

"Go up, Bruce, help your Alpha secure the Pack. I'll see you later."

"But how will you get in the room, again?"

Silas stepped back to the door, placed his palm on the wall and the door opened.

"That is…great, Sir," Bruce said sounding confused. He bowed and left as Silas re-closed the door.

Now to deal with Angus and Brix. Something weird was going on with those two. Tyrese nor Tyrone mentioned Angus on the dock. The fight surrounded them as if they were invisible but Silas saw them plainly. Full of questions, he returned to the dock. When he reached the deck, the stack of humans and breeds were gone. Inhaling, the scents were still in the atmosphere but dissipating. A wolf would pick up the smell but humans would not.

As he made their way to Angus, Tyrone stepped out of the second boat with an opened box on his shoulder. "Look at this, Sir."

He changed directions. Once he reached Tyrone, he placed the box on the ground. "Inside are new collars in sealed bags. There are quite a few more boxes stored inside. What should we do with them?"

"We take them with us." Silas called out to Tyrese. *"Did you order a vehicle to take us to the plane?"*

"Yes, Sir, a four-wheel SUV."

"Good, I want to take the boxes from the boat with us."

"Yes, Sir. How many boxes? Do I need to get another truck?"

"How many boxes?" Silas asked Tyrone who was stooped over the box.

"At least twenty. We'll start carrying them to the opening so all they need to do is get them up and loaded. Maybe we can rig something to make it go faster," Tyrone said standing. He returned to the boat.

Silas informed Tyrese, pleased that they had made a small dent in his enemies' pocket. "Where's Leon?" Silas asked.

Tyrese jogged over and followed his twin inside.

"On the other boat, going through boxes," Tyrone said as he placed five stacked boxes on the ground.

"*Leon?*" Silas called while looking at the boat. "*What have you got?*"

"It's weird, Sir. These boxes have dirt and rocks. They must have some value. I'm bringing a few on deck so we can take them as well." He walked out of the small cabin area carrying boxes. Tyrone and Tyrese took their boxes up the stairs to place in the truck once it arrived.

"*Silas what's going on?*" Angus asked and this time there was a sound of authority in his voice that had not been there before.

"*Just cleaning house.*" Silas watched as the twins returned and took up the last of the boxes.

"*You are almost out of time,*" Angus said slowly, his tone serious.

Silas turned to face the wolf and saw two men. One was a tall dusky complexioned man with long wavy back hair draped over his wide shoulders. Standing next to him was a man who could easily have passed for a Viking of old. Tall, blond, and fair. Curious, Silas strode forward, stopping short of the glowing energy cage to get a better look at both men. Angus' emerald green eyes gleamed in the low lighting of the cave.

"*Time? What do you mean?*" Silas asked taking in the way Angus' lean frame shivered as if his wolf wanted to resurface.

"There are only twenty minutes on the clock," Angus said in a deep, halting voice as if it were rusty from non-use. He pushed his hair behind his ear and waved toward his cellmate. "This is the last day he will use that old form since his cover is now blown. He was an excellent operative who will be missed."

Brix nodded.

"We did not know you would be here today, La Patron. If we had, perhaps things would have ended differently. I apologize for the terrible mix-up," Angus said meeting Silas' gaze. "Tell him, Brix."

"First tell me what form was he in before and what form is he in now? Did he use some sort of masking device to alter his appearance?" Silas asked. Amazed by the drastic changes in the wolf, Silas stared into a pair of ice glacier cold blues eyes. This wolf would always require special handling, like Tyrese. His wolf was leashed, but barely. How had he infiltrated the organization? Anyone could see the man was a predator.

"The core of the gift is in our line. You have the ability to change as well. I am surprised you have never felt the need to use it. Your position is a public one, your face well known," Angus said.

Since he did not want to admit he did not know the gift he nodded and met Brix's gaze. After a moment or two, the wolf bowed. "Permission to speak, Sir."

Silas nodded.

"There are three bombs located beneath the lab floors. There are approximately fifteen minutes left before they blow. You have wasted time on the decoy." He held up a small device. "I control that one from here."

"You changed the time?"

"Yes, Sir, I did."

Silas stared a moment longer before speaking to Angus. "You tell me you came to observe, now you say you have three bombs to blow up the lab? What happened to not interfering? So…What is your plan? You plan to blow the lab, kill innocents above? It seems my instinct to not trust you were correct."

Angus held up his hands. "We had hoped to rob the lab and then destroy it. Neither of those things happened the way we planned. For one thing, we are still here," Angus said his nose narrowed as he glanced at Brix.

"True." Silas looked over his shoulder, the twins were heading in his direction along with Leon. "Time to go."

His mate monitored Asia and would alert him when she woke up; they needed to be on their way by then. With all the data Bruce gave him, Silas considered the mission a success except for Asia's death, resurrection and kidnapping. He was done with this place. If it blew, it blew. He would help Samuel deal with the fallout.

"If you leave I will push this button now and everything will explode," Brix said staring at Leon in a way that made Silas pause. He glanced at Leon. The young wolf appeared thunderstruck as he turned away from Angus and Brix.

Shit. They did not have time for this. Silas's gaze flicked to Brix again. The blond wolf stared at Leon as if he were lunch at an all-you-can-eat buffet. Leon wasn't much better. He kept licking his lips and peeking over his shoulder in Brix's direction.

Silas shook his head at the bad timing and acted on his suspicions. "Let's go guys."

The twins, followed by Leon stepped in front of him. Leon looked back over his shoulder periodically. When they reached the opening, he whispered. "Sir, are you going to leave them here?"

"Why do you care?" Silas asked as they continued up the stairs.

"I don't. At least I don't think I care. But… what if he pushes the button and the bomb explodes?" They reached the upper area of the lab and headed for the opening.

"He would've done it already." He waved to the steps leading out of the lab. "Go up." Leon hesitated briefly and then climbed the steps.

Once Silas was outside in the clearing he stretched. *"Angus, Leon, and I are up in the clearing where you and I greeted each other earlier. Once you deactivate all of the bombs, you and your boy come up here for a talk."* Silas removed the energy cell.

"We have everything loaded," Tyrone said walking toward him.

"Good, I want you and Rese to take off and load the plane with the boxes and the data disks so we can leave as soon as Leon and I get there. Also, contact Jacques, I want to know if any planes left or are leaving within a hundred-mile radius and everything about it. She already has a head start."

"Yes, Sir. We can pick up something to eat on the way, you want anything particular?" Tyrone asked glancing at Leon.

The thought of food made his stomach grumble. "Double whatever you and Rese get for us. I'm hungry." He paused and decided against telling the twins what was going on, he wasn't one hundred percent sure himself. "Samuel left a car for me, have Rese punch in the address in the GPS to the location for us to meet you guys. We're right behind you."

Tyrone nodded. "Yes, Sir."

Samuel contacted him on their link. *"Do I need to call the bomb squad, Sir?"*

Silas told him everything that happened, except his latest hunch. *"It's up to you how you want to handle it. I left the door open to the bomb site. Bottom line, I want this lab to become unusable for them again. Make that happen."*

"Yes, Sir."

"What's going on, Sir?" Leon asked watching the twins and the others leave.

"I'm not exactly sure, but I suspect you are about to be challenged. And I cannot allow my sons to interfere. This one is all on you."

Frowning, he stared up at him. "Who is challenging me? Why?"

Silas shook his head, not exactly certain how to explain. Mates were beyond him, the fates handled that facet of their lives. Like most wolves, Leon appreciated great sex and wasn't particular whether his partner was male or female. Which was a good thing otherwise things could become messy and they did not have time for messy.

"Come with me." He walked in the direction of the small clearing and had just sat on a large log when a large white wolf flew past him and landed on Leon.

Quicker than Silas could blink, Leon jumped up, shoving the animal hard off him in the process. A blur of white fur slid across the ground and hit the trunk of the tree. Silas sensed Angus' presence but remained silent as the dominant match continued. Leon never shifted to wolf rather he fought the beast in his hybrid form which was impressive.

Leon was almost as fast as the twins. Silas recognized some of the moves were from practice in the gym. Leon's long legs were constantly in motion pushing Brix back. When Brix shifted to his hybrid form, the fight was truly on. Physically, Brix was larger than Leon. But Leon's brawling experience showed as he kept Brix on the defensive, pushing, dashing in and out at such a fast pace it was amazing. With absolute focus he slashed with his claws, punched, and kicked the Viking, leaving Brix bleeding from a multitude of cuts all over his body.

With a mighty roar, Brix grabbed Leon in a bear hug.

Silas tensed. There was no way he would allow the young wolf to be broken. Just as he thought he may need to stop him. Brix groaned, trembling as his arms were slowly pushed open. Silas watched in amazement as Leon used his legs, removing Brix's straining arms as he tried in vain to hold on.

Once Leon maneuvered Brix's arm down partially, he pushed against it and flipped over Brix's head. The momentum helped his upper body slide from beneath Brix's arm as his legs wrapped around Brix's neck.

Silas nodded in appreciation at the excellent maneuver. Brix struggled to remove the thick corded legs from around his throat but could not. Eventually, he fell to his knees as Leon tightened his hold.

"Will you kill him?" Angus asked walking closer to the two combatants.

Silas glanced at the man and then back at the two. Leon continued looking toward the copse of trees and did not respond.

"He would not kill you, or allow you to be hurt in any way; do you understand what that means?" Angus asked as if he were moderating a debate. His long black hair was lost in the shadow of his loose-fitting dark attire. When he received no response, he turned to Silas. "He does not hear me… Is he always like this?"

Understanding the significance of what Angus said, Silas called sharply, "Leonidas."

He stopped moving and looked blankly in Silas's direction. For a moment he simply stared and then spoke. "Sir?"

"I believe you have won the challenge," Silas said, proud of the young wolf's performance. His gaze flicked toward Brix, who lay on his side on the ground, his hand still on Leon's leg.

Leon's gaze followed his. "Oh…oh," he said removing his legs slowly with a small grin. "I did, didn't I?" He looked at Silas and then down at Brix. A moment later he extended his hand and pulled Brix up. The Viking topped Leon by at least a foot in height, but it didn't stop Leon from stepping forward until he was chest to chest with his challenger. "Do you yield?"

Brix tipped his head to the side, baring his neck. Leon pulled him close and bit down between the neck and shoulder. Silas sensed the connection, as Leon's and Brix's links were created and the mating process began. He glanced at Angus, who watched the two wolves with a slight frown. One of the perks of winning a dominance challenge gave Leon the right to make decisions for him and his mate. Silas suspected Angus was pissed.

"Mmmm, you taste sweet," Leon said, licking Brix's neck. He stepped back, shook his head, and then turned to Silas. "Sir, I guess the fates decided I was enjoying my time as a single wolf too much." He smiled and glanced at Brix, who continued to stare at Leon as if he were manna sent from above.

"I present my mate to you." Frowning, he looked over his shoulder. "What is your name?"

Silas shook his head. Leon always had an easygoing, sunny personality, unless he was on an assignment. But mating without any knowledge of your mate was over the top.

"I am Brix. You?"

"Leonidas. Leon for short."

"You resemble a lion, and fight as one," Brix said with pride.

Leon's smile widened. "Sir, I would introduce you to my mate, Brix, and ask that he accompany us to locate Asia. I think he will be useful."

Either Silas allowed Brix to travel along or Leon would remain behind. Newly mated separation would be difficult and Leon was not old enough to handle it.

"Brix do you know where the lab Mélange took Asia is located?" Silas asked.

Brix nodded. "Yes, I will accompany my mate and assist you in this matter. The lab is cleverly hidden with large security measures and safeguards. It would be best to take her before she enters if possible."

Silas hadn't thought of that. "You said the lab was three or four hours away, Mélange has an hour jumpstart."

Brix nodded. "Three hours by air. She has to travel a distance from here first and then board a plane. No one approaches that lab by air. She will disembark and travel the last hour over land. This enables their sharpshooters an opportunity to shoot those leaving or entering the compound. It is dangerous no matter what."

"Where is it?" Leon asked.

"It is near the Superior National Forest near the Canadian border in Minnesota."

Leon nodded and stepped closer to Silas with his head bowed, waiting.

"Yes, he may travel with us, we may need his help." Silas didn't mention that as soon as Asia woke, Jasmine would be able to lead them to her as well.

"Thank you, La Patron," Brix said with another bow.

"Thank you, Sir. Don't know how all this works, I just don't think I can leave him behind. It was hard walking up the stairs a few moments ago and that was before the bite. Anything you care to share regarding this process I would be grateful," Leon said with feeling, his gaze sliding to Brix.

"I could not complete my mission once I sensed you. Five years working in the organization, gone at the scent of my mate. You are not the only one who could not leave your mate behind, Leon," Brix said as he brushed against his mate.

Silas stood, determined to get in the air as soon as possible so these two could have some privacy. Plus, he was hungry and would nap on the way to Minnesota. "I will give you a crash course on the drive to meet the twins. The plane is waiting for us. Let's go." He strode toward the clearing where Samuel had left a small black jeep.

"A word with you, Silas," Angus said as they passed him.

"I don't have time right now." Silas continued walking. Leon was behind him with Brix following.

"I have more things to share with you and would appreciate traveling to this new lab as well," Angus said following after them.

"Call my office, make an appointment and we can talk later, not now."

"This information is critical to the success of your trip."

Silas stopped, closed his eyes, and turned. "I said no..." His mouth dropped open.

"What the hell?" Leon whispered as he stared at Angus.

"That is not a black wolf trick," Silas said pointing.

"No this is not. Typically we can change the color of our wolf to shades of black, or the stockings or tips of ears. However, when the threat of the Liege became known to us, we improved on the chameleon gift that is our heritage," Angus said in a softer, more feminine voice. He held up his wrist, the light hit a goldish-looking bracelet he wore. "Technology comes in handy at times. Brix used it to alter his appearance the past five years. Now tell me you do not believe I can be of assistance in this endeavor?"

Silas shook his head, unsure what to say as he stared in awe at Angus, who now looked like Asia's twin.

Chapter 15

Mélange glanced behind her, checking that her passenger was secure in the steel cage that took up half the small underwater pod. She tapped her Bluetooth to make a call. He answered on the first ring.

"You have her?"

"Yes, Sir. I am nearing the location for the next step." She glanced at the coordinates and realized she should be arriving within ten minutes.

"Good. The van is waiting along with a truck. They will follow you to the main road and then split off. I will give you the coordinates once you have loaded the merchandise. How did it go? Anyone follow or suspicious?"

She thought back. "No, it was a smooth exchange. Sims rolled her on board and then placed her in the pod. Just as he finished La Patron showed up, I left before he got to the boat." She was sure Sims died for his role stalling the Alpha but it couldn't be helped.

"Did you remove the tracking device? It should have still been in her chest."

"Yes, Sir, I removed it." The small chip had moved in the opposite direction, near the surface of her skin making it easy to extract.

"What of Orsis?"

Mélange's feelings regarding her former partner were mixed. Orsis wasn't much to look at, brown hair, average height, and build guy, but he was cunning and smart. More than once he saved her ass. Leaving him behind had been difficult, the man was hot in bed, but when she was approached for this side job she jumped on the opportunity to move up in the organization.

"I told him I needed to check on something. He never questioned. The last I saw of him a huge black wolf was running toward him." For old times' sake, she hoped he survived. Even though he wanted nothing more from her than occasional sex, she could trust him whenever they were on Liege business to watch her back and that was rare.

"His chips blinked out. You are the only one who made it out of there alive. La Patron was thorough."

Her fingers tightened on the control as she processed the news of her former partner's death. "The wolf killed him?" her jaw tightened.

"Could be, or the hybrid or La Patron. I do not know who killed him. He was an excellent operative and will be missed."

Surprised to hear any kind of praise regarding someone other than himself, Mélange nodded. "He was loyal to the Liege." She knew better than to pay tribute to another employee. Everything all operatives did must lead to the success of the Liege Lords. But her thoughts couldn't be monitored, and she wished whoever killed her partner a long and painful death. Later she would mourn his loss; right now she had to deliver the most sought after person in the world to her Liege.

"Yes, he was, so are you, Mellie."

She cringed. His nickname for her grated her nerves. "Thank you, Sir."

"There is an opening in the Canadian office; I think you will be perfect. You will oversee a hundred workers in our manufacturing plant. The hours will be long, but if you do as well as I suspect, financially you will be set for a long time."

Exhaling, she touched the flashing red button on the dashboard. If she could take back the night in Rio five years ago when she allowed him to take her to bed she would. The sex had been over before she was warmed up and he snored like a grouchy bear. The next morning at breakfast she had been politely grille over her past life. When she left later that day, she had unwittingly given him keys that he dangled in front of her whenever he wanted something. Griffith may have been horrible in the sack, but he was one of the geniuses behind the Liege Lords organization.

"Thank you, Sir, for your consideration and the opportunity to serve my Lieges. I will do my best to bring honor to your recommendation, Sir."

He chuckled. "And you want to make a lot of money too. I know that is the driving force behind your actions, you cannot trick me. But since I understand why, it works in our favor."

She nodded. If only he knew. Taking the job with the organization ten years ago, money and the chance to rub her success in her family's face had been one of the reasons she accepted the job without researching the company. Once started, she realized her mistake within the first ninety days, but it was too late. The first of many implants had been slipped beneath her skin.

When she graduated from high school, she joined the military and eventually went to Officer's training. Her family saw her stint as an Army Officer as a desperate move by an unwanted child and mocked her. She thought working for a large corporation would be just the thing to make them see her as more than the bastard child of her deceased mother's lover.

Now they thought she lived an exciting life as a marketing executive traveling around the world. She sent pictures wearing the best clothes and stayed at the best hotels. Instead of acceptance, they asked for more money. Not once had she been invited to any birthday parties, christenings, or Christmas celebrations she paid for. No one ever contacted her to just say hello or ask how she was doing. Pathetic.

"Yes, Sir. I don't ever want to be dependent on family again," she said knowing he expected a similar response.

"Clan is not all it should be these days. You should be at the pickup point," he said.

"Yes, Sir." She wasn't surprised that he knew exactly where she was, the man was a brilliant strategist and never left anything to chance. Death was the bonus for failing this job. Everyone knew Asia was a loose cannon and under La Patron's protection to fail meant termination by several hands. It hadn't surprised her when he sent her, the Liege did not value women, sending Orsis, putting him at risk was a surprise.

"I am shutting off the pod now; the men are securing it to the dock."

"Ah, La Patron's plane has left, they are on their way to Minnesota. I will make sure they are welcomed." He paused. "Let me know when she is loaded and you are ready to drive. Leave behind them and I will give you the coordinates."

"Yes, Sir," she said her mind focused on parking the water vehicle and stretching her legs. When the door opened, she grabbed her backpack and stepped out.

"Bring the cage out and store it in the van. Be careful, I don't want her to wake up." Despite Griffith's assurance that Asia would be drugged and harmless. She had given the woman another shot as soon as they submerged. Asia had the highest body count in the organization, the woman had been around for decades. No one messed with her.

Once her feet hit land, Mélange stretched. Standing in alligator boots near the swirling water, she watched as two men lifted the cage from the pod and handed it off to the two men on the ground. They held Asia between them and headed toward the trucks. One of the men fiddled with a palm-held device and the pod slowly sank beneath the water. Mélange snorted as she followed behind the men. Griffith had always been in control of the pod. If she attempted to do anything other than what he wanted, these men would have given her a different type of greeting.

After the cage containing Asia was locked into place in the back of the van, the men went to two separate trucks. "Sir, I am locked and loaded."

"Good, here are the coordinates."

She typed them into the GPS. "Yes, Sir they are in. I have an arrival time of two hours and forty minutes. Is that correct, Sir?"

"Yes, depending on traffic. But at this time of the morning, the roads should be clear. You should arrive in time for an early breakfast."

She smiled. "Yes, Sir."

He laughed. "Thought you'd like that. Get moving, your clock starts now."

She turned the key and shifted gears. "Yes, Sir, waiting for the first truck to move." The trucks moved into position slowly with her in the middle. "Moving out now, Sir." She had no doubt the drivers in the other vehicles were making similar comments to him. He probably had a video installed somewhere in the van. She glanced around the van but saw nothing glaringly obvious.

Chapter 16

A LOW THROB AT the back of her head greeted Asia as she slowly wakened. Opening her senses, but not her eyes, she thanked the Goddess she was no longer rocking on the waves of the boat. For some reason she had yet to discover, being on a boat terrified her. Somewhere hidden in the deep recesses of her mind lay the reason and one day she would have her answer. A few moments later she realized she was in a car. The smooth motion soothed her.

Sensing she was not alone, she commanded her body to remain in a comatose state while she checked things out.

Inhaling, she recognized the scent from the lab. The female was with Deets when she had been captured. Asia tried to remember what happened, everything was blank after she was placed on the boat.

"Mistress?"

"Asia?... Please tell me you are okay? Well... alive and healthy."

"Yes, I just woke up. They gave me something while I ...after I passed out. I wonder where I am. They removed the tracker. I am not sure who has me this time."

"Silas walked me through how to lock on you so they can come to you. If we're lucky they'll beat your plane at the airport."

"Why are they in a plane? Where are they going?" That made no sense.

"They are headed to Minnesota to the other lab. It was the closest one to Pennsylvania." She paused. *"Are you on a plane?"*

"No, I'm in a truck or van on the road with lanes. Not a back road. Who told them there was a lab in Minnesota? The black wolf?"

"No. Leon's mate."

"What?"

"Yeah, things have happened since you've been out of touch."

"Mistress, I have only been out of touch a couple of hours at the most, what has happened?"

"Let me get a lock on you first so I can tell Silas, I have a feeling they are headed in the wrong direction."

"If Leon's mate told Leon a lab is in Minnesota then that is the truth as far as he knows. One cannot lie to a mate."

"I know that. Boy... do I know. There have been times...but that's not important. Just because there's a lab in Minnesota does not mean that is where you are being taken. Since they're supposed to be rescuing you, I need to tell them where you're headed." She paused. *"Got it. You're still in Pennsylvania, traveling south on the interstate. Shit, that's not good. Hold on, let me tell Silas."*

Asia could imagine La Patron's face when he discovered they were headed northwest when she was headed southeast. Whoever planned her capture did a good job of mixing things up. She kept still with her eyes closed as she looked around. The shaded outline of the driver was no surprise. Opening her hearing to a more sensitive pitch, she took a deeper scan and was unsurprised to see three small cameras in the van. That answered her question as to who had taken her. The cameras were trademarks of her former captors. There was a tiny one, barely visible, in front of her clipped onto the cage. Another small one sat on the dashboard facing the driver. Without her new weird vision, she would not have been able to see it, the color blended so well with the dash. A third tiny camera sat on the passenger seat visor. She was certain it was a panoramic view of the interior of the van. Someone monitored their drive.

"Silas said...well... do you have any idea where you're headed?"

Asia wanted to laugh, but with the camera in her face, she refrained. No doubt La Patron was angry and had been colorful in his expression. *"Not yet, Mistress. As soon as I hear anything, I will let you know."*

"Are you tied up or something? Can you break free and jump out the car?"

Asia thought about it. *"I am being closely watched. I believe if I made a move to do either of those things, there would be immediate retribution. That is the normal way things have been done in the past."*

"Huh?"

"If I tried what you suggest, it would trigger something. It could be anything from explosives to some sort of gas, or a virus ... anything. There is only one other person in the van and that would not happen unless this van has been specially equipped. I have done a few of these missions in the past. I am sure the driver has no idea her life is forfeit if I tried to escape."

"You'd both die?"

"Yes, Mistress. Whoever has orchestrated this is high up in the organization and I would like to meet him or her before I kill them. So I will rest for now. It would be nice to have some back-up," she said not wanting to sound ungrateful for the botched rescue mission.

"I'll tell Silas, but if you are heading somewhere nearby, they may not reach you until later."

"I understand. I will have a chance to test my new body sooner than later. I need to tweak a few things in my arms and leg so the magnet will not work. I will work on that."

"Okay...I wish there was something I could do."

Warmth swamped her, reminding her she was not alone. *"It is good having you here. Tell me what happened to Leon."*

With her body shut down, she began the process of demagnetizing her limbs while listening as Jasmine brought her current on Angus, Brix, and Leon.

She had just finished her leg when the female spoke. "Sir, I am turning off the highway." There was a pause. "No, Sir she has not stirred or made any sounds." Another pause. "Yes, Sir, I gave her a shot once she was placed in the pod because she was fighting to break free and we were running out of time. La Patron had just blown the door."

"Yes, Sir." The van turned down a bumpy road and stopped. The female put the van in gear and grabbed her backpack. Moments later she removed a filled syringe and exited the van. Asia commanded her body to remain in stasis as the needle penetrated her skin. Immediately she determined the composition injected had been saline water. Her captor sought to trick her into waking up. She had done that to many others over the years. When the female started the vehicle again, Asia contacted Jasmine.

"*Mistress, we have turned off the main highway down a rocky road. Can you lock on my position?*"

"*Yes. Silas has sent Alpha Samuel since you are still in Pennsylvania. They are an hour behind you. Any idea who has you, or where you're going?*"

"*No. Not yet. It is someone she refers to as Sir. That can be several people. I am prepared to meet my fate or destiny, Mistress. It does not matter who has kidnapped me, I plan to destroy them.*"

"*Well…okay, I understand that. I just don't want you to be alone. You have Pack.*"

"*I am usually alone, it does not bother me.*"

"*I know that. But you don't have to be… unless you really want to. You and I are linked. I feel your sadness, your acceptance of everything as if there is nothing else in life. I want you to know there is much more, and I want you to experience life to its fullest. I want you to have those margaritas on the beach.*"

Inwardly Asia smiled. "*That sounds nice Mistress. I would enjoy that as well. Perhaps after this is over…*"

"*No Asia. When you leave wherever you are headed, I want you to take a trip to the beach and have that margarita. I want you to lay on the beach and allow the sun to warm you and the sounds from the waves to ease you.*"

Asia envisioned the setting as Jasmine spoke it. "*The waves make an interesting sound as they crash into the shore, it is soothing. The sun warms in ways that man can never fully mimic. I have never had a margarita, but I saw a woman drinking a frozen one and she looked so happy.*"

"*When you leave wherever you are heading now Asia, that is what you will do,*" Jasmine said again, her voice stronger as if she were drilling her words in Asia's mind.

"*Yes, Mistress, and thank you. I will return to the compound first because that is my original vow and then I will leave again to lie on the beach for a few days."*

"Good, I want to see you again. We'll eat and go shopping."

That surprised her. She could not remember ever going shopping with anyone for women's things. *"Shopping?"*

"Yes, for beach things and clothes. Plus it will get me and Mom out the compound for a few hours. I have everything locked down until Silas returns and that won't be until he comes for you. So we'll all benefit from your beach trip."

Asia did not know what to say. Jasmine sounded happy at the prospect of walking in stores searching for items to wear, while Asia would rather have a tooth pulled. *"Yes, Mistress."* She tried to inject enthusiasm into her voice.

Jasmine laughed. It was a good sound, one that filled Asia with warmth. *"You'll have fun, just wait. Shopping is a good thing."*

Not wanting to offend, but unable to lie, Asia remained silent.

"Silas said some wolves are trailing the van and will lead their Alpha to your location."

"Tell them to stay away from the van and not to interfere. They will lose their lives if they do not listen to me. This is an old-school kidnapping, I did them all the time early on. The van is the weapon and it is equipped to take out anyone who attempts to stop it from the mission. Even if the driver dies, someone else controls this van and is monitoring it. If he sees a wolf close by, he can shoot with one hundred percent accuracy."

"Oh...okay, I'll tell him."

Asia tried to relax, but the idea of a vacation kept her wound tight. Damn, she wanted that trip. The more she thought of the sun on her skin, and the sound of the waves the more determined she became to fight for her vacation.

Suddenly the van rocked from side to side and then settled into a smooth ride, leaving the graveled path behind.

The next half hour or so Asia floated in a world of fantasy where she sat on the beach with a drink, basking in the sun. In some dreams she ran on the shore, her toes digging into the sand, and on others, she lay and simply listened. The daydreams calmed her to the point it took a moment for her to realize the van had stopped.

"Pull it forward," a masculine voice said. The van inched forward, reminding her of the abandoned mine, she and Tyrese had been trapped in a while back. That day had been filled with the extermination of the Bennett clan, a lot of blood, and death. Although she suspected bloodshed would be a part of freeing herself, she hoped there were not as many deaths as it had been that day.

Once the vehicle stopped, she heard the clanging of heavy metal doors and then nothing. She was inside her enemy's camp. To fulfill her daydream, she would end his life today.

"You can wake up now. I know you have been playing possum for a while now. I can tell by the twitching in your eyes. Come now, get up."

Asia did not respond to his baiting. For one thing, her body was in a comatose state. If her eyes twitched it was natural to that condition. The stakes were too high for her to show her hand now.

"Open the back of the van slowly." Cool air spilled inside the van as the door behind her creaked open.

"Mistress I am inside the house or garage, not sure which. I have sent my body to sleep and need you to act as gatekeeper. Please make sure anything that is shot into my system does not affect me. No implants, please."

"Yes, I will be with you until you walk out the door to freedom. I have joined my energy with Silas in the past and will do the same today because we are going shopping... damn it."

Hearing Jasmine's voice relaxed Asia and she slid deeper into her body sleep. *"Yes, Mistress. I look forward to it."*

"Silas suggests I enter your system now so that I am aware of what is normal." Warmth eased into her system. Her fingertips tingled. *"I'm in. You okay?"* Jasmine asked.

"Yes, Ma'am. They are wheeling the cage out now. There are two men and the woman from the lab. I have never seen any of these people before."

"Okay, just so you know Silas is listening in so I don't go back and forth."

"Yes, Ma'am. Hello Sir. They are taking me up a ramp into what appears to be a large kitchen." The room was much cooler. Her cage door opened and a sharp blade plunged into her chest. Her body arched and then slumped.

"What the hell was that?" Jasmine screamed. *"He stabbed you? Why? Who?"*

Asia's body warmed beneath her Mistress's anger. *"It's okay, my body is designed to handle that, please calm down Mistress. I do not want anyone to know I am not alone."*

"Okay, it's her. We are going to move her onto this." Hands lifted her onto a padded gurney and locked her in. "Take her to the elevator. You..." he said in a commanding tone as he pointed, "clean this mess."

Asia tried to get a better look but was limited to outlines and shadows. The gurney moved slowly forward and stopped. The male stepped forward and placed his hand on the wall. It beeped. He punched something in a keypad, each key made a different sound that Asia stored for later use. A set of doors opened and she was wheeled inside. He punched in a different set of numbers and the elevator moved upward.

"Now you see why she is so valuable?" the male asked. "Imagine if I had stabbed you with that butcher knife. With all your enhancements, your body would not be able to handle it. Notice how she stopped bleeding and her flesh has healed around the blade. To pay five million for her is a mere pittance and has already been placed in your account."

"Yes, Sir. It is impressive. You are a genius."

He chuckled. "I am, but I did not develop the technology. Pity, I must take her apart to discover why she responds so well to the implants in her body. We have searched for others so that we can duplicate her, but have not been successful. Until we do, we will take her off the market."

Doors swooshed open and they walked out into another cool area that smelled like bleach.

"Push her over here." The cart moved slowly and then stopped.

"What is going on?" Jasmine asked.

"They are talking," she said and repeated what she heard.

"Just so you know, Asia, I cannot allow that to happen. I am assuming you have a plan. You are the expert and I am along for the ride, but if you don't want me to lose it, you better kill that bastard before he touches you."

"Alpha Samuel is nearby but not at your location," Silas said in a calming voice. *"We landed to refuel and will be returning to Pennsylvania shortly. I am coming to pick you up, not carry a body home. If you allow it, Jasmine can combine her energy with yours to fight your way out of there. Do not try and fight this alone."*

"Yes, Ma'am. Yes, Sir." She paused as everything about the

whole setup ran through her mind. She cataloged information and cross-verified data until she came to an interesting conclusion. One that made her heart race and her fingers itch for a weapon. *"I think he is one of the Liege Lords. They never surface. Perhaps I can find out more about the organization or where the rest of them are. It would help bring this war to an end and stop the abuse against our Pack."* She added the last for her Mistress. La Patron understood the thrill of the hunt and why she would go after the big game.

No one said anything.

"Mistress?" She had to get her Mistress on board or La Patron might side with his mate and forbid her to do anything other than flee. Her wolf would be hard-pressed to obey that order.

"I am mated to La Patron and his concerns are my concerns, but... right now I don't care about anything except you walking out of that damn place alive."

"But Mistress this is who I am," she said softly, searching for the right words to explain. *"I have pledged to assist in this fight, and this is an opportunity to slap our enemies and gain information. I believe I need to do this."*

"What if they pin you down again, like in the lab and you cannot stop them?" Jasmine asked.

"When I died or rebooted, all of my systems returned online, even things that had been turned off in my previous form. When they caught me in the lab, I was still regenerating. I am at full capacity now and I don't think they can hold me unless I allow it...but just in case, I have you to assist me." She did not want to offend her Mistress, but this opportunity to strike a blow to their enemies was important.

"Okay, I will be here and remain silent unless your body goes into distress or you seek my help. That is the best I can do," Jasmine said.

"Thank you, Ma'am, Sir. They are sitting at a desk talking now. The woman is the same from the lab, but I do not know her. Perhaps Leon's mate can give us some information on her. She is a breed with enhancements, but not much."

"I will talk to Brix," Silas said. She heard relief and excitement in his voice.

"Sit here," the man said to the woman. "I'm going to take her inside and prep her. There are Pack wolves outside, which means the state Alpha and La Patron knows she is here. I'm not sure how that happened. I scanned her before she entered the van and when she exited. She has no implants or devices. The van is clean as well."

"Is it possible La Patron can locate her as her Alpha?" the woman said.

"If that was the case you wouldn't have left the lab alive. And he wouldn't use her as bait, too valuable." He tapped his finger against his chin. "Something is off about that."

The woman took a seat, pulled out a weapon, and placed it on the desk.

"Put that away," the man snapped. "If you use anything like that in this building it would destroy everything. There is a button beneath the desk...do you feel it?"

"I apologize, Sir."

"If there is an emergency, flick open the tab and press the button and then leave. Don't try to find me, I will know what's happening and leave another way."

"Leave here? How?" she asked.

He moved to another section of the wall. "Come here."

The woman met him. Asia strained to see what they were doing but could not. A door opened.

"Go down these stairs, don't stop. Go all the way to the bottom; take one of the cars and drive. Someone will contact you later. If this door opens, leave immediately. It will be my warning you something happened."

She nodded.

"I see your collar, good. If La Patron comes I do not want him to take control of you."

"You think he is on his way here? I thought he left for Minnesota." The woman returned to the desk.

"If the Pack knows the Alpha knows, which means Silas Knight knows. We have at least four to six hours before they arrive and attempt to storm the building. I will make sure they are welcomed appropriately." He chortled as he grabbed the gurney and pulled it into another room.

The door locked behind him and he pulled her down a long well lit corridor. They stopped and she heard the familiar beeps signifying he had punched in another code. The lights came on overhead.

"Got to get you strapped in so I can show off my prize," he

murmured. "They didn't want me to do this, did not think it would pan out, they say I am old-fashioned and work too hard. Nothing wrong with working with your hands. Them gadgets do not have all the answers, sometimes you gotta use your mind and your hands."

It was his comment regarding showing her off that stopped her from killing him then. She suspected he would contact others who were high up in the organization. If she could not open her eyes to see them, hearing their voices would be just as effective. She never forgot faces or sounds, both were her signature calling cards.

When she lay limp in his arms, he snorted. "How much drug did she give you?" He hefted her across his shoulder. He wasn't that tall, not like Tyrese or La Patron, but he had a wide barrel-shaped chest and thick, strong arms. They walked a few feet and he laid her on something padded. The next moment, cold metal secured her ankles and then her wrist.

He patted her shoulder as if they were old friends. "I've got to check in with me boys and then we will know what direction we are going in."

She wondered what he meant by that, but not before the import of what he said hit. He was going to contact the group now.

"Mistress, can you hear what I hear?"

"No. Yes, sometimes, it comes and goes. I don't have full control of this yet. What's going on?"

"He is about to contact the other members so they can see me. It would be easier if you and La Patron could hear it firsthand."

"Damn it. I don't hear anything."

"It is usually a gift between mates and in some cases siblings. If we were linked I could hear as well, I do not understand why Jasmine cannot hear through your link," La Patron said.

"He is greeting someone on the monitor, telling them I am secure and knocked out on drugs." Listening intently, she knew when the men on the other end of the call picked up.

"Hola comrades."

"Griffith, it is good to see you. I hear you were successful in your endeavor. Well done. Where is the bitch?"

"She is here, Gordon, strapped to the table in titanium cuffs..." There was some sort of shuffling noise. "Can you see her now?"

"Yes. Why is that knife in her chest?"

"Verification."

"Ah, simple and effective."

"A scan would have been just as effective and less messy. I am sure you left a trail of blood."

"Perhaps, Boris," Griffith said in a low grumbling voice.

"Where is Mélange?" Gordon asked into the silence.

Griffith chuckled. "She is on guard duty above."

"Everything is in place?" Boris asked, his tone speculative.

"Yes, in twenty minutes I will signal her to leave. When she reaches the ground floor, she will take one of the cars and drive off. There is only one car with keys. She has instructions to just drive until someone contacts her."

"Good, I will monitor her vehicle, there can be no screw-ups on this job. You sure she can handle it?" Gordon asked.

"What is there to handle? She does not know about the bodies in the trunk. If she is stopped her fingerprints alone are on everything," Griffith said.

"So they were able to lift her prints from the pod?" Gordon asked.

"Yes."

"Good... Your hit today cost us a good, loyal man. Orsis will be missed," Boris said.

Asia wondered if Orsis was Leon's mate.

"Yes," Griffith said, sounding aggravated. "Sometimes there are casualties. It is a part of this business. However, I have recovered Asia. We can begin our experiments again."

"We will discuss that in a few moments, it is important to tell you we believe Angus has found La Patron," Gordon said in a somber tone.

"What? How did he escape?" Griffith asked. "Is that the black wolf who killed Orsis?"

"Could be. There was a black wolf at the lab?" Gordon asked.

"Mélange saw a black wolf running toward Orsis, that is the last time she saw him alive."

"Damn it. Angus complicates matters," Boris said with feeling.

"Yes, he does. What kind of damage did he do when he escaped?" Griffith asked in a low voice.

"Body count? He wiped out ten or twelve, a whole wing of staff, damaged some of the equipment beyond repair. We had to order new parts for others. That lab is shut down for a couple of months;

everything is being shifted to the other ones. Which brings me back to Asia," Gordon said.

She tensed.

"Lock her down for now; we don't have space or security in any of the labs to hold her. Now was not the best time to reacquire the bitch. We are short doctors and test subjects. You released the last test wolves to La Patron and they are now dead. In some areas we are starting over, in others we need to fill the orders we have. The last shipment from the lab has been lost as well?"

"Yes," Griffith said tightly. "La Patron arrived before my men could secure it."

"So this venture of yours was more costly than we thought. How long before we can replace those collars?" Boris asked.

"A week, no more than that with staff working overtime," Griffith said.

"You convened a meeting with us to show us your expensive prize, Griffith. We urged you to wait and allow La Patron to take the lab. He would've used his resources to close a facility no longer of value to us. Yet you went ahead and cost us a high-level operative, our test stock, our inventory and now we must pay thousands of dollars in overtime to fill orders for our customers. And all you show us is Asia who has been with us for decades," Boris said.

"We wanted her off the streets," Griffith said defensively.

"Yes, but she is her own enemy and would have eventually resurfaced. One of the bounty hunters would have ultimately caught her and brought her in with no loss of our resources. We need to think more twenty-first century if we are going to survive my brother," Gordon said.

"We have survived just fine and will continue to do so. But I will use my hands as well as my mind. I am not given to trust equipment one hundred percent. My gut told me it was important to remove her from La Patron. Just as your gut told you to capture Angus," Griffith said.

"Angus is a problem to be solved. Asia is not. We already know what she is capable of. Angus and this whole black wolf element is a new threat. His uncanny ability to hear thoughts and mimic human attributes is unusual. And that makes him a wild card," Boris shot back.

"Should I leave her here for La Patron?" Griffith asked in a snide tone.

"Hmmm, that is something to consider. That is one of the smaller satellite locations…easily replaced. If you did that, we could leave the bodies there as well," Boris said.

"What of Mélange?"

"What of her?" Boris asked.

"She has served as well as Orsis. Loyal and obedient," Griffith said.

"She is a woman," Boris said dismissively.

"Ay," Griffith said.

"Women are not to be trusted in positions of power, you know that Griffith," Gordon said.

"It was you who said we needed to operate in the twenty-first century. I am agreeing with you."

"That is something to be discussed later. As for Asia, transport her to your private lair and imprison her until later. Mélange has indeed served us well and if she lives through this assignment, we can consider using her in some other capacity. Women are not equal to men and she will never be allowed to rise to the same level Orsis would have, do not forget that, my brother. For now, we will continue to monitor ongoing experiments and provide our clients with top-quality products. The others are busy in other areas; we do not want to mess this part of the operation up. Research will start up again in three months. Any questions?" Gordon said with a snap of authority.

"No," Boris said.

"No," Griffith said.

"Good, we come together at our regular time, unless another emergency meeting is called," Gordon said.

Chapter 17

FOR A FEW MOMENTS there was silence in the room and then the sound of something smashing against the wall filled the room.

"Condescending bastard. Always got something to say." Another object splattered against the wall. "I would gut the swiggling fop if he ever stepped outside that damn castle of his. I am not the only one either. Guttersnipe always smarting off at the mouth." Another thud against the wall and then he roared. "Mutherfucking bastard." He heaved in air and then sat in the chair next to the table with the computer.

"Wonder what he would say if I gift wrapped you and set you on his door, I wonder how he would respond to that?" He mumbled and sat quietly for a few moments.

Asia wished he would. But for that to happen, he would need to live to see the sunrise and she could not allow that.

"Mistress the meeting did not go as well as he hoped and he is enraged, be prepared for anything."

"What happened?"

"I will tell you later, now I must be on alert. He is a wild card at the moment."

Asia watched as he slumped forward with his head in his hands, breathing hard. Moving slightly, she tested the metal around her wrists. It gave a bit. Waiting in the silence of the room with a knife protruding from her chest was one of the more difficult things she had done in a long time.

The smell of his anger stung her nostrils. The sound of his heavy breathing sent adrenaline crashing through her system. Her wolf stirred sensing prey. He sat in the chair for another ten minutes until his breathing calmed.

"Fuck it," he said, standing and glancing in her direction. "I'll do my own experiments; don't need their lab to handle that." He walked toward a door and entered it.

Asia exhaled.

"Gordon, Boris, and Griffith, those are the names of the three men. Griffith is the one with me and he is upset," Asia said and then told Jasmine about the conversation.

"Angus didn't mention he had been a guest of the Liege, he is full of secrets and surprises. Did they say when he escaped?" La Patron asked surprising her. She had forgotten he was on as well.

"No, Sir, but I got the feeling it was recent. They know he is with you. But did not know he was the wolf who attacked Orsis, sorry I mean Brix or at the lab. Is there a way to verify the wolf who is with you is Angus?" Her gaze slid to the door Griffith entered as she heard the commode flush.

"What's your plan when he comes out the bathroom?" Jasmine asked.

"I plan to terminate him and leave this place."

"Sounds solid, like a good plan," Jasmine said.

Asia moved her ankle and lifted slightly, feeling the metal move. Low humming noises reached her ears as she opened her eyes and looked around the large room. Immediately in front of her was a sitting area with three large leather chairs and a long polished mahogany coffee table. A portable computer desk with a large monitor and keyboard sat on top. Further ahead was a long glass and marble conference table with a multitude of chairs. A roll of cable lay nearby on the floor and a large screen filled the wall. To the right was the door Griffin entered and a row of wood cabinets. The left side mirrored the right except for a couple of blank spaces.

His humming stopped. Next, she heard the water turn on. Was he taking a shower? Seriously? She glanced down at the protruding knife and then looked toward the bathroom. She looked hard. He stood in the middle of the bathroom gazing upward, no doubt watching her through a monitor.

Determined to give him a show, she tugged on her cuffs as if she were trying to escape. After pulling and jerking for a while she collapsed backward as if out of breath.

"Stupid bitch," he muttered.

Inwardly she smiled and waited for him to come closer. A few minutes later the shower turned off and he walked out the door with a towel around his waist wiping his reddish-blond curly hair and full beard. "Glad you decided to wake up and join the party, Asia. Welcome home, we have missed you. How are you feeling?"

"Like there is a knife stuck in my chest. Who the hell are you?"

"I am your new lover, call me whatever you like."

"Asshole? Bastard? Dick?"

"Master or Lord, either of those will be correct," he said darkly.

"Really? You're joking." She baited him, hoping he would lose it again so she could take him off guard.

"No, you have been given to me as a reward for faithful service. And you will obey me."

"Okay." She continued to meet his glare while planning his demise.

He laughed.

She smiled.

"You are a feisty bitch. I have heard many stories about you. I begin to believe they are true." He crossed his massive arms over his chest. "How does one win your loyalty? Or does La Patron control that as well?"

"He is Alpha of the continent."

"But you are not linked to him, why is that? Too hardhead? Too stubborn? Or are you such a mutt he wants nothing to do with you?" He sneered.

She did not bother responding; instead, she used that time to plan the steps for his execution. It would be quicker than she would like, but time was of the essence. She was sure this place was like another place she had worked briefly and would collapse without him to key in the correct codes. She could pull out the blade and throw it at him, pinning him to the wall and then break his neck. That would take about ten seconds, she thought.

"Not that it matters, we will be leaving here soon and you will be off the radar to him and the rest of the world." He moved to a wall and slid open a door that led to a closet. He stepped in and a few moments later he stepped out fully dressed. He glanced at her with a frown. "You're no fun today at all. I keep giving you opportunities to escape...well to try and escape anyway. But you don't use them. How am I supposed to have any fun with my new toys when you won't play?"

"Sorry, I did not know the rules of the game. Perhaps you can explain them to me," she said dryly.

He laughed. "I suppose I should. Otherwise, this could go on for hours and we don't have that kind of time." He paused and picked up a briefcase.

She continued planning. Looking at the titanium cuff on the table, she could pull it off and throw it with such force that it would split his scalp in two. That was another possibility she thought while watching him pick up a goldish-looking band.

"This is one of our newest devices, doesn't work on everybody though. But it is powerful." He replaced it in the briefcase. "We won't use it on you, you have enough going on. What I do have for you is this." He held up what looked like a plastic water pistol. "It is an interrupter. Supposed to shut down your system, not quite sure how it works, I just know that it does."

She looked at the device and then at him. *"Mistress I am going to need your help."*

"You have it."

"He has a device that may short-circuit my brain."

"What?"

"I am not explaining it correctly. It is an electrical device that interrupts the commands from reaching their proper location. For instance, I want to remove the knife, my arm lifts and carries out the command. The device stops my arm from obeying me because it does not get the message of what I want to do. Does that make sense?"

"Kind of. What do I need to do?"

"When he shoots me can you absorb it? If that is the only weapon he has, I will kill him once he discharges and thinks I am harmless."

"Okay, Silas is going to help with this... we have you covered."

Asia did not have time to respond before he fired. Heat raced through her body, causing her limbs to violently shake. Her head rose and hit the back of the table a few times as a cool stream shot through her, sucking in the heat. Gasping for air, she continued to shake as she watched him smiling at a distance.

He glanced at his watch and snapped the briefcase close. Every few seconds she exaggerated a twitch while waiting for him to come closer. He pulled something from the table and snapped it around his neck.

Recognizing the collar he wore, she realized the game had changed. With a hard pull, she snapped the metal holding her arm, grabbed the knife from her chest, and sent it whizzing through the air into his shoulder. He hit the wall behind him with a loud thunk. She pulled her other arm free and then grabbed the cuffs from her legs. The hole in her chest had healed by the time she was free and he struggled against the wall. When he saw her coming toward him, he hulked up, except he wasn't human or wolf. He resembled a jackal, which was fitting.

"Bitch," he hissed as he pulled the knife from his shoulder and threw it at her. She didn't bother replying; instead, she threw one jagged metal cuff into his eye and the other into his crotch. His scream of pain and outrage rattled the windows. Moving at a steady pace, she grabbed the long knife from the floor where it had clattered and threw it toward his other eye. He blocked it with his forearm. It clattered to the floor across the room. Blood dripped from his eye down his chin. Baring long incisors, he moved in her direction.

"Kill you," he hissed, his one good eye locked on her.

The only way to destroy him while collared was to separate his head, which was now doubled in size, from his body. Sprinting forward, she dropped and slammed her fist into his crotch. He doubled over and reached for her. She slid between his legs and jumped up behind him.

He swung wildly, his meaty fist flying over her head spinning him around. She punched him in the jaw and then the eye that had been destroyed by the cuff.

His head snapped backward and he stumbled. He roared as he swung blindly at her again.

She ducked and jumped back, kicking him hard between his legs again. This time he fell to his knees.

Asia kicked him in the face, spinning him around. He hit the ground with a loud thud. She looked around for the knife. It was on the opposite side of the room. Pissed, she kicked him again. He rolled himself onto his stomach to protect himself.

She jumped onto his back, grabbed his head, and twisted until she heard it snap. Exhaling, she continued twisting and then pulled until the head separated from the spinal cord. When she was done, she tossed his head across the room; it rolled beneath the conference table and stopped at the wall. Wiping the sweat from her brow with the back of his shirt, she looked around to see if he dropped anything and then searched him. There was nothing in his pockets, not even a set of keys.

She went to a bank of security monitors and turned them all on. He had said something about the female sitting at a desk. Asia searched the monitors until she saw the female was on the move and it looked as if she was attempting to enter a room. Grabbing his briefcase she ran into his closet searching for a weapon. She had been stripped at the lab before boarding the boat and had nothing.

There were rows of male clothing. She put on a pair of pants and shirt, stuffing the shirttails as she looked around for a pair of shoes. In the back of the closet, there was a long coat hanging at an odd angle. She pushed the coat aside, intent on taking it, and heard a whirring sound. A small panel opened on the wall behind her. Inside were some disks, passports, cash, and a pistol. Asia put everything in the briefcase, except the weapon, she put that in her pant pocket. She heard a sound and fell to her knees. Crawling toward the door, she heard someone opening drawers and closing them.

"Where is it?"

Asia recognized the female's voice and stood slowly at the closet entrance. She placed the briefcase on the top of the shelf and then eased out the door coming face to face with her captor.

"Hello, Asia. I'm Mélange. My business is not with you, but it can be if you make it that way. I just want his briefcase that's all and then I'll be on my way."

"You tried to kill me. Even collected a reward." Asia's gaze swept over the petite Asian assassin.

Mélange snorted as she narrowed her short pointy nose and squinted dark eyes. Her long inky black hair hung in a long braid down her back. Asia was taller than her by at least a foot but she had been in the field long enough to know size was not the most important factor. If it was Griffin would still be breathing.

The woman waved down her concern. "It was business nothing more. I would have gotten here sooner to terminate his ass if he didn't have so many different combinations on each door. He had serious trust issues."

Asia's brow rose. "Do you blame him?"

Mélange shrugged. "I don't care. Where is his briefcase? Do you have it?"

"Yes."

No one spoke. Whatever Mélange wanted from that case, Asia was just as determined she did not have it. The woman had no allegiance to anyone.

"Can I see it? I need one item and then I am gone."

"What item is that?" Asia asked although she was fairly certain it was the bracelet Griffin had shown her earlier.

"Circular, like a bracelet. Kind of small. It belonged to my client and he would like it returned."

"The bracelet is a test object from the lab; it did not belong to anyone else. Your client has acquired your services to steal the technology that is all. You don't lie very well."

Mélange shrugged and pulled out the small primp. "I shoot better. I rarely miss. The bracelet. Now."

Poised to flip out of the way of the discharge, Asia shook her head. "I cannot do that. La Patron wants the bracelet and since he is Alpha…that trumps you and your client."

The weapon discharged before the last word left her mouth. Asia jumped and spun in the opposite direction landing to the side of Mélange, who spun as well. Asia kicked the weapon from Mélange's hand and then stepped forward to add another kick.

Mélange flipped up and backward out of the way. Asia stepped forward, jumped up, and did a roundhouse kick which spun Mélange around but she did not fall. Instead, she did a full spin and kicked out hitting Asia in the chest, sending her flying back against the wall. Dust flew around her head and shoulders from the impact. She shook herself to get her bearings and shifted right just in time, avoiding another kick. Her opponent lost her momentum and fell to the ground, leaving her side unprotected. Asia took advantage of the opening with a well-placed kick, followed by another. Mélange arched and then curled into a fetal position.

Asia fell on Mélange's back, driving her elbow between the shoulder and neck area. The other woman's body jerked and then she morphed into her hybrid form shaking Asia from her back like a rag doll.

Asia's wolf went into a frenzy at the dominance challenge. She slid into her hybrid and jumped back, missing the fast double punches that had been aimed at her head and chest.

The other woman screamed in frustration as she ran toward Asia. At the last moment, Asia stepped to the side, ducked, and plowed her fist into Mélange's stomach sending her flying backward. Jumping up, Asia was on her attacker in a flash landing blow after powerful blow in her face, chest, and belly.

Sounds of rapid-paced punches, flesh hitting flesh, filled the air. Mélange threw up her hand to protect her face as she lost control of her hybrid and returned to her normal state. Asia picked her up and threw her across the room into the wood cabinets. The cabinet door opened as the wood cracked. A tray of empty glass vials fell from the cabinet and broke on the floor. Mélange slid to the ground, gritting her teeth and holding her back. She glared at Asia and stood slowly, looking around.

"You bitch, I just wanted the one thing so I can quit this life," Mélange hissed taking a step to the side.

Focused on her mission, Asia did not respond, instead, she continued forward, determined to exterminate the threat.

"They just use us. This is what they want... for us to kill each other, you can bet they are watching right now, laughing." Mélange kept moving, her eyes darting around the room. Asia knew the moment Mélange saw something she could use as a weapon. The woman dived forward. Asia leaped forward and kicked, her foot connected with Mélange's jaw, sending her backward. She slumped to the ground. Asia looked over her shoulder and saw the butcher knife. Unsurprised that had been the weapon her challenger would go after.

Asia picked up the knife and forcibly threw it into Mélange's shoulder. The blade sliced through her flesh as if it were butter and lodge into the wall behind her, leaving just the wooden handle visible.

"Ow, argh," Mélange hissed at impact.

"Alpha Samuel has arrived, he and his pack are waiting for you, are you done playing with the enemy?" Jasmine asked with a smile in

her voice. Asia fought through the haze of battle so she could process her Mistress' words.

"I am almost done, Mistress."

"Okay."

Asia watched as Mélange struggled to remove the knife. Now that her wolf settled, she looked at her opponent with a critical eye. "Your freedom was supposed to be a part of your reward for bringing me in."

The woman's pinched face reddened. "They are a bunch of old, misogynistic, arrogant assholes. If I were a man, I would have been released from my duties or given a promotion. But as a woman I am incapable of surviving on my own," she spat her disgust.

"And that has been proven time and time again. Women cannot be trusted," a masculine voice piped into the room. Asia spun around seeking his location.

A moment later the large screen on the wall blinked and a shadowy outline of a male filled it. "A murderer and a thief. Griffith was wrong to turn his back on you Asia and wrong to think he could trust you to carry out a simple assignment, Mélange. All you had to do was drive the damn car."

"Fuck you, and your damn games. You sons of bitches set me up to take the fall for some bullshit. Not happening. I am done," Mélange sneered.

"Indeed you are. I will make sure of that." His voice held a note of promise.

Asia recognized the voice of Boris, one of Griffith's partners. She ignored him and headed to the closet to retrieve the briefcase and stopped. Those assholes had been watching the entire time. Why didn't they assist Griffith? Did they see that fight? Was there a trigger somewhere?

"Mistress, Liege is aware of Griffith's death. Have Alpha Samuel and his pack move back a good distance, I believe they are going to destroy this place."

"Get out of there now," Jasmine yelled.

"Yes, Ma'am, my thoughts exactly."

"Where do you think you are going, Asia? I have deactivated the door in that closet, you cannot use it."

She frowned. What door? Opening the briefcase she took the disks, bracelet, passports and stuffed them into her pockets, leaving the cash inside and relocked it. Giving the closet one last look, she exited holding the briefcase.

"You are not leaving," Boris said as if he were actually in control.

Without looking at him, Asia pulled out the gun and shot Mélange repeatedly until she emptied the gun. The woman fell forward in a slump. Next, she pulled the knife from the woman's shoulder and headed toward Griffith.

"What the hell do you think you are doing? I will track you down and tear you apart," he said in a low tone, which she ignored.

"Stooping, she raised the knife and whacked off his hand in one blow.

"Stop that you cunt! Do not touch him, he is a Lord. A man far above your station."

Asia picked the briefcase and the hand up.

"You are dead. I will destroy you personally. How dare you… how dare you desecrate him in this manner? I will track you to the ends of the earth you hideous bitch."

Heading for the door, she ignored the threats Boris hurled at her. She placed Griffith's palm on the identification pad and punched in the numbers based on the sounds she heard earlier. The door opened, she stepped out into the corridor and closed her eyes to remember the directions she had come earlier. Turning, she strode down the hall and repeated the security process. Once she reached the office area, she flicked the button beneath the desk. The door opened and she raced down the stairs.

Yellow warning lights flashed above her head. She jumped over the railing to the stairs below and kept running until she reached the bottom level. There were five cars in the parking level. She ran to the first one and looked in. No keys. By the time she reached the third car, she saw keys in the ignition. Opening the door, she popped open the trunk, inside were three dead bodies. She pulled them out, left them on the pavement, and closed the trunk.

Asia re-entered the car, turned on the ignition, and drove forward. She came to a security gate and placed Griffith's palm on the scanner, the gate opened. She drove through and continued to the next checkpoint. Using his palm again, she was able to leave the grounds. Once off the grounds she pressed the accelerator and shot forward trying to put as much distance between her and the building. When she saw wolves running alongside the car, she exhaled and slowed a bit.

"Mistress I am out and see the pack. Is there a place I can meet the Alpha and get rid of this car?"

"Thank God. Hold on, I'll find out."

Asia nodded.

"He is in a red truck and is on his way to you now. Silas said you should see the truck at the next intersection."

"Thank you…yes, I see it." She stopped the car and waited for the Alpha to exit the truck. When he stepped out, five wolves ran up to him and then surrounded his truck. He stood still waiting. Asia inhaled, recognized his scent, and left the car with just the briefcase.

"Good to see you again," Alpha Samuel said as she moved briskly to the other side of the truck.

"Same to you, we should leave this area quickly. I don't trust the car or the building. I am sure the only reason it has not blown yet is they did not think I could escape so quickly," she said glancing out the window toward the concrete structure while snapping her seat belt.

"Okay." He spun around and took off down the road in the other direction.

"Mistress, I am with Alpha Samuel and we are heading back toward Alpha House. When will La Patron arrive?"

"He says they should be there by the time you and Samuel arrive. Can you rest? Or are you amped up?"

Asia smiled. *"Amped up? That is an interesting term for it."*

A booming noise in the distance shattered the silence in the truck. The ground shook as they continued speeding down the road.

"What the fuck?" Alpha Samuel growled as he pulled over on the shoulder. They both stepped out and looked in the direction they had come. A dark plume of dust filled the air. "Bastards blew the place. Good thing it was so far out of town and away from everything. Was there anyone in the place when you left?"

"I am not sure." The bullets would have slowed Mélange, not ended her existence. The bodies that had been in the trunk were already dead. Asia had no idea what happened to the man who assisted Griffith when she first arrived.

A moment later there was another mini popping sound accompanied by smoke. They had blown the car she had been driving as well. She met Alpha Samuel's grim look with one of her own. Two bombings in twenty-four hours, that had to be a record.

Chapter 18

SILAS WALKED TO THE front of the plane leaving Leon and Brix in the back area. He questioned Brix extensively about the female, Mélange, and had a better idea of the young bitch.

The twins were further up in the main cabin resting. Angus sat up as he approached. *"He knows anything about the girl?"*

"Just that she hated the job, was disloyal and a good person to have at your back." Silas stared at Angus who had reverted to his first form. *"How do I know you are who you say you are?"*

Angus met his gaze and then shook his head. *"This is my original form. I am BlackWolf and have a hybrid of this form."* He morphed into a figure resembling Tyrese. Silas sat back amazed at the technology that allowed such seamless transformations.

While in that form, Angus took off the bracelet. Immediately he returned to his former form. *"This is my true form. I do not know what else to tell you. I am Angus BlackWolf."*

"You did not mention you had been captured lately..." Silas watched for any signs of discomfort or subterfuge.

"Is that something you tell someone you just meet? Someone who refuses to tell you anything? Someone you do not trust?... No, it's not."

Silas nodded, point well taken. *"I agree. How did you become their guest?"*

Angus snickered. *"Guest? Not by a long shot."* He eyed Silas for a moment. *"Let's do this, we each ask a question, get that answered, and move to the next. So far I have been the only one releasing pertinent information and that is not fair."*

Silas eyed him for a moment and leaned forward so Angus could see how serious he took this matter. *"Perhaps, but this is my country, I am in charge here. You stay or go by my word. I do not need to be fair. You are not my guest. You are an intruder, possibly a spy. So I'll ask the questions and you'll answer. If I feel sharing my knowledge with you is beneficial to my pack, I will do so."*

Angus stared at him for a few moments and then leaned back in the seat. *"I told you someone was researching Asia and came to the continent looking for answers. That was ten or twelve years ago. Whispers of an organization seeking black wolves reached our ears. Later, we set Brix up to work on the inside to gather information and things were working smoothly. It took years before he learned anything of substance, but it was beginning to pay off. Recently, inquiries arose again regarding Asia. It was strange hearing that someone searched that intensely for information on one wolf. Fearing they were researching Brix, I got involved. One thing led to another and then I allowed myself to be caught so I could see what was going on."*

Silas nodded. That made sense.

"Imagine my surprise at learning this huge organization committed the atrocities against my brethren in the name of science. That is where I heard about Asia's specific abilities. The doctors were in awe and afraid of her, there was some jealousy as well. They claimed she was a walking miracle with the Midas touch if they could duplicate her."

Silas understood Angus' shock. He had a similar experience when he met his mate. *"Did they run tests on you?"*

Angus nodded. *"Yes, which was okay, because they talked when they thought the drugs knocked me out. That's when I learned most of my information. But when they took me into an operating room to gut me like a fish so they could see my innards, my wolf took exception. We left."*

Remembering Asia's report, it sounded like Angus left in a big way. *"You get any data from that place?"*

"No, just what I had seen or heard. All I left behind was my calling card. They will always remember their visit from a black wolf." Angus chuckled. *"There was one bit of disturbing news. While I was there I discovered they owned one of our chameleon bracelets."*

Silas glanced at the one on his wrist. *"That is unusual I take it."*

Angus nodded. *"Yes. First off it only works with members of our pack, black wolves, or their descendants. Second, if the person it has been made for dies, the bracelet dissolves, returns to the earth. Third, it is the death penalty to share the secrets of the BlackWolf clan. Yet they were aware of what the bracelet can do."*

Neither spoke as the ramifications settled. *"Someone betrayed your clan."*

Angus nodded. *"It seems that way."*

"First time?" Silas asked skeptically.

"That I know of and I have been around as long as you have."

"Then count yourself lucky. Something will surface, it always does. Just hope that it is not someone in your inner circle that makes it personal."

Angus eyed him for a moment.

"Do not ask, I am not sharing that information," Silas said sharply. *"Brix is part black wolf?"*

"Yes, a few litters down from pure. He was raised by the clan, been around us all his life. This assignment was tailor-made for him; he rose through their ranks at a steady pace."

"What happened to the implants and chips they put inside him?" Silas asked, leaning back in his seat and taking a sip of water from the bottle.

"When he removed his bracelet, everything regarding the chameleon died, short-circuited, ceased to exist..."

"Okay, I understand. That's a handy tool then." Silas looked at the bracelet with appreciation. *"Who makes them for the clan?"*

"Me."

Silas met his wary gaze. *"Seriously? You are the only one who makes these? What happens if you disappear...like now? What does your clan do?"*

"They wait or go without. If I had been able to get my hand on the bracelet I might have been able to discover which bracelet was taken and trace it back to the traitor." He exhaled. *"Even then I am*

unsure if I can do that if the bracelet has been used multiple times."

"Have you alerted your Alpha?"

"Yes...he is aware of what is going on." He paused. *"Actually, there is a bit of fuss going on right now. Some of us want to continue to follow our original Alpha..."*

"The dead one?" Silas asked with a raised brow.

Angus frowned. *"He is still amongst us, just in spirit, that is all."*

"Okay." Silas nodded, knowing exactly where this was headed.

"Others want a new Alpha. The usurper has delivered a challenge for the position."

Silas laughed. He could not help it. He had heard all manner of weird things in his position over the years. But challenging the dead for a position? That was a first. When he could pull it together, he met Angus' glower. "Did your Alpha accept the challenge?" He laughed again at the absurd notion.

"It is not funny. I thought you would understand since you are an Alpha. But once again, I am mistaken about you."

"I would require my Alpha to be alive as well. I already have a spirit being in my life. I follow the Goddess, but she is not involved in my day-to-day activities. I vote with the challenger, a Pack needs a physical Alpha in the den. Not one hovering nearby in the clouds."

"You only say that because you have no idea of how great he was...is. There has never been an Alpha of his caliber." He sighed. "I miss the old days."

Silas eyed him for a moment while various thoughts ran through his head. "Who are these Liege Lords and why did they come after me? Is it because my wolf is black or do they want my position? I do not understand the reasons for their attacks." He asked to get the conversation back on track. There was nothing to be gained by mocking Angus' memories.

"Power. Money. Prestige, those are the normal reasons, but I am not sure these Liege Lords have a reasonable reason for doing what they do. At some point, they stumbled across a dual-natured man and took an interest. No question they are making a lot of money, but they have been doing this for centuries. I also wonder with you what their end game is. Their actions make little sense."

Silas nodded. "How many Liege Lords are there? Do they recruit? Are they all from a previous century...Liege is an old title."

Angus shrugged. "I only saw one and heard his name by

accident. One of the doctors called him Sir Roderick and he slapped the man to the ground. Using names was against the rules."

That was not one of the names Asia mentioned. "What did he look like?" It seems they had their work cut out for them if they wanted to eradicate this group from American soil.

"Average chap. My height, slim build, fair complexion, dark brown hair and eyes."

Silas pointed to the bracelet. "Can you…do that thing…show me what he looks like?"

Angus closed his eyes. The next moment a tall male with pockmarks on his face sat in the seat across from him.

"Hold that position I want the twins to see this so we will all know who to look for."

Angus nodded and crossed his hands over his belly reclining in the chair.

"*Rone, Rese, come here*," Silas said through their links.

A moment later the twins walked into the area where he and Angus sat. "What the hell?" Tyrone said staring down at Angus. Tyrese simply stared but stood ready to move in an instant.

"It is important that you keep this information to yourselves. I do not want anyone to know we have access to this new device. If you did not know, this is Angus wearing a chameleon device that is unique to his clan. Most importantly, I want you to memorize this face and build of the person he is mimicking. The man is Sir Roderick and he is a Liege Lord. I have not seen this person, but I want us to all be on the lookout because he can be anywhere," Silas said watching their expressions.

Tyrese nodded slowly. "Because we don't know what they look like they could be living in the town and we wouldn't know. This is good. We can go on the offensive."

"Do we know how many Liege Lords there are?" Tyrone asked.

"We only know of four, now three thanks to Asia. She eliminated the one who kidnapped her. His name was Griffith." Silas watched Angus, whose eyes widened at the name.

"He is the one who had the bracelet. I hope she was able to recover it from him. Nasty piece of work. I never saw him but heard him over the microphone. Sir Roderick called him Griff, but didn't realize he was one of them." Angus returned to his natural form and the twins gawked in amazement.

Silas was happy he wasn't the only one impressed. "We were trying to determine what the end game is for this group. They do not want to rule the world, not overtly anyway. From what Angus says, they already own a lot of politicians around the world and their fingers are deep into the global economy. In relation to that, my pack is small potatoes," Silas said using one of his mate's quirky sayings.

Tyrone sat down in the chair in front of Angus. Tyrese continued to stand. "That's true, but here's the difference. You have an organized force that you command at a moment's notice. If there was a real threat to the United States, there is a real threat to the Pack. No outside force would ever be allowed to enter the US and survive. Our pack would never allow it. Just because the government has turned a blind eye to our existence does not mean they aren't happy to know you would never allow the annihilation of our nation."

"Which exists inside of their nation, the US. So if an enemy had any hopes of conquering the US in any shape they would need to be prepared to meet two Presidents. I use that term to make a point," Tyrese said when Silas's brow rose. "One President the world knows and sees rules the human race in this country. The other is unknown and consequently more deadly. Because you can call every wolf in this country, bitches and pups included, your army is larger. With the new technology, your force will be harder to destroy."

Silas thought over everything the twins said. He had not thought along those lines, but as an offensive measure, it made sense. And was on point because his people lived everywhere, not just on Pack lands. So if there was an attack from an outside enemy he would get involved to save his pack.

"That is an interesting observation. I had not thought of it in those terms," Angus said sitting up. "Here is another possible reason. These are bored old men. Chances are they have overcome every challenge presented and are looking for bigger game. Kind of like that movie where the billionaire brothers made a bet for one dollar that they could make a beggar a millionaire…"

"Trading places?" Tyrese said.

Angus shrugged. "I do not remember the name of the movie only that a friend brought it to teach the pups about greed. It is a movie, but the lessons are real. Some do things for no real reason or deep purpose. These men could be like that."

Silas nodded. Who knew why this group operated? Or if they

had a purpose. In the end, none of that mattered. They could no longer operate in this country.

"We will be landing in twenty minutes. Please return to your seats and put on your safety belts," the pilot said over the speaker.

Tyrone stood. He and Tyrese returned to their seats. Silas continued to think over his options. He had a lot of data to go over and teams to put together. He watched Brix and Leon come from the back, take their seats, and buckle up.

"I have the tape of the discussion you had with Brix, Sir," Leon said. *"There is also a disc of everything he learned about the Liege Lords. Over the years he has composed reports and turned them into his Alpha. We will send those to Jacques when we land and have access to a computer."*

"Thank you, Leon, Brix. That is most helpful," Silas said, feeling better about this mission.

"I would ask your permission to travel with you to your compound. I would like to stay in the states and offer my services to assist in destroying the Liege," Angus said surprising Silas.

"I do not trust you."

"I would pledge my loyalty to you."

Silas stared at the man. That was a big step and one that could not be broken. Silas would hold Angus' life in his hands. *"Why?"*

"I do not like the changes going on at home. The new Alpha-challenger and I disagree on several issues. It was suggested that I leave and find a place where I fit in better. I am comfortable with my kind and thought to visit the states. And I have already sent a report to my brethren, so there is no rush to return."

"They kicked you out?"

Angus frowned. *"No, they did not. I left. I can return at any time and pledge fealty to the new Alpha."*

Silas understood. Angus and the new Alpha did not get along. Being an old wolf who had seen much sometimes it was hard to accept change. If his mate had not come along, Silas would still scoff at the idea of family and everything that defined a home. Those were things he could not live without.

"I will think about it and let you know before we take off. I am hesitant to bring anyone new into my compound because my mate and pups live in my den. You have said I cannot kill you and that leaves me wondering what my options would be to protect my...family."

Angus' eyes widened. *"You have more pups? Other than the twins? How blessed you are."*

Thinking of his pups, Silas grinned. *"I am blessed indeed. They are a rambunctious handful, but I would not change anything about them."* He glanced at Angus and could tell he was truly excited on his behalf. *"I have two boys, Adam and David."*

"Good solid, strong names. No doubt showing traits of leadership already," Angus said with genuine interest.

"Yes…yes they are. Renee and Jackie are my princesses, although they are just as tough as the boys. My genes run strong in all of them, although the boys have eyes the same color as my Sweet Bitch."

"You are doubly blessed my brother. The Goddess has smiled upon you twofold. May they live a fruitful life full of love and laughter."

Warmth filled Silas at the old blessing. *"Where were you when the Battle of Waterloo was fought?"* Silas asked. It had been decades since he had conversed with someone who had seen some of the same things or lived through the changes of times that he had. It was refreshing to listen as Angus' replied while the plane declined to land on the private airstrip.

Chapter 19

JASMINE SAT SLUMPED IN her chair, with her head in her palms. Sleep called with an unerring urgency. Her bones were tired. She had expended energy from somewhere deep inside that she had no idea existed.

"*Sweet Bitch.*"

"Go away, Silas, I am so…" she yawned. "*I'm too tired to talk to you.*"

He chuckled. His deep voice flowed over her skin like warmed honey. She shivered. "*I will talk, you listen.*"

She stood and walked into their bedroom. "*Umhmm. Okay.*" Without turning on the lights she zeroed in on the bed and fell across it, inhaling his latent scent. "*Mmmm,*" she murmured as she pulled his pillow close and curled around it.

"*What are you doing?*"

"Laying down."

"*Missing me?*"

"Yes."

"*I miss you too. Asia is on her way to the compound; you can release her and get some rest. If she needs you, she will call.*"

"No, she won't. She is as stubborn as the boys."

Silas chuckled and the sound rubbed against her skin. Goosebumps exploded across her arms. *"You are right."*

"She had a long day, the sun is coming up and none of us got much sleep. When will you get home?"

"I am home."

She shot up in the bed and looked around. *"Where? I don't see you."* She fell backward missing him more now that he was here.

"In the lab below, installing Angus in Asia's old room. She has taken a room in your old wing near Tyrese. Then I will drop off these disks to Jacques. There is a lot of information to weed through over the next few weeks. I am anxious to hear first-hand from Asia about this group. I think we may soon be on the offense against them, instead of defense. That is exciting."

Jasmine rolled over and pulled the cover over her face. Her mate's idea of excitement and hers were vastly different. She wanted to talk to Asia, but decided to leave the young woman alone so she could rest. Tomorrow they would have lunch and go shopping.

"Okay, when you are done, wake me up, we need to talk about some things that happened here." She yawned.

"Okay, Sweet Bitch. I will see you in a few minutes."

Jasmine pulled down the cover, eyed the clock, and snorted. *"More like an hour."*

An hour later the bed dipped and warm hands caressed her back. Her body shivered at the contact. After he told her he was in the compound she had been unable to sleep, instead, she watched the clock, waiting.

"Baby…"

She rolled over and stared at him. "What did you call me?"

He laughed. "Baby. What's wrong with that? It is a sexy name humans call their mates."

She snorted missing his normal endearment. "Yeah, when they cannot remember the woman's name."

"Ah…I see." He pulled her close. The warmth of his skin chased away the goosebumps that rose from the sound of his voice. Her eyelids drifted close. "I missed my bitch." He pressed a kiss against her forehead, her nipples hardened as if there were a magical connection between the two.

"I love you, Jasmine. You are my sun. I take you with me to keep me warm and grounded wherever I am." He kissed her closed eyelids and each cheek. Her greedy core throbbed in preparation for his taking.

"Love you, too, baby," she whispered.

He slapped her ass lightly. "Say my name."

"I love you, big daddy." She grinned.

He laughed harder and pulled her tight. "You are my joy and my delight. I thank the Goddess for your love and your care."

She smiled. He was in a rare mood tonight. "Love you, Silas. You brought me something?" She looked up at him with a sly grin as her hand rested between his muscular thighs.

"Everything I have is yours…baby. Whatever you need I will provide." He covered her hand and pressed it against his thickening rod. "This belongs to you, anytime, anyplace."

She inhaled his woodsy scent, allowing it to fill her. An ache formed deep in her belly. She hadn't known love like this existed, not until Silas Knight strode into her life. She craved his touch. Needed to hear his voice and see his face. Nothing in her life prepared her for a connection this deep. She searched her mind for an appropriate response and settled for the unvarnished truth.

"I'm yours, Silas."

His hold on her tightened as he took deep breaths against her chest. She stroked the back of his head to calm him. Her man had been through a lot in the past 48 hours. His job…no his calling was not easy, but he was capable of handling the task the Goddess assigned him.

He moved slightly and slid his mouth over hers, deepening the kiss, taking full control. Her arms tightened around his neck, she never wanted to let him go. They broke apart on a gasp, sucking in the air. Their foreheads touched. A tremor of need shook her frame as she pulled her scattered thoughts together.

His palm stroked her back with the same slow caress she had given him earlier. His fingers slipped beneath her shirt and gently lifted it over her head. She leaned back as he removed it from her arms and tossed it to the floor.

The rough pads of his fingertips grazed across her nipples, sending zings of pleasure straight to her core.

"Mmmm," she moaned, lost in a blaze of need mixed with lust he created in her.

"Beautiful," he murmured as he rubbed and pulled the pert nubs.

Feeling as beautiful as he proclaimed, she leaned back in his arms, offering herself to him. When his lips latched onto the base of her neck and sucked hard, her body shuddered, needing more.

"Silas…" she groaned, feeling the proof of his desire against her stomach. "I need you," she murmured.

"I need you, Sweet Bitch," he growled after pulling away from her neck. Sharp teeth protruded from his mouth. He tore off her panties and slid her beneath him.

"No. I want to ride," she said pushing against his chest.

He rolled to the side, and she climbed on top. Placing one hand on his chest, she positioned his stiffness to her entrance with the other and eased down on him. He grimaced as she took it slow. Sweat popped out on his brow as he opened and closed his fist beside them.

She grinned as she tortured him by easing up and down, tightening her muscles on every other stroke.

"What's my name, baby?" She purred watching his jaw tighten.

"Bitch."

A peal of laughter spilled from her lips as she tightened her vaginal walls around him while pulling up slowly.

"Argh, Jasmine you are killing me. Is this how you greet your man when he returns from war?" He exhaled as his body shook beneath her. He would not come before her, it was some unwritten code of manhood he had. It had become a challenge for her to break him and that rule.

"No baby, I am just loving on you nice and easy. Good and slow. I like the way you fill me up. How you throb inside me. I feel every ridge of your dick. I love it. I love you."

"I love you too, Sweet Bitch. That is why I am allowing you to torture me in this manner, but the game will change in a few moments. My beast is riding me high and hard."

She creamed at his words. Tomorrow she may not be able to walk a straight line, but she would gladly deal with the aftermath for him to take her hot and hard right now. "Oh…okay."

"Okay?"

"Yeah."

He flipped her over before she could blink. Holding one bent leg beneath the knee, he slammed into her repeatedly. Eyes closed, she absorbed each thrust as her body spiraled higher, and grew taut.

"Oh no, sweetness. Look at me. What's my name?" he growled

through a crowded mouth of sharp teeth.

She met his emerald green gaze and saw a shadow of his wolf as he pounded into her. Licking her lips she spoke on a gasp. "Baby daddy."

He howled and pulled both her legs straight up and entered her again with a powerful thrust.

"Mmmm, oh yeah," she said huskily loving the new position. She grabbed her nipples and pulled.

"Fuck yeah, like that. Pinch them….yesss," he growled. His words garbled as his excitement grew.

His pleasure fed hers. When he pulled out, flipped her over, and pulled her ass up high she spread her legs. Her man was going to bring it all home and she was ready to fly with him. He slid into her from behind and held her close for a moment. His forehead dropped to the base of her neck.

"Goddess, you are so damn tight, and sweet. I love you. I love this with you. So good, always good."

She warmed beneath his praise and wiggled her ass. "You do this to me. I cannot get enough of you, so get with it, Silas."

Lifting, he smacked her ass, sending a curling warmth between her legs. She wiggled her bottom again.

"Demanding bitch." He slid in and out of her steady strokes. Wanting more, she pushed against him. He spanked her again.

"Oh yeah," she murmured.

He chuckled and sped up his thrusts, taking her hard, deep, and fast. She was in heaven. Closing her eyes she forgot everything except what he was doing to her. Her walls tightened around her. She could no longer keep up and remained still allowing him to drive without assistance. He changed the angle and hit her spot.

She gasped as her walls clenched. He hit it again and again. Her body tightened. His sharp nails scraped against her nipple. Screaming her pleasure, she shattered, arching her back while her body shook like a leaf in the midst of a storm.

His roar filled the room as he hurled over the cliff with her. Through their link, she felt his satisfaction. The shining beacon of his love for her never failed to excite and calm her. This man was all hers.

Breathing hard, they laid side by side on the bed. Absently, she stroked his chest while corralling her thoughts. Now that her immediate needs were taken care of there were some other things they needed to deal with.

"You are amazing, thank you for welcoming me home. I love that." He pulled her close and kissed the top of her head. "I checked on the pups on my way here. Is everything okay with them? No relapses?" He asked.

"No. They are back to normal, fighting, playing, and trying to get into everything." She paused and then went ahead. "Mom spends a lot of time sitting in the chair watching them." If he had a problem with her mother around the kids, she wanted to know now so they could deal with it. Under no circumstances would she tell her mother she could not see her grandkids. Silas would need to get over the past and move forward.

"That's good. I would not be surprised if she and Jacques had a litter. He has always wanted a large den."

Jasmine stared at him, surprised at his response, but not willing to question her luck, she nodded. "That would be odd, having a younger brother or sister at my age. But life as I knew it has changed." She shrugged. Later, when she, her mom, and Asia met for lunch, she might bring it up to see if her mom would consider having more babies. It would be an interesting conversation.

There were other matters to discuss. She proceeded to give him an update on the mid-morning crisis.

"Tomas ran away. Davian called while I was monitoring Asia to say the boy was missing. He wanted permission to go to the Alpha house. I told him Cameron was his Alpha and he could discuss anything with him."

"You talked to him? How? I was linked with you."

Jasmine gritted her teeth at his irrelevant question. "I stepped to the side for a moment to handle a crisis. I multi-tasked. Anyway, the important thing is Tomas was at the Alpha house. He and Thorne left together. Lilly says she had no idea Tomas was there."

"He masked his scent?"

"Don't know. I let her know I am concerned about their abilities to manage the state if they cannot manage their home."

Silas chuckled. "Ouch. That hurt. They are new at this Sweet Bitch, be nice."

"Humph. Not with all the disrespect I had to deal with these two days."

He leaned back and looked down at her. "Disrespect?" He asked in a serious tone. You? ... my mate has been disrespected? By who?" The grittiness of his voice said his wolf had risen near the surface again.

"I took care of it. You may notice some voices are mere whispers. Some may have challenges with their posture. They are bent over and unable to stand fully erect. Do not abuse them further. I want the punishments I deliver to be remembered. Beatings fade, but the loss of certain abilities is a part of long-lasting memories."

He chuckled and pulled her close to his chest, rubbing his chin against the top of her head. "I make no promises. No one disrespects you."

She wondered how he would take this next bit of news. "After Tomas and Thorne left the Alpha house, Davian went searching for them. He found them with a remnant of Griggs followers."

He stopped moving. "Did he now? I told Cameron to seek those individuals and detain them. Where are they now?"

Jasmine was not fooled by the calm question. Silas was pissed. It could be because Davian was the one to discover the remnant of rebels and he would need to thank him. Or because Cameron did not find the remnant and Silas would need to chastise him, she did not know.

"From what Rose told me, Davian fought some of the guys and a couple ran off. Thorne ran with them, but Davian went after Tomas and took him back home. Rose is worried over what will happen to her brother."

"She should be concerned. He has chosen sides against me. I do not take kindly to that behavior, not even in pups. Strange his two sisters had no idea he sympathized with Griggs and her cause."

Jasmine stretched and threaded her legs through his. "That is part of the reason Rose feels so guilty. She has been so busy with work and Rone's family; she hadn't spent much time with her own. She thinks she would have noticed something if she had been around him more."

"Perhaps."

She wasn't sure what that meant but did not have the energy to pursue that thread of the conversation.

"Or perhaps she is regretting her interference on my choice of Alphas. She probably realizes her mate would have picked up

Thorne's leaning and put a stop to them before his life was jeopardized. I am sure there is a thread of guilt running through her mind."

Jasmine snorted. "Not in my mind. I did not want that position for him either."

"You are his mother, not his mate. It is different. Plus… Cameron has not reported this infraction to me either."

Thinking of the arrogant Alpha, Jasmine was not surprised. "He wants to prove he is as good as or better than your first choice. His words, not mine."

"You and Cameron had words?" Hearing the fake calm in his voice she trod carefully.

"I explained to him that we did not want Tomas and Thorne to be together. He had a few questions, which I answered. I believe we have an understanding now." Her hand rested on his chest.

"When did this happen?" He didn't bother to hide the aggravation in his voice this time.

"Yesterday morning before the lab blew."

"You did not tell me."

"Was I supposed to?"

There was silence and she snuggled into his chest.

"No. I guess not. Was he disrespectful?"

"Not really. I handled it, Silas. Either you let me handle things my way or I won't do this again. We are different. I can't and won't fight physically for the right to run things with you, but I am not a doormat either. You, do you and I will do me."

"I do not care if he is my godson. If he disrespects my mate, he disrespects me and I will kick his ass. You know this and he knows. Do not attempt to cover for him or anyone else. I will do me later today. No one disrespects you," he growled, pulling her tight.

Needing space she pushed back a bit and met his confused gaze. "A lot of people don't even know who I am, you cannot get mad if they don't respect me in the way you think they should."

He frowned. "What do you mean? Everyone knows who you are."

She thought about the Alphas who she corresponded with yesterday with questions regarding grant applications. Many had asked impertinent questions before realizing she was his mate.

"No, Wolfie. Everyone does not know who I am." She explained her experiences in his office and he lapsed into silence.

He rolled over on his back pulling her with him. She lay on his chest, listening to the steady beat of his heart. "You make a valid point. We have put it off too long. I will announce our mating ceremony to the Alphas, so that preparations may begin. We will visit the four points of this country, starting in West Virginia. All Alphas and betas will attend a celebration where I present you and my pups. I would like the twins to be presented as well."

His announcement affected her like a jolt of caffeine. "Not the children, Silas. I don't want them exposed."

He looked at her with a raised brow. "What do you mean? They are my pups. My pack expects to see them, to watch them grow into leaders. I will not hide my pups, Jasmine."

She heard the steel beneath his words and cringed. "What about what Griggs said? There is still much we don't know."

"True, but Knights do not run or hide. I will not allow my pups to hide from their enemies, I will teach them to win against them." He paused. "Our pups must learn and understand what a Pack is, and the benefits of Pack. They are now walking and soon will start school. I want them prepared for the challenges they will face as my pups. More will be expected of them, that is only natural. My pups are leaders, each of them strives to excel. Jackie will not move to another puzzle until she masters her current one. Renee fills each book with art, growing better and more vibrant with each page. Adam is athletic and can throw a ball with accuracy. David is a manager and dabbles in all of the others, mastering none but is good in all."

Jasmine sat up against the headboard wanting to yell. "They are not a year old, Silas. They are still in diapers. They have their whole lives to be looked at under a microscope, why do they need to start so young?"

"Because I am La Patron and they are my first litter." He sat up and turned to her, his face granite hard. "According to my mate, they will be my only litter. My people have waited decades, not only for me to mate, but also for my offspring. I understand this is all new for you, but it is normal for Pack. I ask you to trust me in this."

She exhaled. The thought of sleep now replaced with the dread of the ceremony. "Can you just split the country in half and have two celebrations?" She asked hoping to lessen the exposure time.

"It is a fair compromise. It will be similar to an inaugural ball."

Frowning, she leaned back wondering what he was saying, "What?"

"Yes, that is a good idea," he said nodding. "I am similar to the president, but of the Wolf Nation. We will have an inaugural ball to introduce my den. It is appropriate and will be appreciated by the Pack. It has been a long time since anything like this has occurred so I will tailor it to something familiar. An inaugural ball." He smiled so brightly she didn't have the heart to tell him she would rather jump off a cliff than attend something so formal.

"Sounds interesting, Silas. What made you think of that?" Someone had to have mentioned the president or something along those lines because her mate never thought in terms of human events.

He waved down her question. "Thank you Jasmine for not fighting me on this. I must follow Pack protocol and present my entire den to the Pack. To do anything less sends a message that I am ashamed of you or my litter. I will not have anyone think less of you for not being wolf."

Her brow rose. He had done the christening and had not invited any of his Alphas. She really couldn't complain about what amounted to a large party. But she had to tease him just a little.

"Hmm, but I am a descendant from the almighty BlackWolf clan, they should respect that," she said dryly. "Especially since it was a wolf who started the whole half breed process. We are all one big happy family."

Silas tweaked her nose. "You are being silly with that fairy tale."

She grinned, happy to get off the subject of being introduced on such a grand scale. It would take a little more time for the idea to marinate before she could embrace it fully. "Perhaps, but since it is the only explanation for the merging of wolf and human, I'll take it and run with it."

He chuckled. "We will need to arise soon. I left Jacques running a lot of the disks, checking for bugs and security issues. He will let me know what is on them. Plus Asia recovered some information from Griffith's closet. Passports with names and addresses. More threads to pull."

She yawned as she slid down beneath the covers. "I need to get more sleep, Asia and I are going to lunch later and then shop for her vacation."

"Vacation? What vacation?"

Jasmine rolled over to face him. "She is going to the beach for a couple of days to chill and relax. She has never had a margarita."

"What?" He sat up frowning down at her. "A margarita? What does that mean?"

Closing her eyes, she prayed for patience. "I told her that she could take a vacation if she fought her way out of that situation with the Liege guy. I told her she could drink margaritas on the damn beach and listen to the waves. She needed something to focus on and that is what I gave her. So..." She sat up and matched his glare. "We, Asia, Mama, and me, are going shopping for her a bathing suit because she never had one before."

"She needs to debrief."

"She needs a damn break. You cannot just work her like a damn machine, Silas. That is what they did to her. We are not like them and she will see the difference."

"You do not understand..."

She jumped up and pointed at him. "Don't talk to me like that. Like I don't know what she went through... because I do, damn it. She died, Silas. She stopped fucking breathing and walked into the light. When she rebooted, she contacted me. I saw...I saw the darkness of her burial. I tasted her pain. It was fucking unbelievable."

She wiped the moisture from her face. "And she is alone." She closed her eyes at the remembered pain and wrapped her arms around herself. "I have never felt anyone who was so dry in places that should be wet with emotions. She has no attachments, no expectations of anyone or anything. Being joined with her was painful, not in the sense of physical pain. But just knowing she has known none of the joys life has to offer." She met his gaze with a sardonic twist of her lips. "So, yeah. I placed a carrot in front of her. Praying like hell she would take it. The only reason I can think that she and I are linked is that I do care and want more for her. And if anyone deserves some happiness, Asia Montgomery damn sure does. So..." she inhaled deeply and released it slow. "If you need to debrief her make it fast because she will be leaving for a vacation within 24 hours."

"Jasmine...I did not mean you are unaware of what the young bitch suffered. I know you went through a lot of it with her. If I could have carried that load for you I would have. What I am saying is she alone has vital information regarding what she saw at the Liege compound. She recovered a chameleon bracelet which will assist us in placing more pieces of the puzzle in the correct place. Even more importantly, she killed a Liege Lord. There is a huge bounty on her head. Everyone will be searching for her."

Jasmine did not want to hear that it could not be done. "There are beaches all over the world. She has no tracking devices and I pity the person who interrupts her vacation. Chances are they would end up the same as the others."

He sighed.

"I hear what you're saying, Silas. But you need to hear and respect what I'm saying and what I have done. She has my word and I am not going to break it. I will remind her of the bounty and tell her everything that you've said. The choice to stay or go then is hers. I want you to back me on this." She met his frown with determination.

Neither spoke for a few moments and then he nodded. "You are right. Your word carries the same weight as mine. How long will she be away?"

"I don't know. I will find out when we have lunch today." She looked at his disgruntled face and smiled. "Thank you for not fighting me on this Silas. Asia is Pack and should be treated as such. She has never had anyone in her corner who didn't expect anything from her."

He nodded and lay back on the bed with his hands beneath his head. "Until now. She has you."

Jasmine shrugged and crawled beneath the cover, ready for sleep. "Yes, maybe that's my mission. To keep her safe."

He pulled her close and they snuggled beneath the blankets together. "Could be, we shall see."

Chapter 20

Silas took the elevator to the computer room, eager to hear any news regarding the discs. He strode into the room, ignoring Victoria's naked streak to the back room and the slamming of the door. Jacques walked out of the kitchen area with a large cup of coffee and a huge grin.

"You should put on clothes, you scared your mate," Silas said heading into the kitchen area for a cup of coffee.

"Wasn't me that scared her. She loves all of this," Jacques whispered, smiling.

Silas chuckled and looked at the closed door. "Why are you whispering she is awake and can hear you."

Jacques stopped smiling, placed his cup on a table, and knelt before Silas. "I spoke out of turn to Mistress and she took my voice."

Stunned, Silas stared at his oldest friend for a moment. This is what Jasmine had done. "You disrespected my mate?" He couldn't believe it. Jacques knew better.

"We had just mated and I interfered with something you told her to do," Victoria said coming out of the room. "I told her to leave him alone to let him sleep. She dragged him from the bed as a wolf. He growled when he saw me on the wall and she took his voice. It should've been mine; I was the one who mouthed off at her."

Silas' gaze swung from his mate's Mom to his friend. He could not believe Jasmine pinned her mother to the wall…on purpose… to carry out his instructions.

"She pulled your wolf?" he asked to be sure. He did not realize she knew how to do that. His mate was full of surprises.

"Yes, Sir. I was asleep, the mating sleep is deep as you know." Silas nodded.

"I did not hear your summons or her entry. When I came out and saw my beloved against the wall, I growled. A mistake never to be repeated, Sir."

Silas smiled. He could not believe she had done that. Women fought on a whole different level than men. He would have beat Jacques and then been done with it. But this discomfort was a constant reminder of his transgression.

"How long are you to sound…scratchy like this?"

"Until you restore my voice, Sir."

Silas laughed. It was pure genius. With her implementing the punishment with the stipulation that he be the one to end it, everyone would deal with both of them as a well-oiled unit. He liked the way his bitch thought. But the scratchy sound was displeasing, and they had a lot of work to do. He restored Jacque's voice. In deference to Jasmine's mother standing nearby watching him closely, he spoke to him through their link.

"I restored your voice because you were in the mating heat and not thinking clearly. I will kill you if it ever happens again."

"Yes, Sir. Thank you for your kindness and your mate is my daughter-in-law. I will never disrespect my mate's child." He stood with a smile.

Silas had not realized the connection, and cursed, knowing he would never fulfill that threat. *"I may not kill you, but you will beg me for death,"* he said with less heat as they moved toward the bank of monitors.

"Thank you, Sir. You are most generous. My mate and I both thank you," Jacques said aloud gazing at Victoria, who ran and hugged him tightly.

"Thanks, Silas, I appreciate it. That sound drove me crazy," Victoria said with an earnest expression.

Silas nodded and took a seat in front of the monitors.

"I have to work now sweet. What time are you meeting your daughter for lunch?" Jacques asked.

Silas left Jasmine rushing to get dressed while fussing at him for making her late with their extended shower.

"Oh, I need to get dressed. We are going shopping afterward. You need anything?" she asked from the doorway.

Silas refrained from making a smart remark. Newly mated couples could not see ten feet in front of them. He did not expect to see Leon for at least a week. Brix had taped a lot of information regarding Liege operations while he had been in the back of the plane. Tyrone and Tyrese were handling that information.

"No. Just for you to return happy. Buy whatever you want."

"Thanks, baby. I will." She closed the door.

Jacques met his amused gaze. "What?"

"Was I like that with Jasmine?"

"I missed that part. But you were a grizzly bear in denial mode before you accepted her as your mate." Jacques took the seat next to his.

Silas nodded. He had been an ass. "What do we have so far? I want to do a debriefing in two hours with everyone except Asia who has already submitted her notes. She is going shopping…for her vacation."

Jacques spit out the coffee and hurriedly wiped it up." When he was done he looked at Silas. "What? A vacation? Now?"

Silas leaned forward and read the information on the monitor. "Yes, it was a way my mate talked her into fighting to live to see another day. Asia was tired and had no real reason to continue."

The more he had thought of his mate's defense of her actions, the prouder he became. She dealt with the root of the problem. Asia needed to belong and she needed to learn to trust. Those things transcended words. They had to be married to actions. The lunch, the shopping trip, and even the mini-vacation to an uncharted island he owned were all designed to show this damaged bitch that they were not all the same. In the long run, his mate's handling of the matter would reap the larger harvest.

"She deserves a vacation. It's the timing that sucks. Who is going with her? How long will she be gone?"

Silas laughed. "Asia decided to make it a weekend trip. She flies out tomorrow and returns in a couple of days. Tyrone and Rose never took a wedding trip." He glanced at Jacques with a grin. "They have decided to take one now to the same beach. Leon and Brix have also asked for permission to go as well."

Jacques laughed. "Which beach is it? Hawaii? Bahamas?"

"No. I own an island near Bermuda. I have an Alpha stocking the large villas now. There is plenty of room and lots of privacy. Most importantly, she can sit on the beach and have a drink," Silas muttered.

His friend chuckled. "Is Rose going shopping?"

"No, she and Lilly are putting their heads together over Thorne. Tyrone refuses to help search for the boy. Cameron has a team looking now." Silas thought over his conversation with his godson and hoped he never had to deal with Cameron on that level again. Either he ran the state as the Alpha or he would be removed. As of this morning, Cameron was on probation. There was no excuse for Thorne to have left the Alpha house and connect with enemies of La Patron.

"The young pup has too much free time on his hand. Best to find him something constructive to do, like scrubbing the gym," Jacques said grinning.

"Yeah, I heard about that. Quite effective too. My mate has full-bloods quivering and rushing to fulfill her commands. It is because she looks soft and sweet while whipping out retribution. It confuses them," Silas said and then pointed to the screen. "What is that?"

"These are the schematics of the equipment utilized to experiment on wolves. These over here are the notes that were taken. They spent the next couple of hours going over a decade's worth of data. Some they scrapped, others were set aside for a more intensive evaluation later on. After two hours, Silas called for a break.

"Let's grab a bite to eat. Send the information we already cleared to storage. I'll make assignments at the meeting." Silas stood and waited while Jacques stored the data. Together they left the area, locking it behind them.

"We are on our way down to the lab conference room, have lunch sent there for nine people," Silas said to Hank. *"Make sure someone covers for you while you are in the meeting."*

"Yes, Sir."

"Has Davian arrived with Tomas?"

"Yes, Sir. I placed him in the cell personally as you requested

and barred all visitation requests. Jarcee will take him his meals and will be the only one allowed inside the cell until you change the order, Sir."

Silas nodded. He planned to allow the young breed to see what the absence of Pack felt like since he did not appreciate their help before. In a couple of days, he would have a heart-to-heart talk with the youngster and take it from there. *"Good, see you in the meeting."*

"Have you heard from Jasmine?" Jacques asked as they turned the corner to the conference room.

"Not directly. I am monitoring her, but we have not spoken, why?"

"Just thinking about Thorne and the rebels that escaped, you don't think they would go after the women, do you?" Jacques asked as they reached the door.

Silas stopped and gave it some thought. And then he laughed.

Jacques looked at him puzzled. "What?"

Silas stepped inside the empty room. They were the first to arrive. "Can you imagine the looks on those fools' faces if they attempt to interrupt my mate's shopping spree? She has wanted to do this for a while. Asia's vacation is just an excuse." Silas shook his head, smiling. "I pity them if they approach Asia or Jasmine. They will pay big time. Poor Thorne…" Silas took a seat at the table and placed his ankle on his other knee.

Confused, Jacques sat next to him. "Why, poor Thorne?"

"Remember, he lived with my mate for a while. She treated him like a son. Well, she will probably continue to treat him as such. Plus, he has no idea she can and will pull his wolf."

"Oh yes. That is true. I see why you pity the fools. I hope they are bold enough to approach the women. No telling what Asia will do."

Silas shook his head. "Jasmine will not allow her to do anything, just as before with Mark. My mate is capable of handling things, but I will alert her to the possibility."

"Should I alert Victoria as well?"

"She is your mate; however, this is not the time to go into lengthy explanations. I see the twins, Matt, Davian, and Angus. Hank will be here shortly." He leaned back in his chair greeting everyone as they entered.

"Jasmine?"

"Yes?"

"I am just alerting you to the possibility of Thorne and those rebels approaching you ladies while you are out shopping."

"Oh, okay, thanks, Wolfie. I got this."

"What do you mean? Have they contacted you already?" Silas covered his eyes with his hand. The love of his life, mother of his coveted litter would be the death of him.

"No, they haven't. But Asia saw some suspicious dudes when we arrived. It might have something to do with stepping out of a limo that drew attention, but I am not too sure," she said in a dry tone. He did not want her behind the wheel of any vehicle. It made her an easy target. They had gone back and forth over their method of transportation until she finally gave in.

"Could be," he said before chuckling. "I hope you are picking up a few of those frilly things you promised to wear to bed. I am still waiting."

Her laugh flew through their link, warming him. "You'll just have to wait and see. I am getting a bikini as well. Maybe one day you'll take me to a beach or a place with a private pool. Who knows? A girl can dream."

Silas nodded and put her request on his to-do list. "Yes, and I am your dream maker. It is my honor to make your wishes come true. The food is here and we are about to start our meeting. If you come across the rebels, do not kill them Sweet Bitch. I would enjoy talking to them first."

She laughed. "Okay, baby. We will play with them and then leave them somewhere for pick-up, will that work?"

Sitting up, he pulled his plate of food close. "Yes, sounds good and works perfectly. Love you."

"Love you too. Just so you know I'm spending a lot of money today."

"Good." He disconnected and dug into his food. Hank was the last one to enter and he sat in the empty chair and tore into his food.

When Silas pushed his plate away, someone took it and placed it on the cart to be removed later. He glanced at the men surrounding the table and settled on Angus. Before they could go any further, Silas needed to receive his pledge.

"For those who have not met him." Silas pointed toward Angus, who placed his fork down and met Silas' gaze across the conference table. "This is Angus BlackWolf. I met him a couple of days ago and he has asked to join me in my quest to drive our enemies from our land."

The twins clapped. Matt and Dr. Passen nodded. It was obvious they were ready to hear about the new technology. Davian and Hank did not respond, they merely looked at Angus. Silas introduced each man at the table. When he got to Jacques, Angus brightened.

"There was a Jacques Meridian who served in Rome…"

Red-faced, Jacques waved him down. "That was a very long time ago; we can talk about that later. Now… now is not the time."

"Yes, yes of course. It is nice to meet all of you," Angus said, his gaze touching each person briefly.

Silas stood.

Angus stood, walked to Silas, and knelt in front of him. "I pledge my life, my loyalty, and all that I am to the Goddess and her servant, La Patron." He tipped his head to the side. Silas bent forward as his incisors lengthened and bit into his neck. The link between them stretched. Silas pulled back and licked the marks surprised at the strength of the connection. A whirlwind of Angus' memories raced through him. He saw snatches of black pups playing in a large field. There was a large black wolf seated on what appeared to be a ledge watching over them. Memories of a group of black wolves standing around a Pack kill, waiting for the Alpha to finish eating his portion. Flash after flash, snapshots of Angus' life flew before Silas' eyes. When they slowed down, Silas realized everyone watched him. Angus remained on his knees with his head down.

No one spoke.

"He is old, Sir. Older than me," Jacques said.

"Yes, he is from the BlackWolf clan. He says we cannot kill each other, I have never heard of such a thing."

"Well, David cannot kill Adam or Jackie or Renee. Littermates cannot kill each other, but Pack mates kill each other all the time," Jacques said.

"What?" Silas looked at Angus again. *"Litter mates as in from the same bitch?"*

"Yes, that is what it means. If the Mistress was here she would say he is your brother."

Silas stepped back and searched through the memories he had just received. Nothing looked familiar other than black pups with green eyes. He had very few memories from his early years. That was a part of the price for his position as La Patron. The Goddess proclaimed he would have one Pack, one family, and most of his earliest years were forgotten over time.

Shaken more than he wanted to admit by Jacque's words, Silas took a step back. "Stand up."

Angus stood and met his gaze.

"Are we littermates?" Silas asked.

"Yes."

"You knew all along?"

"Yes, I have always known."

"Where the hell have you been? Why didn't you tell me?"

"For some, it makes no difference. I have come many times and saw you from a distance. A few times I thought you saw me."

"I did. At least I always thought I saw a black wolf, but I was never sure. You say you have come to see me before?"

"Yes. At least once every five years. I stayed and watched."

Silas could not wrap his mind around that. *"Why not say something?"*

Angus shrugged. *"Like what? You left a long time ago and never returned. I heard about a black wolf in this country and came to see for myself. You were busy training Alphas that first visit. You seemed okay. And things were changing for our clan. We moved to the continent and staked our land."*

"How many remain from our litter?"

"Two male pups."

Silas met Angus' gaze and realized his wolf accepted Angus from the beginning. Not once had his wolf gone berserk and tried to kill the man. They fought hard, but it was never with the intensity Silas would have for an enemy. Unable to fully process what it meant to have his littermate serve him, he patted Angus on the shoulder and spoke. "Welcome Angus, I am proud to have you with me. We will talk further, later."

Angus smiled and nodded. "Okay."

Silas shook his head and returned to his chair. "Now let's get this meeting started."

Chapter 21

THEY HAD BEEN MEETING for three hours when a call from the gate came. "Sir, the Mistress has returned with some breeds walking behind her car. She wants me to process them and place them in the cells below. We don't have enough cells, she told me to ask you where to put them."

Shaking his head, Silas stood. "My mate has returned with the rebels no doubt. It seems she has succeeded in capturing my enemies where others have failed. I need to locate additional jail space for them. I must be excused. We covered enough material that Matt and Passen can leave now since they have been chomping at the bit to do that for the past hour." The two men stood so fast, even Davian chuckled.

"Thank you, Sir. I am excited to get started," Dr. Passen said as he picked up his pad and headed toward the door.

Matt stopped by Davian for a brief hug and then moved quickly to the door behind Dr. Passen murmuring, "Goddess bless the Mistress."

"I just got a call that there are six of them. They are in the outer court being scanned again. The driver scanned them before tying them together and stuffing them in the trunk," Hank said.

Silas nodded, having received the same report. He eyed Hank.

"How long did it take to scrub that gym?"

Hank laughed. "It took four full-bloods all night, Sir."

"Okay, I want security on rotation to watch them around the clock as they clean the gym. They do not deserve the hospitality of a cell." Silas turned to Davian. "Are you sure you want the responsibility of Tomas? I can send him to an Alpha."

Davian and Matt had formally petitioned for guardianship of Tomas during the meeting. Silas had been surprised, but as Matt discussed the abuse the young pup experienced at the hands of his mother, he knew Jasmine would agree with his decision to allow the pup to return after his punishment.

"Yes, Sir. I believe we can help him. He's not a bad kid, just confused. In time he will be alright," Davian said.

Silas nodded. "Okay, as long as you understand that I hold you and Matt responsible for him and his actions from here out."

Davian nodded. "Yes, Sir."

Silas clapped him on the shoulder. "Okay, work with Hank on that security detail. I will have Rose contact you next week when I release him."

"Thank you, Sir." He followed Hank out of the room.

"*Silas?*" Jasmine called.

"*I am on my way. Where are you?*"

"*In the office, I have Thorne.*"

Silas frowned as he headed toward the door. "*Take him to the gym with the others, he gets no special treatment.*"

"I am off to meet my mate to see what she has for me from her shopping trip," Jacques said with a wide grin. He turned to Angus and offered his hand. "I am glad you are here and after you are settled, I would enjoy sitting and talking with you. I am sure we have some interesting memories to share."

Angus took his hand and smiled. "I am sure you are right."

Silas looked over his shoulder and called out. "Angus, Rone, and Rese, let's go. Your mom has Thorne."

"Oh, oh," Tyrese said moving briskly.

"That's why Rose is upset," Tyrone said, coming up behind them.

"*Who is Thorne?*" Angus asked.

"*I'll explain the family dynamics later,*" Silas said punching the floor into the elevator keypad.

"Like Davian? Your mate's former husband and these are his sons?" Angus looked at the twins and then met Silas' gaze.

"Yes, like that. For now, just observe, hold your questions," Silas said as the elevator opened.

"Yes, Sir," Angus said with a grin as he followed them out the elevator. The rebels were arguing with the guards, refusing to obey the task set aside for them. One second they were speaking English, the next they were whispering in that awful scratchy voice Silas detested.

"First off, you never raise your voices at me, ever..." Jasmine said. "Second, if I tell you to scrub this gym with a toothbrush you will do it and be glad to do it." The next moment he heard yelps of surprise. Curious, he stepped into the gym and looked up. Jasmine had pinned every one of the rebels to the second-floor railing, their feet dangled in the air. Asia stood next to her smiling. The two women were enjoying themselves.

He looked around. The twins stared up in amazement. Hank and Davian stood to the side laughing. Angus stared at Jasmine as if she were the virgin mother.

"Hello, Sweet Bitch. You brought home a little extra from your shopping trip I see." He stepped close to her and tipped up her chin for a kiss. "You taste good. What did you have for lunch?"

"I had a strawberry daiquiri and a margarita," she said, her eyes gleaming with merriment.

"Hello, Asia. Is your Mistress drunk?"

Asia giggled.

He blinked, surprised at the change in the young bitch. Her face softened when she gazed at Jasmine. She looked...happy.

"I don't know, Sir. We all had a few of those fruit drinks," she said grinning.

Tyrone and Tyrese stepped closer. "Mom? What do you plan to do with them?" Tyrone waved toward the young pups hanging above them.

"They are going to scrub the gym." She dipped them a bit. They screamed and begged her to allow them to clean the floors.

Silas laughed and wrapped his arm around her waist. "You were right. They are going to clean the floors."

Jasmine lowered the young pups to the floor. As soon as their feet hit the ground they fell to their knees and grabbed the buckets.

Silas waved at Hank to take over as he guided Jasmine out of the gym.

"Hello," Jasmine said, smiling at Angus.

"Hello Mistress," Angus said bowing.

"Have you met Asia?" Jasmine asked, looking over her shoulder.

"Yes, I met her on the plane. She is a delightful woman."

"Awww, you have manners. I like that. Welcome to our home. Has Silas released you from the dungeon yet?" she asked in a giddy tone.

"Yes, I believe he has." Angus laughed as he walked alongside them.

"Tyrese, walk Asia to her room. The plane leaves in six hours, that should be enough time for everyone to dry out," Silas said walking his unsteady mate toward the elevators.

Tyrone joined them in the elevator, turning his back on his brother-in-law, Thorne. "Rose is finishing our packing. I am looking forward to the beach."

"Good." Jasmine cupped his cheek. "She is sad and worried about her brother. I could not promise her he would be spared this time. This time he went too far."

Tyrone nodded as he released a sigh. "I know, mom. We can only do so much; he will learn or pay the penalty. His choices are his own."

The elevator stopped. Tyrone brushed a kiss across Jasmine's cheek and nodded to Silas and Angus as he exited. Moments later, they exited on their wing.

Jasmine's brow rose when Angus stepped out behind them. Silas had been thinking about how to broach the subject of his littermate when she stopped and looked at him. Her gaze swept to Angus and then back at him again.

"Do you have something to tell me, Silas?" She crossed her arms and met his gaze.

He cleared his throat. "Yes…Angus is my littermate."

She frowned for a moment and then smiled widely. "Angus? You are a Knight? You're his brother?"

"Well, er…no, I am not a Knight…I am BlackWolf. That is my surname to be correct."

She waved him down. "That is a description, not a name." Turning, she grinned at Silas. "So you have a brother…how does it feel to have more family?"

He shook his head at her teasing and looked at Angus. "My mate makes fun of my inability to understand the human relationship structure. She forgets I have claimed her as my mate and wife. Her mother and sister are my relatives. Her sons are my sons. And we have ...children." He turned toward Jasmine, seeing her glassy-eyed stare touched his heart. "She has changed me... brother..." He glanced at Angus seeing his surprise. "I am now a family man and would not have it any other way."

Jasmine smiled and took his hand, warming him. She took Angus' hand and walked between the two men. Silas was unsure how he felt about his brother holding his mate's hand but since his wolf did not respond neither did he.

"Are you mated, Angus?" Jasmine asked.

Silas groaned and looked straight ahead. His mate was on a mission to see Asia mated with a litter of pups.

"No, Mistress. I have not been blessed as my...uh, brother to find my completeness. Some never do."

Hearing the yearning in Angus' voice, Silas glanced at him in surprise.

"You are searching for your mate?" Jasmine asked a bit too excited. Silas thought to warn Angus but let it slide. When it came to family, Jasmine would do as she pleased regardless of his opinion.

"No, not really, if I run across her that would be great, but I serve my people and now La Patron in the meantime," he said with some hesitation as if he sensed where the conversation was headed.

Jasmine nodded as she stopped in front of the nursery. "Our children are napping but if you'd like to see them you can. We'll introduce them to their uncle later." She paused. "They have one uncle and one aunt. Who would've thought..." She looked at Silas and he smiled at the thunderstruck expression on Angus' face.

Clapping his brother on the back, Silas tipped his head toward the door. "Come, I need to get you settled." He entered the nursery behind Jasmine. Angus followed him inside.

A few moments later they stood in front of the cribs. Silas wrapped his arms around Jasmine as she leaned against him.

"I pledged my life to you, La Patron," Angus said in a quiet, yet serious voice. Silas glanced at him, noticing Angus' glassy eyes as the man knelt in front of the cribs. "But I extend that pledge to your litter,

Adam was first and will be well-known and universally liked. Renee will fill the world with color from her internal palette. Jackie will turn the world upside down with her uncanny ability to solve problems and mysteries. And David, who although was not first will have the wisdom and humility of his namesake which will catapult him to the top."

Touched, Silas stared at Angus for a moment and then cleared his throat. "On behalf of my litter, I accept your additional layer of protection for them. Guard them with your life Angus. To do otherwise will cost you yours."

Angus nodded and then stood. "As well it should. I am honored to see the pups, thank you."

"When everyone returns from the weekend, we will begin to sift through all the documentation and prepare teams for counter-attack measures," Silas said as they left the nursery. "I intend to eradicate the Liege from my land."

Angus looked at him with a raised brow. "From the United States, only?"

Silas shrugged and met Jasmine's gaze. "Yes for now."

"Okay," Angus said when Silas stopped in front of the suite he shared with Jasmine.

"I will return in a few moments, Sweet Bitch. I will take him to his room to settle in," Silas said to Jasmine.

She nodded, leaned forward, and kissed Angus on the cheek. "Welcome to our home, Brother."

Silas growled at the innocent gesture but his wolf had not stirred. She slapped him on the shoulder. "Behave, Wolfie."

Smiling, Angus' brow rose.

"No kissing anyone else," Silas said as she strode into their room.

"Yes, Sir," she said in a mocking tone as she waved goodbye and closed the door.

Angus laughed as they strode toward the elevator. "You are blessed beyond measure to have found your mate. I can tell she is your match in every way."

Silas nodded. "Yes, she is. One day I will tell you of our rocky beginning and how I almost lost her. But that is a tale for another day."

Angus nodded. Together they left the elevator and headed to

Cameron's old suite. Silas took a moment to thank the Goddess for his blessings. He had taken some bumps in the past 48 hours, but they were in a better position to fight their enemy than before. He had an explanation, of sorts, how half-breeds came about and met his remaining litter-mate. Now if he could talk his mate into having more pups, he would be the happiest Alpha in the world.

Opening the door for Angus and allowing his brother to precede him, he shrugged. Tomorrow was another day. They would fight for peace and make love until he could not think. As plans went, that was a pretty good one.

End

A Note from Sydney:

Thank you for taking the time to read book five in the La Patron series. I love paranormal books and characters in general and shifter stories in particular. Throw in the romantic element, strong Alpha characters who bend beneath the power of love and I'm over the moon. Sighs...

In BirthStone, I showed a little of Jasmine's power. A lot more was revealed in BirthDate as well as Asia gaining her freedom through death. I enjoyed teaming Jasmine and Asia together to wreak havoc on the Liege as well as set things in place for Asia to discover more about herself. She is a serious weapon, and I love her commitment to Jasmine first and Silas second.

You're invited to journey with me through the six and counting books in this series. If you like fast-paced action, suspense, and great love connections like me, you won't be disappointed. Feel free to drop me a line, SydneyAddae@msn.com, or join La Patrons' Den, my Facebook group where discussions regarding Silas and the Wolf Nation abound.

For more information about Silas Knight and the Wolf Nation, I'd like to give you a *Free Companion PDF Booklet* with personal messages from Silas and Jasmine, as well as their family tree. To receive your Free Booklet and Free Book, go to my website www.SydneyAddae.com and join Knights Chronicles, my reading group, for fresh news on my Works in Progress.

La Patron, the Alpha's Alpha is my first paranormal series and I'd like to ask a favor. When you finish reading, please leave a review, whatever your opinion, I assure you I appreciate it.

Thanks again
Sydney

You've finished this story, get ready for the next! The following books are in the La Patron series, enjoy!

Birth Series
BirthRight
BirthControl
BirthMark
BirthStone
BirthDate
BirthSign

Sword Series
Sword of Inquest
Sword of Mercy
Sword of Justice

Holiday Series
La Patron's Christmas
La Patron's Christmas 2
La Patron's New Year
Christmas in the Nation

KnightForce Series
KnightForce 1
KnightForce Deuces
KnightForce Tres'
KnightForce Damian
KnightForce Ethan
Angus

LaPatron's Den Series
Jackie's Journey (La Patron's Den Book 1)
Alpha Awakening – Adam (La Patron's Den Book 2)
Renee's Renegade (La Patron's Den Book 3)
David's Dilemma (La Patron's Den Book 4)

Rise of the Wolf Nation Series
Knight Rescue - Rise of Wolf Nation 1
Knight Defense (Rise of Wolf Nation 2)

BlackWolf Series
BlackWolf Legacy
BlackWolf Preserved
BlackWolf Redemption

The Leviticus Club (The Olympus Project Book 1)
 Altered Destiny
Family Ties

Booksets:
La Patron Series Books 1-3
La Patron Series Books 4-6
Sword Series
KnightForce Series Books 1-3
KnightForce Series Books 4-6
A Walk in the Nation (Three Stories to Tease Your Imagination

Other Books by Sydney Addae:
Last in Line (Vampires)
Bear with Me (Bear Shifter)
Jewel's Bear (Bear Shifter)
Do Over: Shelly's Surrender
Do Over: Rashan's Recovery
Secret of the Red Stone

www.SydneyAddae.com

Made in United States
Orlando, FL
06 December 2021